◆———— LEGION BOOK FOUR ————◆

FORSAKEN

A.D. STARRLING

AUTHOR OF THE SEVENTEEN SERIES

COPYRIGHT

Want a FREE boxset, new release alerts, and giveaways? Sign up to my newsletter for these and more! Find out how at the end of this book.

PROLOGUE

1951, UKRAINIAN SOVIET SOCIALIST REPUBLIC

The woman crouched over the child, her body taking the brunt of the blows raining down on them. The punches and kicks came erratically, the man delivering them so inebriated he could barely stand. Still, the attack was as savage as it would have been had he been sober.

"Get off him!" the man roared where he towered above them. His spit pelted the woman's nape, so hot she could barely distinguish it from the blood flowing out of the fresh cut on her scalp. "Let me see the ugly freak!"

That's going to need stitches for sure.

She whimpered as the steel cap of his boot connected with her side, denting her flesh with enough force to leave an imprint. Pain exploded inside her chest. She gasped and bit her lip.

She'd suffered enough broken bones to know that he'd just shattered one of her ribs.

The boy let out a low sob. It was the first sound he'd made since her husband had flown into a rage and started beating them, his anger fueled by the cheap booze he'd been drinking all afternoon in their tiny, one-bedroom apartment. Despite the illness that had rendered his body weak, the boy clung ferociously to her with his tiny hands, his tears soaking into her grimy shirt; she had just returned from a grueling shift on the assembly line at the factory and had not had time to change out of her work clothes.

Even though her husband was making enough noise to raise the dead, the woman knew no help would come. Not a single person in their drab and lifeless, red-brick housing block would raise a finger to stop the monster who was currently striking her and her nephew.

"Mama," the boy hiccupped softly.

The man froze for a moment. The woman waited breathlessly, wondering if the sound had somehow finally brought him to his senses.

The blow came from nowhere and sent stars flashing before her eyes. She slumped to the floor, body limp and skull ringing. The object her husband had used to strike her landed with a thump by her head.

It was her Bible. The one she read every night to the boy.

She should have known that the endearment would just infuriate her husband more. He hated that the boy called her mother. Not just because he considered the child a cripple and an embarrassment, but also because she had never been able to bear him his own child.

A hand grabbed the back of her shirt, coarse fingertips digging into the fresh bruises on her body. She was yanked off the boy and cast violently to the side. A choked grunt left her as she struck the edge of a sideboard. The meager porcelain dinner set she had received as part of her dowry rattled on the shelves inside the cabinet.

The boy curled up into a ball on the kitchen floor, his

small frame dwarfed by the monster who loomed over him. The man clutched a handful of his dark hair and started dragging him across the floor.

The boy reached out to her, his crying face and desperate eyes blurring in and out of her sight.

A scream left his lips for the first time. *"Mama! Mama! Help me!"*

Fear gripped the woman when she saw where her husband was heading.

She rolled awkwardly onto her front and tried to push up onto her hands and knees. Her arms and legs trembled. They gave way. Once. Twice.

The woman slammed her palms weakly on the linoleum floor, her tears falling in a hot, steady flow. She sobbed and cursed the frailty of her female body and the cruel fate that had ever seen her cross paths with the monster she had married.

The roar of water reached her ears. Her heart lurched painfully in her chest.

He was going to drown the boy. Just like he had drowned the puppy the child had rescued a few weeks ago.

The face of her late sister swam before the woman's eyes. She'd promised Magda that she would look after her son.

A loud splash came from the bathroom. The boy's screams were abruptly cut off.

The woman pushed up once more. This time, her body obeyed her will.

The room spun dizzyingly around her as she staggered to her feet. She clutched the sideboard and closed her eyes briefly. Then she was moving, her fingers finding a carving knife in the wooden block by the sink.

Her husband had his back to her when she entered the

bathroom. He was on his knees by the tiny copper tub in the corner, his arms elbow deep in the water.

The boy's legs kicked weakly through the surface as he fought to free himself from the monstrous hold around his neck, his shape a blur.

The woman rushed across the room with an animal noise and sank the knife into the man's back all the way to the hilt, right between his shoulder blades. The sound it made as it carved through flesh and bone made her gag.

A low grunt left the man. He grew deathly still before twisting and glaring at her, his face a vicious mask. His pupils flashed yellow for an instant.

The woman froze, terror locking her mind and limbs rigid.

Something else was looking at her out of her husband's body. He turned back to his task as if she weren't even there.

The woman blinked. Awareness returned. She snarled and started pummeling his body with her fists. The monster did not so much as budge.

The turbulence in the water started to abate. The boy finally became motionless at the bottom of the tub.

The woman sank to her knees and started to sob, despair a living entity that choked her very breath. "God, please help us! Help this child! He has suffered so much already!"

A low cackle reached her. It was coming from her husband. The inhuman laughter echoed around the bathroom, an evil sound that frayed her nerves and made her stomach roil.

"*Your God will not help him,*" he growled in a voice she did not recognize.

He let go of the dead boy and climbed to his feet

before turning to face her, water dripping down his arms and a sickening smile splitting his mouth.

The woman gasped, hands moving automatically to make the sign of the cross.

The monster advanced toward her, his grin growing impossibly wide. The whites of his eyes shifted to obsidian. His hand, when he grabbed her neck, was no longer human, his fingers and nails having lengthened to razor-sharp talons that scraped across her skin.

Blood pounded thickly in the woman's ears as she stared blindly into the face of the demon. She knew she would be dead in the next few seconds. She cast a final prayer to Heaven and closed her eyes.

Forgive me, Magda.

A voice came then. One neither she nor the creature who was slowly strangling her to death had expected.

"Let her go!"

The woman's eyes snapped open. She gasped, the sound a wheeze.

The demon paused, his deadly grip stopping shy of crushing her windpipe. He looked over his shoulder.

The woman's eyes widened.

The boy stood in the middle of the copper tub. Steam was curling up from his skin and hair. His wet clothes were already half dry. But it was his face and hands that captured her shocked gaze and the attention of the demon.

Fire danced on the boy's fingertips and blazed from his eyes. The air around him trembled and shimmered, as if struck by an intense heat. A faint aura of flames flickered into life around his body as he climbed out of the tub.

Dark scorch marks stained the marble tiles under his

feet as he came toward them. Some cracked, the limestone warping and bubbling as the blaze licked them.

The demon released her and turned to face the boy.

"*Run!*" the woman yelled, her voice hoarse.

The boy glanced at her.

The demon moved.

What happened next was something the woman never recounted to another living soul and took to her grave when she passed away years later in prison.

The demon swung lethal talons at the boy. The boy blocked the strike with one hand. Fire raced from his fingers and engulfed the demon. First the arm. Then the chest. Then the entire body of the creature was swallowed up by the flames.

As the thing that had once been her husband shrieked and dropped to the floor, skin and flesh blackening while he writhed helplessly, the woman realized that the monsters she had read about in her Bible walked this mortal realm.

A hush fell across the apartment when the demon exhaled his last breath, his corpse a dark husk that was barely recognizable where he lay curled up on the floor.

The boy blinked. The fire went out of his eyes and faded from his fingertips. He looked utterly lost and forlorn swaying where he stood, the weakness in his limbs evident once more.

The woman caught him before he collapsed to the floor.

"Mama!" The boy gazed at her beseechingly, fat tears rolling down his pale cheeks. "I didn't mean to kill him! *I didn't!*"

The woman tightened her hold on the boy. "It's okay, Judah. It's okay, my little *kokhana*." She took a shaky breath, her mind clearer than it had been in years. "Now, here's what we're going to do."

The boy protested when he heard what she said next. In the end, she made him promise on his mother's grave that he would do as he was told.

And so, when the police finally came, the boy stayed quiet. And as she was led away in handcuffs and the neighbors gathered in the corridors of the building and mumbled about what a terrible man her husband had been and how he had deserved what had happened to him, the boy kept his word and remained silent.

"I love you, Judah," the woman called out as she was pushed roughly into the back of a police car. "Remember that."

"I love you, Mama," the little boy whispered where he stood in the entrance of the housing block, a policeman holding his hand.

That was the last the woman saw of him.

CHAPTER ONE

THE BAR WAS QUIET FOR A FRIDAY NIGHT. CONSIDERING the bloodshed of the last forty-eight hours, the man was not all that surprised.

After two decades of fragile truce between the authorities and the gangs that once made El Salvador the country with the highest homicide rate in the world, death had returned to the streets of the capital. Even as he stood on the doorstep of the rundown tavern, squinting slightly while his eyes adjusted to the twilight that bathed the interior, the shrill sounds of sirens reached the man's ears. The noise echoed through the historic downtown district of San Salvador, drowning out the distant screams of people fleeing the latest clash between rival gangs and the police.

Forty souls would perish that night. The man knew this as surely as he knew that the sun would rise in seven hours. And of those forty souls, only thirty-five would be human.

In truth, the man did not really need to squint to see in the gloom. Nor did he need to fear any of the evils that walked the streets of San Salvador. He had faced far worse in his long and wondrous existence.

"You going in or what?" a truculent voice said behind him.

The man looked over his shoulder.

A boy stood frowning at him, his dark eyes unreadable in the shadows. He was dressed in jeans, a leather jacket, a T-shirt that brazenly told the world what it could do with its opinion, and shiny Doc Martens. The only color in his otherwise somber outfit was the wine-red leather belt with the silver buckle at his waist, the intricate bracelet on his left wrist, and his bright diamond earrings.

The man sighed. "Oh. I'd forgotten you'd be here too."

The boy scowled and stormed past him. The man wandered inside the tavern in his wake and followed him to the bar.

The boy plonked himself on a wooden stool that had seen better days and addressed the silent figure in a hoodie on his left. "Here, churros."

He removed an oil paper wrapping from inside his jacket and laid it on the counter.

The guy in the hoodie put down the shot of tequila he'd been about to drink and studied the meager offering. "Was there nothing else?"

"No. It was either churros or two packets of out-of-date chips. The boy sneered. "This place is a shit hole."

The man climbed onto the bar stool on the boy's right and leveled a steady stare above the latter's head at Hoodie Guy. He could see a hint of fair hair under the covering. "Is it me or has your companion grown too familiar with this world? His language has become most foul."

"He's in character right now. And he's hangry."

As if to prove his point, the boy downed two churros in the blink of an eye.

Or the shake of a crow's wing.

"I heard that," the boy muttered.

"You should stop spying on people's innermost thoughts," the man said with a grunt.

"You're not people."

Hoodie Guy's lips twitched.

The man narrowed his eyes at the boy. "May I remind you that I have seniority over you?"

"Eight hundred human years is hardly seniority," the boy countered sullenly.

The man looked at Hoodie Guy. "Let me guess. He's supposed to be a cranky teenager."

"Bingo."

"Can I put him over my knees and spank him?"

The boy bristled at these words, his entire body vibrating as if shaken from within by tremors. His clothes trembled for an infinitesimal moment, the layers quivering like feathers, a hint of golden light flashing between them.

Had he been human, the man would have missed the phenomenon.

Hoodie Guy blew out a sigh. "Stop antagonizing him."

"He started it."

The boy had lost interest in their conversation and was staring hungrily at the remaining churro.

"You can have it," Hoodie Guy said magnanimously.

"Hey, what about me?" the man protested. "No one asked if I was hungry."

The boy flashed him a dirty look and pursed his lips. "We should have asked the chef to make us something."

They followed his gaze.

Framed in the serving window that took up the middle

section of the wall behind the bar was a guy with scars all over his face and arms. He was currently skinning a chicken with a carving knife. Bits of fat and flesh peppered his apron and the grimy T-shirt beneath it like bullets scoring a target.

The man made a face. "I don't think that would have been a wise idea. He looks like a walking advert for salmonella poisoning. Besides, he's gonna be dead in two minutes."

"One minute twenty-eight seconds," the boy mumbled.

The man frowned. "You sure? I'm getting two from him."

"Arael is right," Hoodie Guy said.

The man studied the wisps of darkness that had materialized above the chef's head. They were invisible to everyone but the three of them.

"Well, what do you know? The crow is indeed—"

The tavern door opened. Four figures stumbled inside, bloodied machetes in hand. They were still human. Barely.

The black cloud crowning their heads visibly thickened.

The man scratched his jaw. "Aren't they early?"

A glass shattered on the floor. Someone knocked a chair over.

The few patrons lurking in the tavern's shadows had seen the writing on the wall and were beating a hasty retreat toward the fire exit at the back. The bartender made the sign of the cross and followed them. Fear radiated from his hot gaze as he glanced at where Hoodie Guy, Arael, and the man still sat at the counter.

"*Correr!*" he shouted weakly before vanishing into the gloom of a rear alley.

"I'm afraid there will be no running for us," the man

murmured as the bartender's footsteps faded in the distance. "Tonight or any other night."

Hoodie Guy downed his tequila, winced, and climbed off the stool. "You're being strangely eloquent."

Arael hopped down beside him.

An almighty crash came from the kitchen.

Something was happening to the chef. Something few humans had ever witnessed and lived to tell.

The knife fell from his grip. He grunted, his face flushing impossibly red. His nails lengthened and thickened to dark claws. His eyes rolled into the back of his head before twisting forward again, the whites fading to black and the pupils brightening to a sulfurous yellow. He bowed his spine and let out an animal sound, his body growing in height and girth as the demon who had awakened inside him took over his physical form. He turned his head and glared at them through the serving window, his obsidian gaze filled with loathing.

He knew what they were.

"Wow. He's one ugly sonofabitch, isn't he?" the man muttered.

Hoodie Guy made a tutting noise. "Language."

Arael smirked.

Guttural shrieks rose from the figures in the doorway. They dropped the machetes and headed toward the bar, their deformed bodies now under the full possession of the hellish creatures that lived beneath their skin.

The man turned to Arael. "You take the chef."

The demon in the kitchen smashed through the serving window.

Arael frowned as plaster and wood rained down around them. "Why do I have to take him?"

"Isn't he a friend of yours?"

"I met him an hour ago."

The demons leapt.

Golden light exploded across the tavern.

Arael and the man blinked as the brightness slowly faded.

Choked gurgles escaped the five demons where they lay scattered across the floor, black blood pooling under their twisted, broken bodies.

Arael and the man looked pointedly at Hoodie Guy.

He shrugged. "You were taking too long."

"Spoilsport," the man muttered.

"Show off," Arael mumbled.

They headed over to the dying demons and gave them their final rites.

Black ash filled the air as the creatures' remains crumbled to dust. Hoodie Guy opened his hands and gathered the spiraling cloud into a ball that hovered above his palms. A sad light darkened his eyes for an instant, turning them silver.

He pressed his hands together. *"From dust you were born. And to dust you shall return. Be at peace, my Fallen brothers."*

His words made the very room tremble. All that remained of the ash when he parted his hands was a fading, golden mist.

"That never gets old," the man murmured.

Hoodie Guy arched an eyebrow. "It was you who first brought this prayer to life."

The man rubbed the back of his head. "I must have been feeling sentimental."

Arael's face crunched up. "Why are you always such an ass?"

"Genetics, probably."

Arael sucked in air. "That's blasphemy."

He stepped back and looked expectantly at the ceiling.

"What are you doing?"

"Waiting for the bolt of lightning to strike you."

The man rolled his eyes. "He's not into smiting these days."

Thunder boomed outside the tavern.

The man sobered. "Then again, maybe he is."

Arael grinned.

Hoodie Guy followed them as they headed for the back door. They stepped into the balmy night and strolled to the end of the alley.

Redness filled the sky to the north. Another fire was raging across the city.

"So, you gonna tell me what you guys are doing in my territory? Last I checked, the U.S. border was still over 2000 miles from here, as the crow flies." The man glanced at Arael. "Pun unintended."

The Angel of Crows dipped his chin sagely. He had lost all appearance of the ornery human teenager he had been emulating and had assumed the regal pose in keeping with his station.

"Can't an archangel be neighborly?" Hoodie Guy said lightly.

The man's face hardened as he scrutinized his friend and brother in arms. "No, Uriel. And I strongly doubt the two of you dropped by just to say hi."

Uriel pulled his hood back. His hair shone in the night, his divine power casting a golden glow all around the human form he had assumed to walk the Earth.

And walk the Earth we all have, for thousands of years.

"We bring a message. Do not interfere."

The man frowned. He cocked a thumb at the sky. "Is that from Him?"

Uriel sighed. "It would be nice if you wouldn't point to our Heavenly Father with so little deference. And no. It's not from Him. It's from the rest of Us."

The man stiffened at that. "By Us, I take it you mean the Divine Army? The one I once *led?*"

"There he goes again," Arael muttered. "I told you he'd get like this."

Uriel ignored Arael.

"We all are aware that we won the war against the Grigori because of your strength and leadership," he told the man quietly. "But it doesn't mean we can look away from what you've been doing for the last three decades."

The man straightened to his full height. "And what is *that*, exactly?"

"Interfering."

The man snorted. "Don't give me that crap. I know full well you butted into the fates of your own bloodline. And you still visit those kids."

Uriel sighed and pinched the bridge of his nose. He looked like he was counting to five.

"I did nothing that would directly affect their destiny," the archangel finally said. "And the children enjoy my company, as I do theirs. Nowhere in our edict does it state that we cannot meet with the ones we have bestowed our sacred gifts upon, once they have come into their powers and know of us." He paused and gazed steadily at the man. "It's different in your case. Artemus Steele's very existence is something that has long been called into question. That you were ultimately correct in your suspicions about the Grigori's plans doesn't take away from the fact that you chose to lay with a woman. Technically speaking, you're a Fallen Watcher."

The man smiled thinly. "You forget. She wasn't just a

woman. And I slept with her to save her, and the world, from what that bastard Samyaza was planning."

Uriel sniffed. "I am fully aware that she wasn't just a woman. I can't believe you yourself didn't realize this until, well—" he waved a hand vaguely, "after the fact."

The man's smile widened to a full grin. "I was preoccupied."

Uriel narrowed his eyes at his carefree tone. "There's more than just the fact that you lay with a human. There's also that incident the night the boy turned six. You know, when you grabbed Cerberus from his den and dumped him in that field with the boy and his pet rabbit?"

"That poor kid had nightmares for years," Arael murmured.

"I thought it was the appropriate time for them to meet," the man said defensively. "And I wanted to see what the boy would do." His tone turned maudlin. "Did you know Cerberus bit me?"

"You deserved it," Arael said unsympathetically.

"Oh, and let's not forget the gun," Uriel continued, undeterred.

The man pasted an innocent expression across his face. "What gun?"

"You know full well the weapon I mean," Uriel snapped. "You're not going to stand there and pretend you didn't guide Karl LeBlanc's hand when he made that gun for Artemus? Or deny that you created the barriers that would protect Artemus and his allies in the future? It's bad enough that Gabriel visited Ronald Stone and influenced his decision to auction the Scepter! And let's not even talk about Camael setting up shop in Bangkok so he could sell his sword to Yashiro Kuroda!"

"No, I'm not going to deny what I did," the man said

quietly. "And it was Artemus and Drake's mother who created the divine wall around Karl LeBlanc's mansion." He had rarely seen his friend in such a state. "What's going on, Uriel? Why are you really here? Because this feels like more than just a warning."

Uriel faltered. He exchanged a troubled glance with Arael. "Stay away from Rome."

The man felt his heart grow cold. He glanced to the east. "Why? What's going to happen in Rome?"

A muscle jumped in Uriel's jawline. "Things you should most definitely not interfere with."

The man watched his friend for a timeless moment. "Thanks for the tip."

Uriel sighed. "It wasn't a tip."

The man turned and headed out of the alley. "I hear Rome is nice this time of year."

"Your actions may very well change the course of humankind's destiny, Michael," Uriel warned. "You of all people should know that."

Michael stopped and cast a lopsided smile at the archangel and the Angel of Crows over his shoulder. "That may very well be true. But Artemus is my son. And the burden he will one day carry would unnerve even Heaven's most powerful warriors." He paused. "Have you ever stopped to consider whether our—*interference*, as you call it, was also preordained?"

Uriel ignored his question. "Drake is Samyaza's son. He *will* fall to Hell. And if you keep pushing Artemus, your son may fall too."

"Artemus will save his brother," Michael said coolly. "That, or he will die trying."

He turned and headed off into what remained of the night.

A<small>RAEL</small> <small>SHOOK</small> <small>HIMSELF</small> <small>INTO</small> <small>HIS</small> <small>TRUE</small> <small>FORM</small> <small>AND</small> <small>FLEW</small>
onto Uriel's shoulder.

"That went well."

Uriel frowned at the space where Michael had disappeared. "It could have been worse."

He twisted on his heels and headed in the opposite direction, the crow's feathers warm against his cheek.

"You know that was a tip, right?" Arael muttered.

"No, it wasn't."

"You practically told him to go to Rome."

"I warned him not to interfere." Uriel paused. "Besides, *she's* in Rome. I doubt he'd want to meet her."

CHAPTER TWO

The dream started like it usually did. With her walking toward him. Her features were indistinct, as if he were looking at her through a foggy window.

He could never make out the background of where she was. The landscape was mostly pale, with a hint of sparkling dust occasionally rising under her feet with her steps. The only things he could see clearly were her breathtaking eyes and the lustrous chestnut curls that framed her face. Her gaze had matured over the years, the soft expression from when he first started dreaming of her as a child now focused and hinting at the incredible strength and indomitable spirit of the woman she had become.

Even in the dream, Artemus felt his heart throb with longing.

He had been in love with her nearly all of his life. And every time he saw her in his dreams, he ached to see her in real life. To smell her hair. To touch her skin. To kiss her lips.

"Tell me your name," he breathed.

She gazed at him, her beautiful eyes full of sadness, as if she too longed to be with him. She raised a hand and pressed it against the barrier that separated them.

Artemus drew a sharp breath. This was new.

She looked at him expectantly. He hesitated before lifting his hand and touching the ethereal wall.

Though the barrier kept them apart, Artemus thought he felt a light pressure as their fingertips connected.

Hot light exploded from the point of contact and filled his world, dazzling him.

Images flashed before his eyes, snapshots so fast and dizzying they brought a gasp to his lips. He couldn't make out any of them but for the last one, which slowed and came into sharp focus, as if someone had pressed pause on a hyper-lapse video.

It was a pair of metal gloves. Gauntlets, very much like those wielded by medieval knights.

The objects revolved slowly on their axes on an inky background, their edges glowing as if lit by fire from within. Though the vision only lasted a few seconds, every detail was indelibly etched on Artemus's mind, like a map only he could read.

The gauntlets became brighter, the blaze inside them growing. Artemus took a step back.

The last thing he saw was an incandescent conflagration.

ARTEMUS'S EYES SNAPPED OPEN. A VOICE WAS CALLING his name.

He twisted in the bed. A pair of frightful eyes blinked at him from half a foot away.

An incoherent scream burst from Artemus's lips. He bolted out the other side of the bed and fell on his ass in a tangle of sheets and blankets.

Sebastian straightened on the opposite side of the four-poster. "You are a very sound sleeper."

Artemus released a shaky breath, the adrenaline rushing through his veins abating. Irritation filled him as he untangled himself and climbed to his feet. "What the hell are you doing in my room?"

Sebastian drew himself to his full height.

"Well, excuse me for trying to be a helpful tenant," he said in an affronted tone. "Your ten a.m. appointment is here."

Artemus blinked. "What ten a.m. appointment?"

"The ten a.m. appointment I told you about yesterday."

Artemus scowled. "You never told me about a ten a.m. appointment."

"Yes, I did. It was when you were having that idiotic argument with Drake in the kitchen."

Artemus sighed and ran a hand distractedly through his hair. He'd almost forgotten about that. "It wasn't an idiotic argument. I just don't want him to take on any risky jobs."

He walked over to a chest of drawers and started picking out a set of fresh clothes.

"Your brother is a grown man. He can make his own decisions." Sebastian paused. "Or would you have him live in a gilded cage for the rest of his life?"

Artemus stilled, his hand hovering inside a drawer. He twisted on his heels, his expression growing defensive. "You know full well that his line of work borders on the illegal more often than not. I thought you of all people would be on my side on this."

Sebastian looked surprised for an instant.

"Well, maybe I have changed," he murmured. "The world is not as black and white as I once thought it was. And I know why you are being so protective of your brother."

Artemus studied him silently.

"You are afraid that Samyaza will take control of him one day, when he is not in your sight."

Artemus clenched his jaw. It irked him that Sebastian could read him so easily.

Four weeks had passed since they'd returned from England, where they'd defeated Amaymon, the demon prince who had killed Sebastian's family when he was a child and kidnapped Otis Boone, Artemus's assistant. Sebastian had turned out to be the Sphinx, a divine beast who possessed the key to a gate of Hell. He was also the older brother of Callie Stone, the Chimera, and Smokey, the hellhound Cerberus.

Like all the other Guardians, Sebastian now resided in Artemus's home. He had even moved part of his arcane bookstore from Salem to Artemus's antique shop in Old Town, Chicago. Much to Artemus's ire, the Englishman's new business was booming, this despite the fact that he only opened once a week.

Though Sebastian hailed from another era, the more Artemus got to know the man, the more he realized they had in common. It was only recently that he'd finally grasped why.

Sebastian reminded him of Karl LeBlanc, in many ways.

"So, who's the visitor?" Artemus asked testily as he headed for the bathroom.

"It's Elton and a gentleman I have never met before," Sebastian said. "A clergyman."

Artemus stopped and arched an eyebrow. "A priest?"

"A bishop, to be precise."

The bedroom door creaked open. Smokey hopped inside, stopped, and twitched his cute bunny nose at Artemus and Sebastian.

We're out of Kobe beef.

Artemus stared at the rabbit. "What do you mean, we're out of Kobe beef? Callie and Sebastian bought you tons of the stuff last week."

Smokey shrugged, his chocolate eyes projecting innocence.

Sebastian folded his arms across his chest and studied the hellhound with a stern expression. "Explain yourself, brother. Fifty pounds of prime Japanese meat does not just vanish overnight."

A loud grumble erupted from Smokey's stomach. He burped guiltily.

Artemus sniffed the air. He wrinkled his nose in disgust. "Christ, it smells like something died in your mouth."

"You promised you would not raid the freezer," Sebastian told the hellhound accusingly. He glanced at Artemus. "Maybe we should install padlocks."

"He pees and salivates acid. Those things wouldn't last a minute."

Sebastian's frown cleared. "Ah, but *you* are a metalsmith. And a gifted one at that. That new leash you made for him is practically indestructible."

A worried mien clouded the rabbit's face. He was not a fan of his new leash.

"There's something I need to make first," Artemus murmured as he disappeared inside the bathroom. "I think."

CHAPTER THREE

"Artemus, this is Bishop Irons. He is the Pope's secretary," Elton said smoothly. "Bishop Irons, Artemus Steele."

"It's a pleasure to finally meet you," Bishop Irons said warmly, the corners of his eyes wrinkling as he smiled. "I've heard a lot about your exploits, Mr. Steele."

Artemus shook the priest's hand. The man was dressed in a black cassock trimmed with red cord, with matching, silk-covered buttons. A purple fascia was wrapped around his generous waist and the ruby on his pectoral ring was mirrored by the one adorning the center of his gold cross.

"That's quite an antique you have there," Artemus murmured.

The bishop glanced at his cross, surprised. "You can tell?"

"18th century St. Petersburg, if I'm not mistaken." Artemus arched an eyebrow. "A Keibel, right?"

Admiration brightened the bishop's eyes. "You are correct."

Sebastian looked thoughtfully at Artemus. "There are days when I forget your other abilities."

"Yeah, well, if it weren't for my abilities, Elton's auction house would not be as renowned as it is," Artemus muttered.

"I can't exactly deny that," Elton said candidly.

The bishop turned to the Englishman. "Elton has told me a lot about you too, Mr. Lancaster." He paused. "Or do you prefer to be called Earl?"

"Sebastian is fine, thank you."

Artemus looked from Elton to the bishop. "So, to what do we owe the pleasure of your visit, Bishop Irons?"

The bishop reached inside his cassock and removed a white envelope with gilded edges. "I am here on behalf of Pope DaSilva to issue a formal invitation to you and your companions. She would very much appreciate the pleasure of your company next week for a private tour of the Vatican and to discuss…matters of import to all of us."

He handed the envelope to Artemus. Artemus exchanged a wary look with Sebastian before opening the invite and removing the single sheet of folded paper inside. The official Vatican stationary bore a simple line in an elegant, flowing script that the Englishman would approve of.

"*I look forward to meeting all of you. Signed, P. DaSilva,*" he murmured.

"The P stands for Persephone," Bishop Irons added helpfully.

Artemus blinked. "Really?"

Elton flashed him a warning look.

"What?" Artemus shrugged. "I didn't say anything."

"You did not have to," Sebastian muttered. "Your face said it for you."

"Can I inform her Holiness that you will be coming to Rome?" Bishop Irons asked tactfully.

Artemus studied the invite. "I need to discuss this with my associates."

Lines wrinkled Elton's brow. "It's an invitation from Vatican City. You'd be hard pressed to refuse it."

Artemus frowned at his oldest friend and mentor. "Unlike you, I don't answer to Rome. And I have my suspicions about these 'matters of import' they want to talk to us about."

"Come now, Mr. Steele. We all have a common objective," Bishop Irons said amiably. "And that is to defeat Ba'al, is it not? Surely, it won't do any harm to compare notes and see if we can't get one step closer to achieving our goal by working together?"

The bishop's words were still echoing in Artemus's ears when Elton and the clergyman left a short time later. As he watched Elton's town car disappear down the driveway, Artemus couldn't help but feel the strangest foreboding.

There were several reasons why he wanted to refuse the invitation from Pope DaSilva. In fact, they numbered exactly five. Drake and Otis made the top of that list, followed by Sebastian, Haruki, and Callie.

Artemus was convinced the primary reason behind the Vatican's summons was their interest in the Guardians and their keys.

And they sure as hell won't want to miss the chance to study the son of Samyaza.

A sharp pang of anxiety twisted Artemus's heart as he thought of his twin. It was Amaymon who had revealed to Drake when they were in England that the one who wished to take over his human soul was none other than the demon who had sired him. Samyaza, the Second

Leader of the Grigori and one of Heaven's most powerful
Fallen Angels.

"I sense dark clouds gathering on the horizon," Sebastian said quietly.

Artemus glanced at him. "You too, huh?"

Smokey appeared between them. The rabbit's eyes
flashed crimson for a moment as he sniffed the air.

"That makes three of us, then," Artemus said grimly.
"I'm saying no to that invitation."

The decision was taken out of his hands that very
night, when Haruki and Callie returned from their trip
to L.A.

"So, a business opportunity just came up for Callie and
me." Haruki opened the refrigerator and grabbed a beer.
He loosened his tie and popped the cap. "It's in Italy.
We're heading there next week."

Artemus stilled where he'd been gathering plates and
cutlery from a sideboard. He looked over at the cast-iron
range where Sebastian stood, hand frozen on the ladle he'd
been using to stir a pan.

"That is interesting," Sebastian muttered.

Smokey's ears twitched. They all heard the words he
spoke inside their heads.

Haruki's eyes widened.

Callie drew a sharp breath. "What? We've been invited
to visit Rome by the Pope?!"

"Who's been invited to Rome?"

They turned and stared at the man who'd just appeared
in the kitchen doorway.

Drake stripped the leather riding gloves off his hands
as he walked inside the room, his expression tired.

Artemus frowned. "Did someone hit you?"

Drake touched the red area on his jaw gingerly. "Yeah.

Some asshole landed a punch when I wasn't looking." He took a bottle of water out of the fridge and sat down at the kitchen table. "What's this about Rome?"

Artemus hesitated before recounting the visit he and Sebastian had received earlier that day. The others' expressions grew sober as they listened.

"So, you think this invitation is just an excuse for them to, what—" Haruki raised an eyebrow, "prod and poke us like we're some kind of lab rats?"

"I wouldn't put it past them," Artemus said moodily. "They're gonna want to look at our weapons, at least. And hell knows what they'll do to Otis. With the power he possesses to destroy Hell's gates, they may decide to keep him there."

Otis's transformation during their final battle with Amaymon had shocked all of them. But the fact that his geeky young assistant had turned out to be a powerful seraph, one who stood closest to God, had stunned Artemus the most.

Although it had become apparent since their return to Chicago that Otis couldn't tap into his powers at will like the rest of them, it didn't take away from the fact that he'd done something none of them could do, not even Artemus with his uncanny ability to wield metal.

"The one we should be worried about the most is Drake." Callie studied Artemus's twin with a worried expression. "The son of a demon walking about freely in the Holy See, the very capital of the Roman Catholic Church? I'm sure there'll be a lot of people in the Vatican who won't be happy about that."

Silence fell across the kitchen.

"I still think we should go," Drake said. "We could learn a lot about Ba'al from them."

Artemus glowered at his twin. "We need to decide this as a group."

Haruki raised a hand. "It's a yes from me."

Callie faltered before nodding, her eyes shifting guiltily from Artemus's stare.

Artemus turned beseechingly to Sebastian.

"I vote we go too," the Sphinx said quietly.

"Have you guys lost your minds?!" Artemus snapped. "I mean, Haruki and Callie *both* receiving business invitations to Italy the same day Bishop Irons turns up on our doorstep? Can't you see that this is some kind of trap?! Hell, we all know that Ba'al has a mole in the Vatican! This could very well be the work of that spy!"

His words reverberated across the kitchen.

"All the more reason to accept the invitation, then," Drake said calmly. "If Ba'al really *is* up to something in Rome, then we want to be there too."

"My thoughts precisely," Sebastian murmured.

He opened the oven, removed two roasting pans, and brought them over to the table along with a gravy boat.

Haruki's stomach grumbled. "That smells nice. What is it?"

"Venison and black pudding roast, served with vegetables and blood sauce," Sebastian said proudly. "And there is Eton Mess for dessert." He paused. "What is with those looks?"

"Black pudding?" Artemus made a face. "And, seriously, *blood sauce?* I thought that was wine you were pouring in that pan earlier!"

Smokey leapt onto the table and inhaled the steam wafting off the dishes. His eyes glazed over. Drool appeared at the corner of his mouth.

Sebastian sniffed. "At least the hellhound is a connoisseur of good food when he sees it. And Nate put me in charge of cooking while he and Serena are away, so you had better eat up."

"We need to get their opinions on Rome too," Artemus added stubbornly. "They're also included in the invite." He frowned at Callie. "Shouldn't they be back by now? I thought they were coming home tonight."

"Nate called a few hours ago. Apparently, there was an unexpected complication."

CHAPTER FOUR

SERENA STUDIED THE SHADOWY FIGURES FACING HER.

The men's chests heaved with their breathing. Sweat rolled freely down their angry faces. Their gazes strayed briefly to the bodies of their fallen comrades, aft of the cargo hold.

Serena didn't have to look to know that flies were already buzzing above the fresh corpses. The metallic stench of blood and urine tickled her nostrils where she stood loose-limbed and relaxed, the odor intensified tenfold by the heat.

It was one hundred degrees inside the ship and no better outside.

Blood thumped in Serena's veins, slow and steady. The barest sheen of perspiration covered her upper lip, the nanorobots in her body working overtime to cool her down.

A faint whimper came from the cage next to the dead men.

Serena looked over at the terrified faces of the eighty

or so girls, boys, and women crammed inside their filthy prison. They were bound for a slave market in Uganda, where their wretched fates would be sealed by the highest bidder.

Her team hadn't expected to find a human cargo when they'd done their recon on the arms dealer's ship yesterday.

A memory drifted through Serena's mind. Of a prison deep beneath a desolate landscape of ice and snow. Of rows of tanks shrouded in darkness. Of feeding tubes and intravenous lines that pierced her young body where she lay in suspended animation, a weapon born in captivity and bred to kill.

"It's going to be okay," she murmured to the prisoners in the cage.

The human traffickers' expressions told her what they thought of her words and what they planned to do to her if they won the upper hand.

Rape, sodomize, and, if I'm lucky, cut my throat.

Serena smiled thinly. "Let's do this."

Scowls darkened the men's faces as they glanced at one another. One of them spat on the floor, his eyes gleaming with loathing.

"Cette salope pense qu'elle va quitter ce bateau en vie?!"

His companions laughed raucously.

"Quinze secondes," Serena stated calmly.

The men looked at her as if she had grown a second head and a tail.

"Qu'est-ce qu'elle dit, cette pute?" one of them muttered, his grip tightening on his filthy knife.

This close to the port, the men were wary of using their guns.

Serena untwisted the suppressors on her new Sigs, secured the guns on her thigh holsters, and removed her blades from the harness on her lower back. "This is gonna be over in fifteen seconds, assholes."

A voice came through the receiver in her ear, distracting her for a second.

"Soooooo, is it true there's something going on between you and the Dark Angel?"

Serena frowned as the men fanned out around her. "I'm kinda busy right now, Tom."

"You're a super soldier," Tom Bright said blithely. "Multitask."

The men charged. Serena ducked beneath fists and knives, elbowed a guy in the nose, and drove the heel of her left palm into another one's chest, breaking his sternum. She blocked a strike to her face and kneed a third man in the groin.

"No, there isn't anything going on between Drake and me. Whatever gave you that asinine idea?"

Serena hook-kicked a man in the gut and fended off a fist one foot from her left temple. She twisted the arm of her attacker, dislocated his shoulder, and broke his right femur with an axe kick. The man screamed, bone snapping like a dry twig.

"Lou said he could sense a vibe between you guys when he met up with you and the gang in Chicago two weeks ago," Tom said.

Serena reached behind and grabbed the knife headed for her right loin. A shocked sound escaped the man who'd crept up on her. His eyes widened when she turned, his gaze dropping to the blood pooling on the cut on her palm. She yanked him close and headbutted him in the face.

"I never said that," Lou Flint protested over the comm link. A grunt echoed down the line. "Great. Some asshole managed to hit me 'cause you distracted me."

"What happened to your lightning-fast super soldier reflexes?" Tom asked, unrepentant.

"In case you hadn't noticed, which I'm sure is impossible since you're watching this on four infra-red cameras right now, it's fifteen against one."

Two of Serena's remaining attackers rushed her with loud battle cries. Their shrieks became choked grunts as she jumped into a reverse, spinning roundhouse kick that broke their jaws. By the time they fell to the ground, the wound on her palm was already healing, the flash of gold gleaming at the edges of the laceration the only hint of the divine powers she now possessed.

"Going back to our previous conversation, you said, and I quote, that there was a 'smoldering sexual tension between Serena and Drake,'" Tom continued.

"And I did not say that either, Serena," Lou denied fervently.

Another grunt ensued.

"I may yet reproduce one day asshole, so let's leave my balls alone, shall we?" he snarled at one of his assailants.

There was a fleshy sound followed by a muffled cry from the unseen man.

"I didn't know you wanted kids." Tom sounded genuinely surprised this time.

"Maybe. Someday. I think I'd make a great dad."

Serena bobbed beneath a swinging fist and hook-punched her attacker in the solar plexus, breaking several of his ribs. He staggered backward, tripped over one of his accomplices, and went down hard.

"And I think I'd make a great godfather, so make sure

you name one of the brats after me," Tom told Lou. He paused. "You know who I think would make a great mom?"

Serena scowled as she evaded a wicked knife aimed at her right eye. She could almost see Tom grinning.

"Don't say it," someone mumbled on the comm line. It was Nate.

"Oh, hey, big guy. I almost forgot you were here. How're you doing in the control room? And, whatever you two say, I think Serena would make a wonderful mom."

"I've secured the vessel. The cops are ten minutes out." Nate sighed. "Serena's gonna kill you."

"Not if I kill him first," Lou muttered. "I'm done here. What about you, Serena?"

Serena eyed the four men who'd just climbed back unsteadily to their feet and stood glaring at her from where they stood swaying. She sheathed one blade, took out a Sig, and shot each of them in the leg. They screamed and collapsed to the floor.

"I'm done too."

"Was that gunfire I just heard?" Tom asked sharply.

"It was."

Serena put the gun away and finished off the few remaining conscious men with swift punches to the jaw.

"We said no gunshots without suppressors. The cops are nine minutes out. You still had time."

"I have places to go and things to do. Namely, kill you."

"Oh, come on, it was a joke!"

They stood on the deck of a fishing boat an hour later and watched the Somalian police lead the rescued prisoners and the surviving arms dealer's men off the ship.

"Another job well done," Lou said in a satisfied voice.

He turned to Serena and Nate. "Thanks for helping us out. We didn't know these guys were trading in illegal arms *and* slaves when we came to shut them down."

"No problem," Serena murmured. "Besides, we still owe you for New York."

Lou grimaced. "I'd almost forgotten about that. I don't want to see another flying demon for a long time."

"Those bastards were fugly," Tom mumbled.

Serena and Nate shared a guarded glance.

Lou didn't miss their exchange. "What?"

"Has Gideon said anything to you?" Serena asked the two men quietly. "About our encounter with first-generation super soldiers in Chicago, a month ago?"

Surprise dawned on Lou and Tom's faces.

"No, he hasn't," Tom said, his expression hardening.

"You met first-generation super soldiers?" Lou's voice had turned steely. His smartband chimed with an incoming call. He narrowed his eyes when he saw the name on the display. "Talk of the devil." He tapped the display. "You're on speaker."

"I've got a job for you guys," Gideon Morgan said without preamble.

"We just finished a job," Tom said pointedly. "Like, an hour ago. And why didn't you tell us about the first-generation super soldiers?"

"Because it's on a need-to-know basis. And that mission you just completed was one of our pro bono gigs for the CIA. This one pays." Gideon paused. "We can't say no to this client."

Serena stiffened. She traded a cautious look with the others.

They all knew what Gideon's words meant.

"Is it an Immortal?" Lou said stiffly.

"Yes. He'll be with you in eight minutes. Look to your six o'clock."

They turned and spotted the yacht approaching the fishing vessel.

CHAPTER FIVE

"I HAVE NO IDEA WHAT TO PACK," OTIS SAID ANXIOUSLY. "I mean, what does one wear to meet the Pope?"

"I bet she'd be thrilled if you turned up as The Seal of God." Artemus grinned. "I can imagine the headlines now. 'Metatron causes ripples at the Vatican.'"

"Don't even joke about that!" Otis's scowl faded. His expression grew doleful. "Besides, we all know I haven't been able to transform into the...the seraph since that day."

"I'm sure he'll return when we need him the most."

The heat from the stone forge washed across Artemus's skin as he turned his attention back to the bars of metal on the table.

They were in the smithy at the rear of the building that housed his antique shop and Otis's apartment, in Old Town. Although Artemus had invited Otis to stay with them at the mansion many a time since their return from England, his assistant had refused and insisted on staying put. Sebastian had consequently had to manipulate divine energy to reinforce the barrier around the building as best he could.

With his ability to destroy Hell's gates and the prophetic visions he'd projected to his mother while he was still inside her womb, Otis was bound to be a subject of intense interest to Ba'al.

"What are you making?" Otis asked curiously.

Artemus glanced up distractedly from the pile of metal he was busy considering. "A pair of gloves."

Surprise danced across Otis's face. "Gloves?"

Artemus frowned. "Yeah. Gauntlets, actually."

Half a week had passed since Bishop Irons's visit to the mansion. Artemus and the others had since discovered that Serena and Nate were also on their way to Italy; they and their super soldier friends Lou and Tom had been engaged as security for a consignment of rare artifacts originating from the Middle East. They were presently accompanying the convoy to its final destination.

"They're in North Africa right now," Callie had told them two nights ago. "Nate has been pretty cagey about the whole affair. He only gets this way when Immortals are involved."

Callie and Nate had gotten together when they were in England and were now in a romantic relationship. Fed up with how much they expressed their romance at night, Haruki had moved rooms and was now ensconced opposite Sebastian's chambers.

Artemus had quizzed Elton and Isabelle the day before, but they'd denied all knowledge of the super soldiers' latest mission. Still, Artemus couldn't shake the feeling that it had something to do with the reason they'd been invited to Rome.

As for the gauntlets, they were the only things that had

occupied his dreams for the past few nights. He was now confident he was meant to make them. He selected three bars, picked up his tools, and walked over to the forge and the anvil.

Sebastian popped his head around the door. "You have a customer."

"Oh. Coming." Otis headed back to the shop.

Smokey hopped inside the room. He jumped on the table and silently watched Artemus work, the glow from the furnace reflected in his dark eyes.

DANIEL LENTON HURRIED THROUGH THE ALLEYWAYS past the Piazza Navona, his leather sandals slapping unevenly against the asphalt. He tugged the lapels of his raincoat close to protect the precious package under his arm.

A cool drizzle was falling across Rome, the first rainfall they'd had in over two weeks. It was a welcome sight for the city, which had been suffering from yet another summer heatwave.

Although he'd known the forecast was for rain, Daniel had become distracted when he'd received the phone call from the small bookstore he usually frequented and had forgotten to take an umbrella. Tucked at the end of a narrow cul de sac west of Municipio I, some half a mile from the Tiber, it was one of his favorite places in the capital; it wasn't on the usual tourist trail and its dusty windows kept most people away. Few knew of the treasures that lurked on the shelves inside.

The owner of the shop had stayed late to give him the book he'd been waiting to get his hands on for the last month and which had arrived in Rome that very evening. Daniel had offered to pay him extra for the trouble, but the old man had refused.

"Let it not be said that I have extracted more money than was necessary from a man of the cloth," he'd said wryly. He'd squinted at Daniel in the soft light of the lamps that dotted the shop. "I don't know what they're putting in the waters at the Vatican these days, but you don't look like you've aged a day in the last decade, Father."

Daniel had smiled vaguely and thanked him for the compliment before hastily taking his leave.

He crossed the Pont Vittorio and soon reached the Via della Conciliazione. The dome of the Basilica glowed in the distance, its spire a symbolic beacon in the night. He glanced at the plain leather watch on his wrist, wiped moisture from his glasses, and hurried past the obelisks that served as the avenue's lampposts, his left leg dragging slightly with his limp.

It was almost curfew.

He'd just stepped across the white line that separated Piazza Pio XII from St. Peter's Square when goosebumps broke out across his nape. Daniel stiffened and stopped. He turned and carefully scanned the piazza behind him.

There were still many tourists about despite the late hour and traffic was moderate on the Road of the Conciliation.

It took but a moment for him to spot the one who did not belong.

A woman stood near the northeast corner of the square some hundred feet from him, under the awning of a gallery. She was alone and standing very still, her attention focused on the Basilica.

Above her head danced wisps of darkness.

Daniel knew they would be invisible to everyone but him.

It was too far to see the woman's eyes. But if he had been a betting man, he would have wagered a lot of money on the fact that her pupils likely gleamed with the occasional sulfurous light.

The demon sensed his stare. She looked over to where he stood.

Though he willed himself to move, Daniel found his feet inexplicably glued to the ground. The line at the edge of St. Peter's Square demarcated not only where Vatican City started and the state of Italy ended, but the outer limit of the divine barrier that protected the Holy See from demonic attacks.

He knew he was safe where he stood.

"You're going to miss the curfew, Father."

Daniel startled and whirled around. A man had appeared beside him. He wore dark trousers, a navy shirt, polished boots, and a long coat.

Where did he come from?

The man's gaze shifted from the woman to Daniel. His eyes were crystal blue and as clear as a lake.

"Do I know you?" Daniel asked hesitantly.

The man smiled faintly. "We have not met before. Now, go."

Daniel found his feet moving again, as if the man's voice were propelling his body forward. He froze a moment later.

Wait! Can he see the demon?!

He twisted on his heels. The man had disappeared. So had the woman.

Daniel stared at the spots they had occupied before reluctantly scurrying along.

The Swiss Guard at the staff entrance sighed when he saw him.

"You're late, Father Lenton. Five more minutes and you would have been locked outside."

"Sorry, Federico. It won't happen again."

The guard grimaced. "You said that last time, Father."

Daniel heaved a sigh of relief when he finally entered the private enclave of Vatican City. He'd always felt more at ease within its grounds and tonight was no different. He crossed the gardens to the ecclesial residences and nodded at the few priests who were still circulating through the corridors of the building while he climbed the stairs to his room.

There was a World Cup match on today and most of the clergy had stayed up late to watch it.

His bedroom was cool and dark when he entered it; he'd left the casement window open that morning to get some fresh air. He switched on the light, deposited the package atop the small desk that constituted his office, and walked past his bed. The heady smell of magnolias washed over him when he reached the windowsill.

A light glowed faintly in the distance opposite, in one of the windows of the Papal apartments to the west.

A faint smile curved Daniel's lips.

Persephone must be reading again.

The smile became a low chuckle when he recalled the stack of books he'd brought her last week. International thrillers were not supposed to be on a Pope's reading list. Persephone had ignored that advice since she came into office and regularly had him sneak her all sorts of novels, to her bishops' blissful ignorance.

Had Daniel agreed to her repeated requests over the years, he too would have been living in the Apostolic Palace. He knew Persephone hadn't completely given up on convincing him to move there.

He closed the window, the smile still on his lips.

An hour later, he turned the final page of the book and sat back in his chair, his face somber. A sigh left his lips.

Another dead end.

The stranger who'd accosted him outside the Vatican came to his mind once more. Daniel frowned.

Who was that man?

CHAPTER SIX

THE GLOW ON THE HORIZON GREW STEADILY BRIGHTER as the minutes ticked by. A warm breeze ruffled Serena's hair where she stood on the upper deck of the research ship, bringing with it the smell of the sea.

"Although I have seen this sight many times, from back when the place was still under the rule of the Kingdom of Sicily, I still find it striking. Naples is incredibly beautiful at night, is it not?"

Serena turned and eyed the man who had appeared from the bridge behind her. He strolled to her side, removed a Cuban cigar from a silver case inside his jacket, and leaned against the railing.

"You're not going to light that?" Serena asked after a short silence.

"Nah," Dimitri Reznak muttered. "I'm trying to quit. My goddaughter keeps telling me it's gonna kill me one day."

"That's ironic."

A smile tilted the corner of Reznak's mouth. "Why, because I'm an Immortal and I'm afraid to die?"

"I was thinking more about the fact that you had a goddaughter."

To her surprise, the Immortal's smile widened. "You've met her, actually, although you may not recall it. And you remind me of her."

Serena raised an eyebrow. "Somehow, I think that would have stuck in my mind. And in what way do I remind you of her?"

"In the way you kill."

Serena digested this candid statement with a faint frown. Shadows shifted on the main deck below. The Immortals making up Reznak's guard were patrolling the ship despite the lateness of the hour.

Serena could hardly blame them.

In the six days since she, Nate, Lou, and Tom had joined Reznak and the team of Immortal Hunters transporting the cargo of priceless cultural artifacts currently making its way to Italy from Libya, their convoy had been attacked four times.

Two of those attacks had been by demons.

Despite their use of holy-water-impregnated, silver-leaded bullets and their advanced fighting skills, several of Reznak's men had lost a life during the assaults. More would have perished had Serena and the other super soldiers not been there.

"I'm glad you agreed to accompany us."

Serena eyed him coolly. "We didn't really have a choice in the matter now, did we?"

Reznak sighed. "Gideon does tend to take our Council's word a bit too literally. My request for assistance wasn't an order."

Serena arched an eyebrow. "Are you saying the accord the Immortals forced the super soldiers to agree to before they granted us our freedom thirteen years ago no longer applies? The one that clearly states that we are duty-bound to help the Immortals if they so command?"

An awkward expression danced across Reznak's face. "Not quite. Look, I know your people don't harbor much goodwill toward us, but that covenant was the only way we managed to convince the Immortal societies to let you go at the time."

An uncomfortable hush fell across the deck.

Serena decided to change the subject. "How long have you guys known about Ba'al?"

For a moment, she thought the Immortal would not answer.

"The name of the organization? Only recently." Reznak rolled the cigar between his fingers. "If you mean demons, we've been aware of the rumors for some time."

"Before Turin?"

Reznak eyed her guardedly. "I take it you mean the first confirmed demonic possession, in 2018?"

Serena dipped her chin.

"As far as we know, demons have only ever been able to take over human hosts. As such, our experience of them is limited. After Turin, the Vatican reached out to us. Knowing of our extensive history, they asked us to search our records for any mentions of unnatural phenomena that could be attributed to those creatures."

"Are the Immortals allied with the Vatican organization tasked with hunting Ba'al?"

Reznak hesitated. "No. We have offered our assistance in other ways, but we are not directly involved in the fight against demons."

Surprise shot through Serena at that. She narrowed her eyes. "Why not? Surely, if Ba'al succeeds in their objective, you will have as much to lose as the rest of us."

Reznak's face turned inscrutable.

Irritation surged through her. "I guess your kind really doesn't care after all. Why get involved if you have nothing to gain from it, right?"

Reznak stiffened at her scathing tone. "It isn't that we don't care. It's because—" he paused, as if struggling internally with himself, "it's not our place to stop Ba'al."

Serena stared. "What do you mean by that?"

"I'm afraid I cannot say any more on the matter," Reznak said firmly.

She mulled over the Immortal's words. Somehow, she couldn't help but feel that he'd just given her a huge clue. She turned and leaned her back against the railing. Her gaze found the star-lit sky above the ship's satellite dishes and antennae.

"A friend of ours will be in Rome tomorrow. You should let him take a look at those relics of yours when we get there," she said quietly.

Reznak studied her for a moment. "One of our experts will be joining us there, actually. He's the most knowledgeable person on the planet when it comes to archaeological treasures."

Lines wrinkled Serena's brow. "How much does your guy know about possible demonic artifacts? Because if Ba'al is after what's in the cargo hold of this ship right now, then you can bet it's not because they want to sell it to some art collector on the black market."

Reznak frowned. "You believe that's why they attacked our convoy?"

Serena gave him a grim look. "Ba'al never does anything without a reason."

CHAPTER SEVEN

A JOLT WOKE ARTEMUS UP. HE BLINKED FUZZILY, yawned, and stretched his arms above his head before looking out of the porthole next to him. Their jet was rolling across the tarmac of Rome's international airport. Gray clouds dominated the landscape outside.

It was raining heavily.

"We're finally here, huh?" He turned and startled when he saw Otis's face in the seat next to him. "What the heck happened to you? You look terrible!"

"How could you sleep through that thunderstorm?" his assistant mumbled, complexion pasty and knuckles white where he gripped his armrests.

"Because he's an idiot, that's how," Drake muttered from across the aisle.

Artemus stared. "What thunderstorm?"

"I feel decidedly queasy," Sebastian declared next to Drake.

"I don't think I'm gonna be able to eat anything for the rest of the week," Callie added weakly from her seat behind them, eyes closed and sweat beading her forehead.

"Seriously, though, what thunderstorm?" Artemus looked down at his lap, where Smokey still slept. "The hellhound seems fine too."

"That's because he's an even bigger idiot than you are," Drake said darkly.

Haruki shot to his feet and headed for the lavatory.

The pilot appeared from the direction of the cockpit.

"I'm sorry about that, sir," he told Sebastian apologetically. "That weather front came out of nowhere."

"It's okay, Harry."

Harry glanced at the lavatory door. The faint sound of hurling echoed from the other side. "Is your friend going to be okay?"

Sebastian sighed. "Yes. He has a somewhat fragile constitution at times."

The storm had delayed their flight by an hour. By the time they cleared immigration and left the airport building, the rain had abated.

A stern-faced man in a dark suit stood waiting for them at the curb. "Mr. Steele and party? Welcome to Rome. I hope you had a pleasant journey despite the weather."

"Are you Captain Rossi?" Artemus asked.

The Vatican officer dipped his chin crisply. "I am indeed."

He glanced down at Smokey.

The rabbit was sitting quietly at the end of the leash Artemus had clasped around his neck, his chocolate eyes gleaming with cute innocence.

From the troubled expression that danced across the policeman's face, news of the hellhound had already reached the Pope's guards.

"Mr. LeBlanc and Her Holiness are awaiting your arrival," Rossi murmured. "Please, wait here a moment."

Elton had traveled to Rome the day before to meet with his contacts at the Vatican. Artemus suspected his mentor had gone ahead as much to scope out what their hosts had in store for them as to connect with his allies.

Although Elton was faithful to the organization leading the fight against Ba'al, Artemus knew he would not let any harm befall him or the others. He frowned at that thought.

Not that they would be able to do much against two angels, three divine beasts, a hellhound, and a currently impotent but powerful seraph.

Four SUVs with tinted windows pulled up beside them shortly. They loaded their luggage in the back and were soon on their way.

"How long is the drive?" Artemus asked Rossi as they headed onto a motorway. He was in the lead vehicle with Otis and Smokey.

"Thirty minutes, give or take a few," the policeman replied curtly. "Traffic will be heavier outside the Holy See."

"Wake me up when we're close."

Artemus dropped his head against the backrest and closed his eyes. He'd been working almost non-stop in the smithy these past few days and his lack of sleep was finally catching up with him.

⁓

HARUKI WATCHED CALLIE FIDDLE WITH HER CELL phone. "You heard from Nate?"

Callie glanced at him distractedly. "No. He got in touch when they landed in Naples last night. He said they would be in Rome today."

She chewed her lower lip anxiously.

"What's wrong?"

Callie hesitated. She looked furtively at their escort in the front seats before shuffling closer to him.

"Nate mentioned something when we spoke," she said in a low voice.

"What?"

"He said that their convoy had suffered several attacks in the last week."

Haruki raised an eyebrow. "Is that unusual? They're mercs. I would have thought that that was part of the territory."

"Two of those attacks were demonic."

Haruki stiffened at the Chimera's words. "Are you sure?"

Callie nodded. "Positive. He and Serena want Artemus to take a look at something. They think the collection they've been tasked to guard may contain—" She stopped abruptly. Her eyes widened. "What is that?"

Haruki frowned. "What are you—?"

That was when he felt it.

DRAKE DRUMMED HIS FINGERS ON HIS KNEE AS HE GAZED out of the vehicle's window. They'd been travelling for a while and were now well inside the boundaries of the Italian capital.

Someone sighed next to him.

He looked around. "What?"

Sebastian eyed Drake's restless hand. "That is rather distracting."

Drake stilled his fingers. "Sorry."

Sebastian met his gaze. "I am surprised. Of the two of you, I thought Artemus would have been the more nervous."

"What do you mean? Why should he be nervous?" Drake frowned. "And, come to think of it, why should *I?*"

"Come now. I know you like to keep your feelings to yourself, but your brother is clearly worried about you, as are we all." Sebastian glanced at the two officers in the front of the vehicle. He dropped his voice. "And you know very well the reason why."

Drake made a face. "Don't worry. If the demon takes over, I'm sure you guys can handle him."

Sebastian scowled. "Do not even jest about that. If Artemus heard you, he would be very—" He faltered. "Drake?"

Drake straightened in his seat. He looked around wildly, trying to pinpoint the source of the evil energy that was suddenly making his skin prickle.

Sebastian drew a sharp breath. He was staring beyond Drake's shoulder, to the south. "What on earth is—?"

Drake twisted around. His stomach dropped. His eyes followed the trajectory of the attack. He jerked forward against his seatbelt, one hand reaching out helplessly even though he knew he would not reach his brother in time.

"*Artemus!*"

CHAPTER EIGHT

ARTEMUS HAD BEEN ASLEEP A GOOD TWENTY MINUTES when a hand suddenly clutched his shoulder. He blinked groggily and looked over at Otis.

Beads of sweat peppered the young man's brow. A glazed expression clouded his eyes. He was staring out of the window past Artemus.

Artemus straightened, fully roused and senses on high alert. "What's wrong?"

Rossi glanced over his shoulder at them, a curious frown wrinkling his brow.

Smokey stirred on Artemus's lap. He rose and propped his front paws against the glass, his nose twitching.

"Something...something is coming," Otis mumbled hoarsely.

Goosebumps broke out across Artemus's skin as he felt the temperature plummet around them. Smokey's eyes flashed red. The hellhound started to transform.

Movement outside the window drew Artemus's startled gaze.

Rossi gasped.

A swirling vortex of darkness swooped down from the sky and slammed into the SUV with a sound like thunder.

There was a sensation of weightlessness. Artemus rose out of the seat as they became airborne, the seat belt digging into his stomach while the world rotated dizzyingly around him. His hands found the roof of the vehicle a second before his head would have cracked against it. The pop of airbags and shocked grunts echoed from up front, the sounds carrying faintly through the roar of the windstorm that had smashed into them.

The end came with a fury that stunned him.

The SUV crashed into something with incredible force. It was as if a giant hand had come down from the Heavens and swatted it in an attempt to deliver some kind of divine retribution. Metal and plastic crumpled. An explosion erupted at the front of the vehicle, the detonation an incandescent bloom of light and noise that tore through the darkness shrouding them.

The fire raced toward Artemus, lightning fast and deadly. He reached to the core of his powers, knowing it would be too late to avoid the flames.

Shit!

The fire never reached him.

Artemus blinked, his heart racing.

He was standing a few feet from the blazing wreckage of the vehicle in his angel form, his divine sword in hand. A low, continuous growl rumbled out of Smokey's throat where he crouched in front of him in his dark hellhound shape.

They were in the middle of a graveyard.

How the—?

"Artemus?" someone said on his left.

He startled and looked around.

A faint light shimmered around Otis where he stood uninjured beside them, the only illumination in the twilight that otherwise surrounded them. Their unconscious escort lay on the grass next to a tombstone behind him, the men's wounds seemingly nominal considering what had just gone down.

"What the hell just happened?!"

"I don't know," Otis murmured. "But whatever it is, it has something to do with *that*."

Artemus followed his assistant's unblinking gaze.

It was Otis's powers that had ultimately protected them, the barrier that shielded the seraph from demonic attacks having seemingly ripped them out of the damaged vehicle in the blink of an eye before expanding to form a bubble some thirty feet in diameter.

Outside that barrier, howling like something possessed, was a writhing wall of living darkness. Intangible shapes appeared fleetingly in the boiling mass. Crimson eyes glared at them with hatred. Mouths and talons snapped and clawed at the divine shield.

Artemus clenched his jaw. Whatever the phenomenon was, it was clearly of demonic origin.

"I have no idea what that is." He unfurled his wings and gripped his sword. A white light appeared on the blade as power flowed from his core to the metal. "But whatever the hell it is, it looks like we're gonna have to fight it to get out of here." He glanced at the hellhound. "Let's go, Cerberus."

Smokey shook himself into his final, three-headed form and followed Artemus as he rose in the air and headed determinedly for the dark mass.

"Er, Artemus," Otis started. "I really don't think you should do—"

Something struck Artemus like a two-ton truck when he left the safety of Otis's defensive shield. Air left him in a harsh grunt as he shot backward.

He landed heavily inside the protective circle, his body carving a deep groove in the grass all the way to Otis's feet. A blurred shape flew out of the storm.

Cerberus dropped down on him a moment later.

"Ouch," Artemus wheezed.

The hellhound shook his three heads and rose unsteadily to his feet, his eyes rolling slightly. He whined, stepped off Artemus, and stared at the enemy surrounding them.

Artemus sat up slowly and rubbed his chest. The only thing that had prevented the invisible force from crushing his flesh was his divine armor. He accepted Otis's hand reluctantly and let his assistant pull him up.

"Did you see what hit you?"

"No." Artemus scowled. "But whatever it is, it's stupidly strong."

Brightness pierced the darkness briefly to their right. Another flash came on their left. A third carved the gloom above their heads.

"It's the others," Otis breathed. "They're trying to break through!"

Artemus's blood thumped rapidly in his veins when he sensed the presence of his twin and the divine beasts across the bond that linked them. A jet of flames tore through the demonic cloud. He caught a glimpse of Haruki and Callie in their beast forms through the jagged opening.

They were combining their flames to blast a passage into the storm.

Several of Sebastian's lightning balls zoomed inside the

hole, the spheres slowly carving it wider as they spun and rotated against the pulsing walls of darkness. A shadowy figure flashed into view.

DRAKE FLAPPED HIS WINGS AND GAINED ALTITUDE. THE red flames on his sword grew larger and brighter, the blaze matching the anger and fear twisting through him.

The vortex had carried Artemus's SUV some two hundred feet from the road and into a cemetery next to a church. Horns honked on the avenue to his right, traffic having ground to a halt following the incident; three other vehicles and a motorbike had been caught in the fray, sending debris scattering across the asphalt. He could hear panicked shouts and the distant blare of ambulance sirens as he hovered in mid-air and faced the swirling dome of shadows, the trees in the church grounds shielding him and the others from curious eyes.

The Vatican officers who made up their guard stood helplessly some dozen feet from where Callie and Haruki were attacking the phenomenon with their divine flames.

"I'm going in!" Drake yelled.

"Be careful!" Sebastian called out where he hovered below him, eagle wings thrumming the air steadily and eyes blazing bright with power.

Drake tucked his black wings and dove for the gap the divine beasts had created.

His ears popped when he entered the storm. A sickening sensation gripped him as a corrupt force rippled across his flesh, resonating with the demon who dwelled inside his soul.

This felt different from the demonic energy that normally triggered his dark side.

Drake clenched his jaw, his knuckles whitening on the handle of his blade.

Not today, asshole.

He took a deep breath and plunged into the vortex.

A gasp left his lips as a thunderous wave of pressure crashed down upon him, ripping him from the air and dragging him into the depths of an inky ocean. Ghostly hands snatched at his armor. Distorted faces swam in and out of view around him. Garbled voices howled in his ears.

It was like being attacked by an enemy without substance.

As he was tossed violently about by the supernatural power at the heart of the storm, Drake realized the manifestations were staying well clear of his sword.

He blinked. *The flames!*

Drake gritted his teeth and reached inside himself, his heart hammering against his ribs. The runes on his shield flared crimson and gold as his power expanded. Fire exploded on his broadsword, lighting up the gloom.

He clamped down on the bloodlust rising from the depths of his soul and swung the weapon.

The flames carved through the apparitions. They shrieked and warped violently before fading to shrinking tendrils of darkness.

A savage smile twisted Drake's lips.

Hang in there, brother! I'm coming!

He started to clear the darkness, foot by slow foot.

By the time he and the divine beasts had destroyed the vortex, the rain had started to fall again. It doused the fires in the wreckage of the SUV and the vehicles burning on the road, sending black smoke spiraling into the gray skies.

CHAPTER NINE

"NEWS REPORTS ARE COMING IN ABOUT A SUSPECTED terrorist attack on the Via Aurelia, just over two miles from Vatican City. Our reporter Gianni Greco is in the air over the area where the incident took place an hour ago."

The man sipped his Chianti before carefully slicing off a piece of the tender venison on his plate and popping it in his mouth. He chewed slowly, a sliver of blood oozing from the rare meat and slipping down his gullet as he watched the TV on the wall ahead of him.

The news reporter and the studio background were replaced by the camera feed from a circling helicopter.

"This is Gianni Greco reporting live from the scene of the mysterious attack that happened this afternoon on this busy avenue."

A chaotic scene unfolded across the screen. Ten firetrucks and half a dozen ambulances came into view. They were blocking the road outside a church. The darkened carcasses of several vehicles dotted the asphalt around them.

"Witnesses report seeing a large, black cloud descend from the sky before lifting a motorbike and several cars across the road. One of them crashed into a nearby cemetery."

The helicopter moved closer to the church.

"If you look carefully through the trees, you will see the giant circle impacted in the ground, along with what remains of the vehicle. Despite the ferocity of what happened here today, there have miraculously been no fatalities. So far no terrorist organizations have laid claim to the attack."

The man smiled faintly at that. He waved a hand. The TV switched itself off.

The cell phone next to his glass vibrated with an incoming call. Amusement darted through the man when he saw the number on the display. He tapped the screen.

"I take it you were behind that attack?" the voice at the other end of the line said without preamble.

The man took another sip of his wine before replying. "Yes, I was. I'm surprised you didn't call earlier."

"The Vatican has been somewhat busy." The caller sighed. "I suspected you might try something like this." He paused. "So, how did you find them?"

"They were...interesting," the man mused. "I doubt they knew what was going on, but it didn't take them long to realize how to fight the spirit cloud."

"They used fire," the caller murmured.

"Yes. And the seraph was most intriguing. Although he did not manifest his full form, his divine shield protected Artemus Steele and the hellhound from my attack."

"Have your guests arrived yet?"

"They should be with me within the hour. The Via Aurelia incident caused a bit of traffic on the ring road.

What about you? Any further insight into who our mysterious Guardian might be?"

"Not yet," the caller said with a grunt. "But I have no doubt that what you're planning will draw him out." A low mumble of voices came in the background. "I have to go. They just got here."

ARTEMUS STEPPED OUT OF THE BACK OF THE VATICAN Gendarmerie van.

Drake and Otis came out after him. The others joined them from the second van. They studied the four-story building surrounding them with wary stares.

They were in the courtyard of the Apostolic Palace. A dull roar came from St. Peter's Square to the west, where crowds of tourists and the faithful circulated despite the drizzle soaking the city.

Artemus wondered whether some were there to try and peek at the VIPs who had just been escorted inside the private Vatican enclave. A weary sigh left him. Of all the ways he'd thought they'd be making their entrance to the Vatican, being ushered in by a cavalcade of police cars wasn't one of them. His gaze found the group of men standing under a portico up ahead, their purple cassocks bright in the gray light.

"That's a lot of bishops," Drake muttered.

Artemus ignored the clergymen for a moment and observed what he suspected was an inordinate number of Swiss guards and police officers around them. Security had evidently been tightened up since news of what had taken place an hour ago had reached Vatican officials.

Haruki had overheard Captain Rossi on the phone as

the man was being wheeled away on a gurney and into the back of an ambulance at the scene of the attack. The captain and the driver of their SUV had no recollection of what had happened after the storm had struck their vehicle, or the battle that had subsequently been fought to rescue them. His men, however, did. One of them had filmed the entire thing on his cell and shown it to Rossi before he was taken away.

From the guarded expressions on the faces of the guards and officers around them, the news of their prowess had already spread among the corps.

Artemus grimaced.

I'm not sure whether it's respect or fear that I'm seeing on their faces.

Even though Drake had told him that the only way he and the others had managed to win the fight was by using the divine flames that formed part of their powers, Artemus was still shaken by the fact that he and Smokey had had to be rescued at all. He was aware that Callie, Haruki, and even Drake's fiery abilities were different from the light that wrapped around his weapon in its ultimate form. Unlike them, or even Sebastian, whose lightning balls mimicked their blaze, he could not generate divine flames on his body.

Artemus could tell from Smokey's subdued demeanor that he too felt the sting of having had to be saved by their friends. They were both powerful in their own right. Today, they had both been helpless in the face of their enemy.

"The barrier around this place is impressive," Sebastian murmured.

Artemus startled. "There's a barrier protecting the palace?"

"Not just the palace," Sebastian said thoughtfully. "I believe it covers the entire territory of Vatican City." He paused. "It is as strong as, if not stronger than, the one that surrounds the mansion in Chicago."

Someone came out of the building and marched rapidly past the bishops.

Elton slowed as he drew close to their group.

"Are you okay?" he asked stiffly, his anxious gaze roaming their faces.

Artemus rubbed the back of his head with an awkward expression. "Yeah. We're fine. The only thing that's bruised is my ego."

Relief and guilt darkened Elton's eyes in equal measure. "I'm sorry. If I'd known this would happen, I wouldn't have pushed you to come to Rome."

"It's not as if you put a gun to our head, Elton," Callie murmured.

One of the clergymen came forward. Elton made the introductions.

"Artemus, this is Archbishop Holmes. He's my main contact at the Vatican."

"It's a pleasure to finally meet you, Mr. Steele."

Artemus shook the elderly man's hand. "The pleasure is mine. Elton has told me a lot about you."

The Archbishop smiled. "All good things, I hope." His gaze wandered to the figures behind Artemus and the rabbit by his feet. "Pope DaSilva is most keen to meet you all. Come."

They were introduced to the rest of the clergymen who formed the welcome party before being led inside the palace. Artemus's tension eased as he observed the breathtaking interior of the building. The sheer scale of the priceless Renaissance features and furnishings around them were making his fingers itch. He sensed faint traces of divine energy from many of the artifacts crowding the rooms they passed and wondered at their origins. He could tell from Elton's expression that he was similarly yearning to explore the religious relics on display around them.

They came to a gilded elevator and were soon on their way to the top floor of the palace.

The Pope's private apartments were more welcoming than he'd anticipated. According to Elton, each pontiff was allowed to decorate the formal residence according to their personal tastes once they came into office.

Pope DaSilva evidently liked bright colors.

The antechamber outside the Pope's study was as heavily guarded as the rest of the building.

Bishop Irons stood waiting for them at the door, his expression solemn. "If you'd like to follow me."

A sudden bout of nervousness shot through Artemus as they headed after the bishop. Although he'd tried not to dwell on it, he knew the invitation to Rome was a serious attempt by the Vatican to get to know their most powerful allies in the war against Ba'al. And the woman they were about to meet was the leader of that organization.

His first impression of the room they entered was of soft light bathing pale walls and a cream, marble floor dotted with dark wood furniture.

Seated at a desk on the opposite side of the expansive floor, her figure nearly dwarfed by the enormous chair upon which she sat, was a wiry woman with a shock of gray-peppered auburn hair pulled up in a bun. She was dressed in a white cassock and was bent over some paper-work, her ink pen moving swiftly as she wrote. She paused when she sensed their presence and looked up.

The faint frown clouding her brow cleared and her green eyes brightened. "Ah. You're finally here."

CHAPTER TEN

THE POPE'S GAZE SHIFTED TO BISHOP IRONS. "THANK you, Bishop. You may leave us. Father Lenton, do stay."

Bishop Irons bowed his head and exited the room. Artemus blinked and looked to the left.

He hadn't noticed the dark-haired, bespectacled man in the black cassock sitting quietly at a desk behind an arrangement of cream, silk-lined, cushioned chairs.

Elton cleared his throat and took a step forward. "Your Holiness, this is Artemus—"

The Pope waved her hand and smiled. "Bah. I told you to call me Persephone, Elton. I don't want us to stand on formalities when we're in private."

Artemus's eyes bugged out slightly.

Elton flushed. "I'm afraid that's impossible, Your Holiness. I cannot be so forward."

The Pope's smile faded. "Goodness, don't tell me you're going to act all prim and proper, like those bishops out there." She sighed. "I swear, there are days when I wish they'd remove the giant stick they have shoved up their collective bottoms. I bet some of those old codgers would be right fun if only they'd let their hair down once in a while."

Sebastian made a strangled sound. Callie and Haruki's jaws dropped open. Drake's lips twitched. Otis gaped. Elton stared, his expression a mix of shock and horror.

Father Lenton sighed. "Perse—I mean, Your Holiness. Maybe you should stand on formalities after all. Your guests look, well—" he glanced their way, "—traumatized, for want of a better word."

Surprise bolted through Artemus at his casual address.

Are they close?

The Pope looked momentarily guilty. "What? I'm only saying what you think too."

The priest's face grew pinched. "I have never said anything about sticks and their nether areas."

"Just be grateful I didn't use the word ass, Daniel."

She rose and came around the desk.

Artemus's gaze dropped. It stayed there.

The Pope slowed to a stop in the face of their frozen stares. She looked down. "Oh. I forgot to change them for the official slippers." A sheepish grimace twisted her mouth. She scratched her cheek lightly. "Ah, well. It's too late now. The bunny is out of the bag. At least Irons isn't here. He'd tell me off for sure."

She wriggled her toes. The ears of her pink rabbit slippers danced with her movements.

Instinct made Artemus glance to his right. Smokey had straightened on his haunches and was staring intently at the Pope's footwear.

She registered the hellhound's keen interest. "Does he like the slippers?"

Smokey's thoughts drifted through Artemus's mind. He made a face. "In a way, yes."

"Wow," Haruki muttered. "That's one sick rabbit."

"Maybe it's jetlag," Callie mumbled, abashed.

Drake rolled his eyes. Otis looked mortified.

"What?" Elton asked, puzzled.

Sebastian folded his arms across his chest and glared at the hellhound, his eyes flashing faintly with a hint of his power. "I swear on everything that is holy, brother. If you hump her feet, I *will* disown you."

The Pope stared before bursting out laughing.

DANIEL SAT FROZEN AT THE DESK, PERSEPHONE'S chuckles ringing in his ears. His heart throbbed wildly in his chest.

For a moment, he was back in that small apartment in Kiev, on the day his world had changed forever. The day he had briefly become something else. Something that didn't belong to this plane of existence.

The creature whose presence he had felt so keenly during those breathless minutes in his aunt's bathroom when he'd defended her against his uncle had disappeared just as swiftly as it had manifested itself.

In the years that had followed, as he was moved from one orphanage to another across the country, his every relocation taking him farther and farther away from the prison where his aunt had been sentenced to life imprisonment for the manslaughter of her husband, Daniel had tried in vain to summon the beast he'd transformed into that day so he could save her again.

For a beast it had undoubtedly been. And he knew it was capable of doing things he could only dream of.

The raw, savage power that had filled his frail, eight-year-old body that day still echoed in his consciousness, a memory that was as sweet as it was bitter. Because in that timeless moment, he had been in full possession of his disease-ridden limbs. As fire had consumed the monster who had taken possession of his uncle, Daniel had caught the briefest glimpse of the creature whose wondrous energy had swept through his human form. He should have been terrified of the shape he'd discerned. Instead, he'd found himself utterly enthralled.

The beast was as beautiful as it was terrifying.

But when his aunt had finally died all alone in her austere prison cell, her body ravaged by cancer brought on by the chemicals she'd been exposed to at the factory where she'd worked, Daniel's fascination with the creature had slowly turned to resentment. And as decades passed and he aged with a slowness that defied time, his resentment had turned to loathing. For he knew the beast was at fault for his aberrant lifespan.

Now, for the first time in almost a century, Daniel could feel the creature's presence again. He realized two things in that shocking moment.

The beast had never left him.

And the reason it had made its existence known to him again just now had everything to do with the men and the woman who had been personally invited to Rome by Persephone. The ones who had fought demons one-on-one and who were considered Ba'al's greatest threat.

Artemus Steele, Callie Stone, Drake Hunter, Otis Boone, and Sebastian Lancaster. Their names, which he'd memorized as part of his duties in anticipation of hosting Persephone's guests, now resonated in his mind.

The rabbit, whom he knew was named Smokey, turned his head, his chocolate gaze locking unerringly on him.

And then there's, well—that.

"Now, show me your weapon."

Daniel's attention focused sharply back on the conversation. Persephone was staring somewhere south of Artemus's belt.

The blond man opened and closed his mouth soundlessly, his face so horrified Daniel found himself biting his lip to stop from laughing out loud.

"What's wrong?" Persephone's puzzled expression gradually cleared. "Good Heavens. Young man, I will have you know that I swore a vow of chastity when I was seventeen. You may be a handsome fellow, but not enough for me to break two hundred years of celibacy." Her gaze moved. "Your brother, on the other hand..."

Drake's eyes widened with something akin to terror.

Callie turned slightly, her shoulders trembling. Haruki covered his mouth with a hand and stared intently at the floor, his shoulders similarly shaking. Otis gaped. Elton looked like he was going to pass out any minute. Sebastian scowled disapprovingly.

"I'm pulling your leg." Persephone smiled. "That stiff Englishman over there is actually more my type."

The color drained out of Sebastian's face.

"No offence, Mr. Kuroda, Mr. Boone, Mr. LeBlanc," Persephone added with diplomatic aplomb.

"None taken," Haruki managed in a strangled voice.

"Er," Otis mumbled.

Elton waved a hand vaguely, too speechless to utter a single protest.

"Now, let's see the weapon," Persephone repeated.

"What weapon?" Artemus asked hoarsely.

Persephone sighed and gave the blond man the look

she usually reserved for imbeciles. "The Sword of Michael, obviously."

Artemus blinked, as if something had just sunk in. Suspicion darkened his eyes the next instant.

"Wait. Did you just say two hundred years of celibacy?!"

CHAPTER ELEVEN

THEY TURNED ONTO THE ACCESS ROAD BEHIND THE exhibition center, checked through security, and pulled to a stop inside a large delivery area.

Serena climbed down from the cabin of the lead truck with Lou, her gaze sweeping the courtyard around them. They were joined by Nate, Tom, Reznak, and the Immortal Hunters, the latter fanning out to stand watch over the precious cargo in the back of the trucks.

Reznak had overseen an agreement between the head of his security team and Lou a few days ago. The Immortals would defer to the super soldiers during an attack; otherwise, they would command their guard when it came to defense measures around the artifacts they were protecting.

To Serena's surprise, the Immortals had not begrudged her and the others leading their team during the assaults they had so far suffered. It was evident she and Nate had the most experience fighting demons of all of them and it appeared the Immortals wished to learn those battle skills. They were also keen to know more about the nanorobot, liquid-armor tactical suits Gideon had made for them.

From what Reznak had briefly mentioned, it seemed the Immortal societies were interested in commissioning Gideon to mass-produce the suits for them.

It was a strange situation to be in, as Tom had commented the night before.

"It feels weird," he had murmured across their comm link.

He, Serena, and Nate had been standing guard on the grounds of the property where they were staying the night, in Naples.

"We've spent all of our lives resenting the Immortals for what they did to us. We've always believed they regard us with nothing but contempt. But these guys are...well, they're kind of okay. The fact that they want us to teach them how to fight demons is pretty damn flattering."

Serena had stayed silent at that.

"It's because of him," Nate had finally said.

"Who do you mean?" Tom had asked quizzically.

"He's talking about Reznak," Serena had muttered. "I get the feeling that man could charm a snake. He's a born diplomat if I ever saw one." She had paused then. "He's careful about whom he employs. He's not into douchebags."

"One of his guards told me something last night," Tom had said, his tone unusually serious. "Apparently, Reznak is one of the people who brokered the treaty that ended the war between the two Immortal societies during the four-teenth century. I think that's why his men respect him so much."

"So, he's a peacemaker," Serena had mused. "That role suits him."

"He's also one of the Immortals who argued vocally for our independence," Nate had said.

"He is?" Tom had sounded shocked.

"Yeah. Their team leader mentioned it to me a couple of days back."

"So did our father," Serena had said brusquely. "It still took the Immortal societies years to come to that accord."

"To be fair, most of us were still kids at the time," Tom had said. "They couldn't exactly kick us out into the world without looking like utter bastards."

Serena had frowned. "I'm not denying that Reznak is one of the good guys. But I can't help but feel that he's hiding something from us."

"What kind of something?"

"The kind that has to do with demons."

A voice called out to them, bringing her sharply back to the present.

"I'm so glad to see you made it safely to Rome. Welcome to our fair capital."

Serena turned and studied the elegant man crossing the courtyard toward them.

"Mr. Bach, I presume." Reznak shook the curator's hand. "This is quite the place you have here."

He indicated the enormous steel, concrete, and glass complex rising around them with an admiring look.

The exhibition center was nearly as big as the Metropolitan Museum of Art and covered just over six hundred thousand square feet of prime real estate in central Rome. A decade old, it had already hosted some of the most extensive art and archeological shows the world had ever seen under one roof.

"Thank you." The man smiled. "And, please, call me Lionel. Would you care for a rest and some refreshments before we look over your consignment and talk about the exhibition?"

"Sure. My men will stay here, if you don't mind."

Bach glanced at the super soldiers and the Immortal guards. "Of course."

"Is Professor Jackson here yet?"

Bach dipped his chin. "He arrived an hour ago."

Footsteps sounded to the right. A man came out of a loading bay door and jumped lightly to the ground. He was tall and handsome, with dark blond hair and ice-blue eyes.

Serena stiffened.

Reznak brightened up. "Zachary. You should have called." His face fell as he studied the man's dusty boots. "Don't tell me you were still in Nepal? I thought you packed up and went back to New York a week ago."

The man gave Reznak a quick hug and a hearty pat on the back. "Yeah, well, something came up. If it wasn't for Alexa reminding me of my flight, I wouldn't have made it today."

Serena glanced at Nate and Lou. She was unsurprised to see the shocked expressions on their faces. Tom had only been eighteen months old when they were rescued in Greenland. She and the other two had been old enough to recall all that had happened on that ungodly night.

And there, standing in front of them, looking not a single day older than he did twenty-two years ago, was one of the men who had been directly involved in their rescue.

～

"You're the offspring of a pureblood Immortal and a human?" Artemus said leadenly.

"Yes."

Persephone's attention returned to the Sword of Michael. It was currently devoid of flames and looked disarmingly safe.

Drake was surprised the coffee table hadn't collapsed under its weight.

"Can I hold it?" Persephone asked.

"It's heavy," Artemus warned. "So, what's a pureblood Immortal?"

A grunt left Persephone as she tried to lift the broadsword. "It *is* heavy." She sighed and let go of the weapon. "A pureblood Immortal is one whose bloodline can be traced directly to the original Immortals. They are Immortal royalty, in a sense."

"I didn't realize the Immortal societies had such a complex hierarchy," Sebastian murmured.

"Oh, their history is quite fascinating," Persephone explained enthusiastically. "The first Immortals ruled over one of the largest empires in the world. They built their kingdom on the skulls of thousands of their enemies and shed enough blood over the centuries to fill a sea."

"That sounds gruesome," Callie mumbled.

"An offspring of a pureblood Immortal and a human is also an Immortal?" Haruki said, puzzled.

"Not quite. We are as mortal as any human. But we have a longer life span."

Persephone glanced at Daniel.

Drake did not miss the exchange. *Ah.*

"Are you the same?" Sebastian asked the priest before Drake could voice the very same question.

"That's a bit bold," Elton told Sebastian with a frown.

Daniel's face remained inscrutable.

Persephone looked unperturbed by the query. "What makes you think Daniel is the same?"

"One, you're talking about this in front of him. Two, his limp. He suffered from polio as a child, did he not?" Sebastian observed Daniel with a shrewd expression. "Polio was eradicated from Europe over four decades ago. He does not look a day past thirty."

The priest narrowed his eyes slightly at that.

Drake stared. *Not so emotionless after all.*

He wondered if the others could sense it.

Daniel Lenton was a man who was trying his damnedest to fade into the shadows. To make himself as inconspicuous as he possibly could. His impassive face and muted demeanor helped him accomplish this to a large extent, to the point Drake doubted he would remember the man if he passed him in the street. Still, he couldn't help but feel that there was more to the priest than met the eye. That somebody else existed behind the wooden facade, and the black cassock and crucifix.

"You are correct," Persephone admitted with a dip of her chin. "We suspect Daniel's father was a pureblood Immortal too."

Drake arched an eyebrow. "Suspect?"

"I was born out of wedlock," Daniel replied in Persephone's stead, his tone cool. "My mother never revealed the name of my father to my aunt before her death."

His words echoed uncomfortably around the room.

"Why don't you have a rest before supper?" Persephone said brightly to Artemus and the others. "Daniel, I hope you will join us."

Surprise flashed on the priest's face for a moment. He masked the emotion in the next instant. "I don't think that's a good idea."

"I believe you meant to say, '*Yes, your Holiness. As you wish,*'" Persephone said sharply. "Considering you're going to be their guide this week, don't you think it would be best if you got to know one another?"

The priest gaped.

He recovered his composure, his mouth thinning to a disapproving line. "I'm afraid I will have to decline that request. I am too busy with Holy See affairs to—"

"Daniel," Persephone warned in a voice laced with steel.

The priest stopped. For a moment, Drake thought he would argue his case and refuse a direct order from his superior.

The man's eyes grew inscrutable once more. "Yes, your Holiness. As you wish."

CHAPTER TWELVE

SERENA AND NATE WATCHED THE STAFF TAKING inventory of the artifacts Reznak had brought for the exhibition that would be taking place in three days. It was late afternoon and the crates containing the relics Reznak had unearthed in Libya a month ago had finally been moved from the trucks to one of the processing areas at the rear of the exhibition center.

"I didn't think we'd ever see him again," Nate murmured.

Serena followed his gaze to Jackson, who stood talking animatedly with Reznak and Bach some thirty feet away. "Neither did I."

Tom had been stunned when they'd told him about Jackson's presence in Greenland twenty-two years ago.

"So, he's an Immortal?"

"Sure looks like it," Lou had said. "I'm kinda surprised, though."

"Why?"

"He doesn't give off an Immortal vibe."

Serena knew what Lou meant. Immortals had a certain demeanor and a look about their eyes that often gave them away. Their faces usually held a wariness that spoke of years of experience and lifetimes lived, not all of them good.

Jackson displayed none of that. He was fresh, in a preppy kind of way, and his passion for his work was evident in his clear gaze and his smile.

"I guess he doesn't recognize us," Nate said.

Serena thought she detected a trace of disappointment in Nate's voice. "Well, we were children at the time."

What she didn't tell him was that she'd caught Jackson looking at them furtively on several occasions. The man was reputed to have an eidetic memory. She'd be willing to wager a lot of money that he knew who they were.

Her smartband dinged with an incoming message.

"Is that Drake?" Nate asked.

"No." Serena frowned as she read the words on the display. "It's Gideon. He wants to talk."

Nate studied the crowd. "You might want to take this somewhere private."

Serena strolled out of the processing bay, found a quiet spot outside, and called Gideon. "What's up?"

"How's the mission going?" Gideon asked.

Serena pursed her lips. "Is that really why you're calling?"

"I was trying to make small talk."

"You suck at it. Get to the point."

Gideon sighed. "Someone I know just spotted some first-generation super soldiers."

Serena tensed. "Where?"

"Well, seeing as I'm calling you, I thought the answer

to that would be obvious," he said drily. There was a pause. "Serena, you still there?"

"I am. I was counting to five." She narrowed her eyes. "So, they're in Rome?"

"Yeah. Something tells me it's got to do with why you're there."

"You mean the exhibition?"

"Possibly. But I mostly meant your friends at the Vatican."

"How do you know about that?" Suspicion made Serena scowl. "Goddammit, Gideon! You had better not be monitoring our calls!"

"That accusation offends me highly."

"Then how did you know Artemus and the others were in Rome?"

"Shockingly enough, I have contacts in the Vatican too. Let Reznak know about the super soldiers. And, Serena?"

"What?"

"Be careful. We know how Ba'al operates. Our EMP devices may no longer be effective against them."

Unease stirred inside Serena as she headed slowly back inside the building. She checked her messages. There were no new ones.

Where the hell are you guys?

~

"I REALLY DON'T THINK WE SHOULD BE DOING THIS," Daniel protested stiffly.

"Relax," Artemus said. "We'll be back in time for dinner. Besides, you're supposed to be our guide, aren't you?"

They were in an SUV with tinted windows, headed into the center of Rome.

"Where are we going?" The priest's gaze moved briefly to the busy scenery unfolding outside before locking on Drake's reflection in the rearview mirror. "And how did you manage to convince one of the gendarmerie officers to lend you this vehicle?"

"I can be quite persuasive," Drake said from the driver's seat.

A dubious look came over Daniel. "I don't believe any amount of persuasion would convince an officer of the Corps to give you his car keys."

Callie smiled where she sat on the other side of the priest.

"There is nothing funny about this situation, Mrs. Stone," Daniel said coolly.

"Oh, I'm not smiling about that." Her eyes sparkled with mirth. "You just remind me of Sebastian when we first met him. He was prissy as hell."

"I was not prissy," Sebastian protested from the front passenger seat.

"You still are," Drake drawled. "If you were any more straight-laced, we could use you as a lightning rod."

Artemus grinned.

Now that they were out of Vatican City, he felt more relaxed than he'd been all afternoon.

Maybe it's all that religion concentrated in a small space.

There was a heaviness inside the Holy See, as if centuries of solemn duties and rigid adherence to protocols had rendered the institution stale. Persephone was the only breath of fresh air in the place. Although he'd wondered at the fact that a female archbishop had been elected as the head of the Catholic Church, meeting her in person had made Artemus realize that she was exactly what the organization needed to fight Ba'al. He had little doubt in his mind that it was thanks to Persephone that the Vatican group leading the battle against the demons had been formed in the first place and had gained allies so quickly.

The woman was a force of nature.

Otis had elected to stay in Vatican City while Artemus and the rest took a road trip, the seraph keen to talk to the Vatican experts who'd been studying his mother's journals. Artemus had asked Haruki and Smokey to keep him company. They still didn't know who lay behind the attack earlier that day and Artemus had decided it would be wise if none of them were on their own while they were in potential enemy territory, especially Otis whilst he was still unable to draw on the formidable powers of the seraph at will.

Artemus frowned.

We may already have crossed paths with Ba'al's mole for all we know.

He'd asked Persephone earlier about the Vatican's investigation into the identity of the person leaking vital information to the demons. Since most of the clergymen who made up her immediate council and her close staff were the offspring of an Immortal and human coupling, the Pope had been pretty adamant it wasn't someone in her innermost circle of confidants.

The fading sunlight glinted on the walls of a glass structure some half a mile ahead.

Surprise dawned on Daniel's face. "We're going to the exhibition center?"

"Yeah," Drake replied. "Some friends asked us to meet them there."

He turned onto a narrow one-way street.

"By the way, what does the J stand for?" Artemus asked the priest curiously.

He indicated the initials on the simple crucifix hanging around the man's neck.

Daniel hesitated. "My middle name is Judah."

They were almost at the end of the road when a black van suddenly pulled across the exit.

Drake stepped on the brakes, sending them rocking forward against their seat belts as the SUV screeched to a stop.

"What the hell is that guy doing?"

The back of Artemus's neck prickled. He'd just sensed a subtle change in the air pressure. From the way Callie stiffened, so had she.

He turned and looked back the way they'd come. "Drake?"

"Yeah?"

"We're blocked in."

His brother glanced at the side mirror and cursed.

A black van had parked across the entrance to the street. The side doors of the two vehicles slid open. Artemus's stomach lurched when he saw the figures who stepped out.

"Bugger," Sebastian said leadenly.

"I believe the expression you're really looking for is 'Fuck,'" Callie muttered.

Daniel cast a disapproving look her way before turning to Artemus. "What's going on?"

Guilt twisted through Artemus at the confusion on the priest's face.

Damnit. If I knew this was gonna happen, I wouldn't have forced him to tag along.

"Stay in the car, Father Lenton."

Artemus stepped out of the SUV with Drake, Sebastian, and Callie.

They reached for their weapons just as the super soldiers started toward them.

CHAPTER THIRTEEN

"THEY'RE LATE."

"It's probably just traffic."

Even though Nate's tone was mild, Serena could see the anxiety coursing through her reflected in his eyes.

"Drake's driving." Her mouth thinned to a disapproving line. "That guy has no respect for road etiquette."

Nate maintained a diplomatic silence.

They were standing at the exhibition center's west security gates, where they'd arranged to meet Artemus and the others.

"So, how are things with you and Callie?" Serena asked after a while.

"They're...good. Really good."

She smiled faintly. "I'm happy for you."

"Thanks." Nate hesitated, his expression uncertain. "What about you and Drake?"

Serena blinked, surprised. "What do you mean?"

Nate studied her for a moment. "Forget I mentioned it."

"That's gonna be difficult." Serena frowned at the gathering twilight. "There's nothing going on between me and Drake. I don't get why Lou and you think otherwise."

Nate sighed.

Serena's eyes narrowed into slits. "Explain that sigh."

Her smartband beeped. She froze when she saw the message on the display. A live video popped up next to it. Her heart clenched with alarm.

"What's wrong?" Nate asked tensely.

Rapid footsteps sounded at their backs. They turned.

Lou and Tom were headed swiftly for them.

"Reznak just got some intel on those first-generation super soldiers Gideon told us about," Lou said grimly. "They're fighting some people a few streets from here."

"It's Artemus and the others!" Serena said.

She removed a black disc from her pocket, slapped it on her chest, and depressed the button in the center. Her nanorobot, liquid-armor combat suit unfurled, encasing her entire body in a handful of seconds.

She was running before Nate, Lou, and Tom had engaged their own tactical suits, the enhanced satellite video Gideon had just sent of the battle unfolding a short distance away driving her forward.

Drake, Artemus, Callie, and Sebastian had assumed their full forms to fight the super soldiers who'd ambushed them.

A flash of light dispelled the growing darkness beyond the rooftops to the right. Serena reached the corner of the street and accelerated in that direction, her pulse hammering in her veins.

The range of the EMP device Gideon had created to neutralize the first-generation super soldiers was five hundred feet. She was still too far away to activate it.

Hang in there, you guys!

CALLIE BLOCKED A DEADLY BLOW TO HER BELLY. Something sliced across the back of her left hand. Blood bloomed on her skin. The snakes making up her mane hissed in anger.

She scowled at the razor-sharp, nanorobot spear protruding from the palm of the blank-faced super soldier demon who'd attacked her, inhaled deeply, and released a jet of fire from her jaws.

Her flames engulfed the creature, searing his skin and flesh. He was still standing when the blaze abated a moment later, his liquid-silver eyes impassive. The burns on his body healed even as she watched, the nanorobots inside him working seamlessly to remake the damaged tissue.

A fiery whip hummed past Callie. The triple cords wrapped around the demon's neck, scorching crimson lines across his throat. Sebastian beat his powerful eagle wings and bore the creature up with a grunt. He rose some thirty feet before casting his prisoner violently into the side of a building.

A boom shook the air as the demon crashed into the structure. The impact carved a ten-foot crater into the concrete and sent cracks snaking along its wall. The creature fell toward the ground amidst a cloud of debris and smashed head-first into the roof of a car.

The vehicle crumpled as if it were made of paper. An alarm pierced the twilight.

Callie stared. "Are you kidding me?!"

The demon was pushing himself back up onto his hands and knees.

Sebastian scowled. "These men are stronger than the super soldiers we fought in England."

"Can you rift us out of here?" Artemus shouted as he dove and slashed at another super soldier.

Sebastian clenched his jaw. "I already tried. Something is stopping me."

The demon climbed off the wreckage of the car and swayed unsteadily for a moment before heading purposefully toward them, his pace gathering momentum.

DRAKE SMASHED SHOULDER-FIRST INTO A SUPER SOLDIER demon and carried him across the road and into the front window of a flower shop. Glass exploded around them as they flew inside. They plowed into rows of shelves, crashed through a plasterboard wall, and fetched up hard against a cold storage unit in a workshop at the back of the store, a trail of broken clay, dirt, and plants littering the ground in their wake.

A whimper reached Drake's ears as he rose to his feet. He glanced at the ashen-faced couple cowering under a table to his right.

"Get out of here!"

Air shifted in front of his face.

Drake cursed and raised his shield. The talons headed for his eyes collided with the dark, rune-covered metal in a shower of sparks inches from his face.

Damn! He's fast!

He swung his broadsword low. The weapon struck the demon's left calf, carving a shallow gash in his flesh.

And he's tough as nails. That should have cut his limb to the bone.

Drake took a step back and appraised the enemy with narrowed eyes. There was no doubt about it. These super soldiers were different from the ones they'd encountered during their last battle with Ba'al.

Drake took a shallow breath.

He had no option but to draw on his full powers if he wanted to defeat them.

TREPIDATION FLOODED ARTEMUS WHEN HE FELT HIS brother's energy surge across their bond, his twin's life force laced with echoes of darkness from the devil trapped inside his soul.

What are you doing?!

Drake's voice reached his mind. *We will not win this fight if we don't use everything we have!*

Shit. Artemus gritted his teeth. He knew Drake was right. *Just...don't lose yourself to that demon!*

I won't.

Artemus bent his knees and shot into the air with a snarl. The two super soldiers who'd been clawing at his back fell away as he rose, their bodies smashing into the parked vehicles that crowded one side of the street.

They were on their feet in seconds.

Artemus flapped his wings and continued to ascend until he reached the level of the rooftops.

The demons' blank faces followed his every move.

At least these bastards can't fly.

He could tell these first-generation super soldiers were unlike the cohort he and the others had fought recently. But it wasn't just that observation that was causing unease to fill his veins.

Despite the violence of the battle that was taking place beneath him and the explosions caused by Callie's flames and Sebastian's lightning balls, he could hear no sounds of panic from the nearby streets, nor police sirens headed toward them.

Artemus frowned.

It was as if the fight were happening inside a bubble.

Is there some kind of barrier around us?

A flicker to his left made his head snap around. He blinked.

A figure in a long coat was perched atop a chimney some twenty feet from where he hovered in mid-air.

It was a man with dark hair and blue eyes. Eyes that bore an uncanny resemblance to his own.

An eerie sensation throbbed through Artemus. His heart lurched.

The man smiled, as if he too had felt their energies connect. He glanced down. "You hold it differently from me."

Artemus's gaze dropped to his broadsword. By the time he looked up, the man had vanished. Shock reverberated through him as the words the stranger had spoken finally registered.

"*Dad?!*" he whispered into the night.

CHAPTER FOURTEEN

DANIEL'S HEART THUMPED VIOLENTLY AS HE WATCHED the battle unfolding outside the SUV. Despite the chaos reigning around it, the vehicle stood unscathed in the middle of the street, as if by some sort of miracle.

Even though he'd heard accounts of the battles Artemus and his friends had been engaged in during the last few months from Persephone, Daniel could still hardly believe his eyes.

Balls of white energy flashed from the Sphinx's right palm as he attacked the demons, the Triple-Thonged Whip of Raguel trailing lines of flames through the air and across the flesh of the figures who stood in his path. Fire gushed out of the Chimera's jaws where she stood braced on his left, the flames swallowing the silver-eyed monsters; the Scepter of Gabriel glinted as it left her grasp at an incredible speed, the weapon drilling holes into the bodies of the enemy before returning to her bloodied grasp.

The ferocious expressions on the faces of the man and the woman who each bore the soul of a divine beast made Daniel shiver.

He knew it wasn't just fear that was raising goose-bumps on his skin.

He could feel the presence of the creature inside him keenly now. It was lurking behind his eyes, clearly fascinated by the battle it was witnessing.

Whatever the power was that was swirling through the Sphinx and the Chimera, it was resonating with his own beast's energy.

And it isn't just them.

Though he'd only glimpsed their forms, their movements too fast for his human eyes to follow, Daniel could sense the presence of the two angels engaged in the battle alongside the Sphinx and the Chimera.

Something landed heavily atop the roof of the SUV. A shocked cry left Daniel's lips. He ducked in the seat, his arms wrapping protectively around his head.

"SOMETHING'S WRONG!" LOU SHOUTED. "WE SHOULD have passed half a dozen police cars by now!"

Serena clenched her jaw as she pounded the asphalt next to him.

Lou's right! What the hell is going on?

They turned a corner and finally came in sight of the street where Artemus and the others were fighting the first-generation super soldiers. A black van stood parked across the entrance.

Cars and people were going around it as if nothing was wrong.

There was movement in the air beyond the vehicle. Serena's stomach dropped when she saw the three figures rising and diving rapidly out of sight in the shadows. She glanced at the pedestrians walking past.

Can't they see what's happening?!

Tom and Nate slowed to a stop beside her and Lou.

"Whoa," Tom murmured. "Is the guy with the eagle wings the Sphinx?"

"Yeah," Nate replied.

Lou glanced at Serena. "It must be the nanorobots in our retina. That's why we can see them and ordinary people can't."

"Let's go!"

She took out her gun and blade and dashed across the intersection, the others in her wake. People startled and moved out of their way hastily as they scaled the van and jumped for the road beyond.

A gasp left Serena as she slammed shoulder-first into an invisible wall. She was knocked back onto the roof of the van and landed hard on her bottom. Lou, Nate, and Tom crashed down beside her a heartbeat later.

"The hell was that?!" Tom snarled.

Serena climbed to her feet, her pulse racing. She stepped carefully to the edge of the van, holstered her gun, and raised her hand. Pressure bore down on her fingertips when she made contact with something she couldn't see.

"It's a barrier."

She spotted Callie and Sebastian amongst the wreckage of several vehicles some forty feet up the road; they were fighting the demons at full power. She removed an EMP bomb from the pouch on her thigh and detonated it.

She might as well have fired off a Christmas cracker for all the effect it had on the first-generation super soldiers.

A muffled shout reached her ears. Someone was calling her name.

Drake blurred into view a few feet in front of her, his wings thumping the air strongly. He reached for her.

Sparks erupted when his hand connected with the wall that separated them. Surprise dawned in his gold-rimmed, crimson eyes. He frowned, drew his fist back, and punched the barrier.

The air trembled. Serena took a step back, her gaze following the faint haze that warped the space before her.

"It's some kind of dome," Nate said beside her.

Lou frowned. "By the looks of it, it extends all over the street."

Drake bared his teeth and attacked the barrier with his sword. Crimson cracks flared briefly into life, the red lines snaking along the inner surface of the divide before fading in the night.

The barrier held.

"Is this thing made by demons?" Tom asked grimly.

"Probably," Serena muttered.

She flicked her dagger into her left hand and stabbed it into the barrier. Red light flared at the tip of the steel blade when it made contact with the surface.

"What are you doing?" Lou asked, alarmed.

"We need to get one of our EMP devices to them." Serena looked into Drake's startled gaze where he hovered opposite her, before glancing past his shoulder at the first-generation super soldiers engaging Callie and Sebastian. "It's the fastest way they'll be able to defeat them."

She took a shallow breath, gripped the handle of the dagger with both hands, and focused all her strength in her wrists.

Time to see if this divine energy I've inherited serves any purpose.

Her muscles bunched. Tendons screamed in her arms and neck as she attempted to tear a breach with the blade.

More. She gritted her teeth. *I need more power, damnit!*

Heat suddenly surged inside her, as if in response to her desperate command. With it came a rush of strength that made her very blood sing.

Wonder filled Serena.

Is this what Drake and the others experience when they transform?

The force flooding her body was so exhilarating she feared she would get drunk on it. A golden haze fluttered into existence across her fingertips. A tiny crack appeared in the wall. Serena gripped the edge of it with one hand and pulled.

Pale radiance erupted beside her. Surprise jolted Serena. She looked over at Nate.

His hands gleamed with the same glow dancing on her skin. For a moment, his pupils glinted with the same light too.

"Together," he said firmly.

He slipped his fingers into the gap above hers. Serena nodded.

The holy energy they had been bequeathed through their bond with the angels and the heavenly beasts flared through their bodies as they ripped through the demonic barrier.

Lou and Tom stared, their faces pale.

The crack slowly expanded. Serena waited until it was big enough before grabbing another EMP device and squeezing her hand through the opening.

Pressure gripped her extremity, the evil power in the barricade fighting the enemy incursion. She bit her lip as she felt bones grind. The nanorobots in her armor resisted the attack, flashes of gold sparking across the surface of the suit.

Serena snarled and pushed through with all her might. A warm breeze washed across her skin as she finally made it past the barrier.

She released the EMP device.

It landed in Drake's waiting hand.

He looked at it before suddenly linking his fingers with hers. Serena stiffened at the unexpected connection. Her pulse spiked when she saw the expression in his eyes. Then, he was gone, his dark angel form swooping toward the battlefield.

She gazed breathlessly after him, her heart pounding and her skin tingling from his heated touch.

"Ah," Tom muttered to Lou. "I see what you mean by the smoldering sexual tension."

A FIGURE DROPPED ONTO THE HOOD OF THE SUV. IT was a demon. Daniel's breath choked in his throat. The demon twisted on his haunches, as if he'd heard the ragged inhale. His gaze found the priest through the windshield.

Daniel blinked.

The demon had vanished.

There was movement to his right. The rear door of the SUV was ripped from its hinges and cast violently aside. Warm night air rushed inside the vehicle. It brought with it the low growl of the demon and the stench of death.

Daniel froze as the creature's enormous figure filled the opening. It stooped and peered in at him.

This demon did not have silver eyes. From the look of the ragged strips of clothing still hanging from his body and the blood and gore coating his chin and chest, he had only just transformed into a monster.

Daniel glanced out of the SUV's rear window. A woman lay motionless in an expanding crimson pool outside a flower shop a few feet away. She was evidently the demon's first victim. And he was going to be the second.

The monster reached for him.

Daniel scrambled frantically backward, terror bringing a rush of bile to the back of his throat.

A figure flashed into view behind the monster. It grabbed the creature by the neck and hurled it away. The demon smashed into the building next to the vehicle and slid to the ground.

Daniel blinked as his rescuer came into focus.

It was the man he'd seen that night in St. Peter's Square, when he'd returned from the bookstore and spotted the female demon outside the Vatican.

The stranger gazed at him steadily. "It's time, Judah."

Then, he was gone.

Daniel's chest heaved with his panicked breaths.

Time?! Time for what?!

"What do you mean?!" he yelled. "*Time for what?!*"

The demon was climbing to his feet. His obsidian eyes locked on Daniel. His lips peeled back, exposing bloodied fangs. He lunged toward the open doorway.

The last thing Daniel saw as he raised his arms and closed his eyes was the yellow glare of the monster's pupils and his wicked claws.

Heat erupted inside him.

"Shit!" Drake cursed. "They're still standing."

Sebastian scowled. "How the devil is that possible?"

Drake had just activated the EMP device Serena had given to him. It had seemed to work at first, the super soldiers halting in their tracks when the electromagnetic wave washed over them.

Now, they were moving once more, albeit erratically.

A muscle jumped in Drake's jawline. "Something tells me they've adapted to the EMP pulse since the last time we fought them."

"Is that possible?" Callie said.

"Anything is possible with Ba'al," Drake said darkly.

Artemus dropped toward them from the sky. "We managed to beat them before, without the EMP device!"

Drake wondered at the agitation he could sense swirling through his twin.

"We just have to—" Artemus continued.

A violent detonation rocked the air, swallowing the rest of his words. They lurched back a couple of steps as a powerful shockwave struck them.

"Oh crap," Artemus whispered, ashen-faced.

Flames engulfed the misshapen shell of the SUV in the middle of the road.

"Father Lenton," Callie mumbled. "He was still inside!"

Artemus landed on the ground and started for the wreckage. He came to an abrupt halt a moment later. "What the—?"

Drake stared.

Something was moving inside the flames.

The left rear door of the vehicle exploded outward. The metal panel sailed through the night and crashed onto the asphalt a few feet from Artemus.

A figure stepped out of the burning wreck. It was dragging a demon by the throat.

They were both on fire.

The monster shrieked, body convulsing as the conflagration consumed his flesh and bones.

Daniel Lenton studied the creature with a curious frown, heedless of the inferno that wrapped around him. He lifted the demon in the air with one hand, as if he weighed less than air.

The monster clutched at the priest's wrist, his ochre gaze filled with terror. The fire in Daniel's eyes and on his fingertips flared white.

Even from a distance, Drake felt the heat radiating off the man intensify ten-fold.

The demon's screams of agony faded as his body slowly crumbled into a cloud of fiery ash. Daniel gazed at the remains fluttering from his fingertips into the night.

"Father Lenton?" Artemus said tentatively.

The priest turned and looked blankly at the angel.

"Daniel." Drake's twin took a careful step toward the man. "It's me, Artemus."

Awareness returned to the priest's face. His eyes grew round. He looked down at his hands, as if he were seeing them for the first time. "Oh."

The blaze enveloping him evaporated into nothingness. The fire went out of his eyes. He swayed and started to fall. Artemus rushed forward and caught him before he hit the ground.

There was movement on the road around them. Drake tensed.

The super soldier demons had vanished. So had the barrier separating him and the others from the rest of the city.

Running footsteps sounded from behind as Serena, Nate, Lou, and Tom headed rapidly their way.

CHAPTER FIFTEEN

OTIS AND HARUKI STROLLED THROUGH THE BASEMENT of the Apostolic Palace, Smokey at their side.

"So, how is it looking?" Haruki asked curiously.

Otis glanced at him with a preoccupied air before studying the thick wad of notes in his hands. They'd just visited the Vatican Library's private archives, where they'd met with the archbishop heading the team of experts attempting to translate his mother's journals.

"It's good. Between the work Sebastian and I did in Chicago and the Vatican group's efforts, I think we're close to cracking the code."

Excitement danced through Otis as they navigated the dimly lit corridors beneath the palace. Though he'd dreaded coming to Rome, the trip was already proving worthwhile.

He grimaced internally. *Well, except for the demon attack on the way here.*

The more Otis thought about it, the more he wondered whether the ambush had been some sort of test. He couldn't help but feel that whoever had been behind it had wanted to see what they could do. If Ba'al had truly wished to hurt them, there would have been more than just that strange cloud about.

Otis had yet to voice his suspicions to Artemus. Somehow, he had an inkling his boss and the others were thinking along the same lines.

They reached a junction. Otis turned right and was fifteen feet down the passage before he realized Haruki and Smokey were no longer with him. He looked over his shoulder and spied them disappearing around a corner in the opposite direction. He caught up with them a moment later.

"Where are you going? This isn't the way back to our quarters."

"I'm looking for something," Haruki said as their footsteps echoed along the corridor.

Otis gave him a puzzled look. "What are you looking for?"

"The Vatican's forge. Artemus asked me to find it."

Otis's eyes widened slightly. "Is this about the gauntlets he's been making?"

Haruki dipped his chin, his gaze sweeping the passage. A narrow staircase appeared on their left. He headed toward it with Smokey.

Otis followed, now more than a little anxious.

"Wait up!" he hissed as they negotiated the staircase. "Do you even know what's down there? And what makes you think you'll find a forge in the Vatican anyway?"

"This place has been here forever. It's survived numerous attacks and sieges over the centuries since the first foundations were laid." They came to a landing. Haruki glanced at Otis before taking the steps spiraling into the bowels of the Vatican. "Besides, you've seen the

Swiss Guards' weapons. There has to be some place where they do the upkeep for all those swords and lances."

They reached the bottom of the stairs. A murky corridor stretched out on either side of them. Yellow light flickered faintly in the distance to their right.

They were halfway down the passage when a pair of guards stepped in their path.

"Halt! Who goes there?" one of them called out, his hand on his rapier.

Torchlight pierced the gloom, dazzling Haruki and Otis. Smokey huffed impatiently at their feet.

"They are guests of Pope DaSilva."

Otis whirled around.

A figure had stepped out of the shadows a short distance behind them.

It was Archbishop Holmes. The man observed Otis and Haruki with an unreadable expression before addressing the guards. "I am showing them our facilities."

"Your Reverence." The guard dropped his hand from his sword and lowered the torch. He bowed his head stiffly. "My apologies. I did not see you there."

"No apologies needed. You were only doing your job." Holmes looked at Otis and Haruki. "The forge is this way."

They hesitated before following him past the guards.

"How did you know we were looking for the forge?" Haruki said quietly.

"Elton told me Artemus was making something before you came to Rome. The only reason you'd be down here is if he asked you to locate the whereabouts of the Vatican's smithy."

Smokey was studying the Archbishop curiously.

Surprise jolted Otis when the hellhound's thoughts reached him a moment later.

"That's interesting," Haruki murmured.

Holmes arched an inquisitive eyebrow at them over his shoulder.

"The rabbit says you're the same as Persephone."

A disapproving expression clouded the Archbishop's face. "I take it Her Holiness has given you permission to address her by her first name?"

Otis flushed. "Sorry. She insisted."

"It's not your fault," Holmes said darkly. "She can be persuasive that way."

"You don't agree with her?" Haruki asked.

"I'm old fashioned when it comes to matters of that ilk."

"Oh. So, you *are* the descendant of a pureblood Immortal and a human, like Perse?"

Holmes's mouth thinned slightly. "That is somewhat of a personal question, Mr. Kuroda."

"Please, call me Haruki," the Yakuza heir said, blatantly ignoring the archbishop's sarcastic tone.

"*Perse?!*" Otis mouthed at him behind Holmes's back.

Haruki shrugged. "Her full name is kinda long."

They descended a second flight of stairs, reached another long, rambling passageway, and turned the corner at the end. An iron-plated door finally appeared before them.

Holmes removed a bunch of keys from inside his cassock, unlocked the door, and pulled it open. "We're here."

A wave of heat washed over them. Holmes stepped across the threshold into the space beyond. They followed and paused on a stone landing.

Otis's eyes grew round.

"Holy shit," Haruki said dully.

Holmes cut his eyes briefly to the Yakuza heir before gazing at the enormous cavern before them. "The weapons room in the Swiss Guards' headquarters is but a smaller, modern version of this one. This is the Vatican's original smithy and armory."

Otis noted the pride in the archbishop's voice as he stared at the veritable arsenal assembled twenty feet beneath the gallery upon which they stood. Rows of medieval armor and weapons stood in wooden racks lining the immense, multilevel floorspace below. Dotting the sizeable gaps between them and three walls of the cave were some dozen forges and anvils of all shapes and sizes, in addition to wells and slack tubs for water.

They descended the stone stairs and were soon on the floor of the smithy.

Otis indicated one of several pits they passed. "What are those?"

The shafts were covered by metal grilles, their depths lost in shadows.

Holmes's expression grew uncomfortable. "They are...oubliettes."

Haruki's eyebrows rose. "The Vatican kept prisoners down here?"

"In the past. When the place was under siege and marauders broke through."

They reached the far side of the smithy and stopped before the largest forge. It was the only one still alight and the source of the warmth flooding the cave.

"This one always stays lit," Holmes explained at Otis and Haruki's curious looks. "It's an unspoken rule in the

Vatican." He paused. "This is the first forge that was ever built on these grounds."

Haruki observed the enormous anvil and the array of tools next to the furnace. "I think Artemus will find this to his liking."

Smokey let out a soft snort of agreement.

A flicker drew Otis's gaze to the left.

An alcove stood in the wall of the cave several feet from the forge. Standing atop the roughly-hewn, stone pedestal within it was a white marble crucible holding a small fire. Figures were etched in the outer and inner surfaces of the vessel.

Otis moved toward it for a closer look. "Are those griffins?"

Holmes nodded and joined him. "You are correct. The crucible and the fire are as old as, if not older than, the original forge. It has never gone out in all the centuries it's been down here."

Otis found himself almost hypnotized by the golden dance of the flames in the vessel. His hand rose, unbidden.

Smokey froze beside him. The rabbit turned stiffly and stared to the east.

"What is it?" Haruki said with a frown.

The Yakuza heir straightened in the next moment. His gaze followed that of the rabbit.

Otis blinked as he finally registered what it was that the hellhound and the Dragon had just felt.

He felt the blood drain from his face. "Is that—?"

"Yes," Haruki muttered grimly.

Concern filled Holmes's face. "Is everything okay?"

Haruki made rapidly for the exit, Smokey and Otis on his heels. "There's been another attack."

CHAPTER SIXTEEN

"You can put him in here."

Artemus looked cautiously at the burly, dark-eyed man who'd spoken, before glancing at Serena.

"You can trust him," the super soldier murmured.

Artemus nodded and carried the unconscious figure of the priest into the room they'd been shown to. He placed him carefully on the couch under the window and stood back.

Lines furrowed Artemus's brow.

Daniel had still not regained consciousness following their clash with the super soldier demons. Although it would have made more sense for them to return to the Vatican, Artemus had thought it best to get him checked over in the closest safe place.

Serena knelt by Daniel's side and ran her hands lightly over his body, examining him for injuries.

The chances of another assault are slim at best, but I don't want to risk another trip across the city just yet. Artemus's frown deepened as he stared at the priest. *Not after what happened back there.*

The man who'd been waiting for them at the security gates of the exhibition center had guided them to a private meeting room in the administrative quarters of the glass and steel complex. He'd paled slightly when they'd first appeared out of the rift Sebastian had created to take them there, but had recovered his composure swiftly.

From what Artemus had been able to deduce, he was the client Serena and Nate had been hired to work for.

"I'm Dimitri Reznak," the man said presently. "This is Zachary Jackson."

He indicated the blond man who'd just joined them. The latter wore a relaxed if unreadable expression.

"Artemus Steele." Artemus shook their hands and introduced the others. He turned to Reznak. "Lou said you tipped them off about the attack?"

Reznak nodded, his face serious. "We have a satellite positioned over Rome at all times. We received intel this morning about first-generation super soldiers having been spotted in Italy, so we've been keeping an eye out for them."

Artemus digested this with interest. "So, you really are an Immortal."

Reznak smiled faintly. "Correct."

"I can't see any obvious wounds." Serena sat back on her haunches and studied the unconscious man on the couch. "So, who is he?"

"His name is Daniel Lenton," Drake said. "He's Persephone's assistant."

Serena arched an eyebrow. "Persephone?"

"He means Pope DaSilva," Callie explained distractedly.

She was staring unblinkingly at Daniel.

Artemus could hardly blame her. The man had pretty much just stunned all of them with his little fiery display.

Lou grimaced. "You're on first-name terms with the Pope?"

Sebastian's pensive gaze was similarly locked on the priest. "She insisted."

Callie stepped toward the couch. She hesitated before crouching next to Serena and laying a hand on Daniel's chest.

"What's she doing?" Tom hissed to Nate.

"She's trying to sense his beast."

Tom blinked. "Oh."

Lou sighed. "Considering the guy just lit up like a bonfire and pulverized a demon with his bare hands, you really shouldn't look that surprised."

"Beast?" Reznak's expression grew wary. "You mean, he's a divine creature?"

A thoughtful light dawned in Jackson's eyes as he observed Daniel.

"Yes. His is still dormant though." Callie lifted her hand from the priest's chest. "That, or it's deliberately keeping a low profile."

"That would not surprise me," Sebastian said. "My beast was the same, and so was the Dragon from what you related about Haruki's awakening. Which means he likely has not come into possession of his key yet, nor been in the presence of his gate."

"So, he's a Guardian." Drake glanced at Artemus. "Do you think he knew?"

Artemus shrugged, as perplexed as his twin. "I'm not sure."

"He knew all right," Sebastian said grimly. "He did not look that shocked by what he had done to that demon.

Which makes me wonder if something like that has happened to him before."

A dozen thoughts stormed Artemus's mind as he gazed at Daniel. Chief among them was the fact that they had been attacked twice by Ba'al on the very day they had arrived in Rome and they'd struggled to come through both battles unscathed.

The second troubling realization was that their paths had crossed that of a divine beast in the last place they'd expected to find one.

Is this coincidence or providence?

Artemus pursed his lips. "Maybe Rome isn't such a crazy place for one of the beasts to be hiding after all."

"What are you mumbling about?" Drake said.

A soft groan drew their attention to the couch.

Daniel stirred. His eyes slammed open a moment later. He stared blankly at the ceiling before bolting upright and scanning the room, his face a mask of panic.

His gaze landed on Artemus. "The demon! Where is it?!"

"You killed it," Artemus replied bluntly.

Daniel blanched. "Oh God."

Sebastian levelled an exasperated look at Artemus. "Your bedside manner could do with some improvement."

Artemus grimaced and rubbed the back of his neck ruefully. "It's the truth."

"You don't remember what happened?" Callie asked Daniel gently.

The priest shook his head. "I recall the attack. And then this—this demon ripped off the rear door of the car and tried to—" he faltered and swallowed convulsively, "tried to kill me!"

"He did not succeed," Sebastian said. "Your beast awoke briefly and disposed of him."

Daniel stared at them, stunned. He looked down at his hands. "Did I—did I burn him?"

His fingers trembled on his lap.

Artemus glanced at Sebastian. The Sphinx had been right. Daniel had barely blinked when he'd mentioned the word 'beast'.

"You did," Drake replied quietly. "It took but seconds for you to turn him to ash."

Daniel opened and closed his mouth soundlessly. "I turned him to ash?!"

"Yeah," Lou muttered. "Even though we were outside the barrier, it still looked damn impressive."

"What barrier?" Daniel said blankly. His face cleared. "Oh. I just remembered something! Did you see a man? He was wearing a coat and had dark hair and blue eyes. He —" the priest stopped and frowned faintly, "well, he kind of appeared in front of me before the demon attacked. And he told me it was time."

"Time?" Drake said, puzzled. "Time for what?"

"Artemus?" Sebastian said in an anxious tone. "Are you all right? You have gone quite pale."

Artemus stared blindly at Daniel, his heart slamming a fast tempo against his ribs. "You saw him too?"

Daniel nodded, clearly troubled. "It wasn't the first time either. He appeared to me a week ago, in St. Peter's Square."

"Who are you talking about?" Drake said with a frown. "There was another man present during that fight? I didn't sense—"

"He was there." Artemus swallowed. Now that he had time to process what had happened, the enormity of it was finally sinking in. His gaze moved from Daniel to Drake. "Michael was there."

Drake's eyes widened.

Sebastian blinked. "Michael? Wait, do you mean to say—?"

"Your father?" Serena said. "As in, the Archangel Michael?"

Callie gasped. Reznak and Jackson sucked in air. Lou and Nate's eyes rounded.

"My goodness," Sebastian mumbled.

Tom put out a hand. "Hold the fort." He gazed at them leadenly. "Goldilocks's father is an *archangel?!*"

CHAPTER SEVENTEEN

"ARE YOU CERTAIN?" PERSEPHONE SAID HOARSELY.

Bishop Irons dipped his chin. "Yes, Your Holiness. The Immortals just relayed the information to our intelligence officers. Mr. Steele and his companions are currently at the exhibition center in the city."

Persephone chewed her lip. "Thank you, Patrick. Please see to it that they have a security escort for their return journey."

Guilt twisted through her as her secretary bowed his head and exited the study. She rose and walked over to the window, her footsteps heavy.

Lights had come on in St. Peter's Square. The bright glow washed across the people still gathered there. Some were holding candles in silent vigil as they prayed before the sanctity of the Holy See.

If only they knew the crimes the Church has committed over the centuries to preserve said sanctity.

Having reached the ripe old age of two hundred and fifty-four, Persephone had witnessed many of those crimes during the long years of her existence.

The calling had come to her late in life. She had taken the cloth at the peak of the Napoleonic Wars, after the Battle of Borodino, one of the bloodiest skirmishes to be fought by the French Emperor during his attempts to conquer Europe. Helping people was something that had always come naturally to her and becoming a nun had seemed the safest way to travel the continent to continue her good deeds. It was in the decades that followed that she discovered just how many offspring of pureblood Immortals and humans had instinctively migrated to the Church, a place where they evidently felt the secrets of their longevity would be kept.

As it currently stood, about a quarter of the clergymen and nuns in Vatican City were the offspring of an Immortal and human union.

Persephone watched the movement of the crowd for a moment and wondered if she had made the wrong decision inviting Artemus and his allies to Rome.

"It wasn't the wrong decision," someone said behind her.

Persephone whirled around.

A man stood by her desk. He was tall, with wavy, dark hair and eyes so blue she felt she was staring into the depths of a clear lake. He was too beautiful to be called handsome.

"You!" she spat.

"Long time no see, Perse," Michael said with a smile.

Persephone scowled. "Less of the Perse, please. I can't believe your nerve! After that stunt you pulled—"

Michael sighed. "Why is everyone obsessed with the fact that I slept with a woman? It was for the greater good."

"I don't mean that, you fool!" Persephone stormed

toward the archangel and stabbed his chest with a bony finger. "I mean the stuff you keep doing to Artemus. Stop teasing your son!"

Michael sobered. "I'm not teasing him." He pursed his lips. "And should you really be addressing one of your superiors like this?"

"Superior my fanny," Persephone said, her words dripping acid. "If it isn't teasing, then what the devil is it? Arael told me what you did to the boy when he was six. Cerberus wasn't impressed either, apparently."

Michael lifted an eyebrow. "You're pals with the crow?"

Persephone shrugged. "We enjoy a game of chess now and again."

"That little tattletale," Michael muttered. "I'm gonna pluck one of his feathers next time I see him."

"Don't you dare," Persephone said between gritted teeth. "Besides, Uriel won't let you."

"You're right. That guy is the perfect choirboy."

"Do I detect a note of sibling rivalry?"

Michael sniffed. "You do not."

Persephone rocked back on her heels. She studied the archangel with a frown. "Why are you here, Michael? Is it because of what happened to Artemus and the others today?"

"I can't tell you that," the archangel replied enigmatically.

Persephone's frown deepened. "You said I wasn't wrong. About inviting them to Rome. I'm not so sure about that. I never wished for harm to come to any of them and they've already been attacked twice in under twelve hours! I should ask them to leave. They'll be safer in Chicago."

"Do you truly believe that?" Michael said.

Persephone hesitated. "I don't know what to believe anymore." A heavy sigh left her lips. Her shoulders drooped. "I just don't want them to get hurt."

Michael laid a hand on Persephone's arm. "Your will to protect them is admirable, as always. But do not forget. They are divine beings. As such, theirs will never be an easy path. The tasks that lie before them are too important for any of us to interfere with, even if we only wish to do so to shield them from harm."

"And yet, here you are, interfering," Persephone murmured.

"I will never do anything that directly affects their Fate. Uriel and the others know this, however much they grumble about it like old men." Michael's eyes grew as flinty as diamonds. "After all, I am the one who commanded the army that cast Satanael and our Fallen brethren to Hell. Do you really believe I would do anything to jeopardize the outcome of the upcoming war?"

Persephone swallowed in the face of the archangel's fierce expression. "No. I don't." Lines marred her brow. "So, *why* are you here, then?"

Michael picked up her quill pen and rolled it nonchalantly between his fingers. "Rome is nice this time of year."

Persephone pinched the bridge of her nose and started counting to ten under her breath.

"All right," Michael muttered when she got to five. "I'm here to observe them."

"Observe them?" Persephone narrowed her eyes. "What, like a Peeping Tom? That's low, even for you. Callie is barely twenty-five and Serena isn't that much older than her."

Michael's expression grew irritated. "I mean, in my capacity as one of the generals of Heaven's Army. Christ, I didn't even intercede when that demon tried to kill Daniel, so give me some credit, will you?"

The blood drained from Persephone's face. "What?"

Michael looked suddenly contrite. "Oh. You didn't know? I thought you might have heard by now."

"Heard what?" Persephone's heart raced as she stared at the archangel. "Daniel is in his room. The Vatican is protected by a divine barrier. How could a demon get—?"

"Your protégé gave you the slip." Michael grimaced. "Or, to be more precise, my idiot son sneaked him out of the Vatican over an hour ago."

"Is he okay?" Persephone grabbed Michael's shirt, her knuckles white. "*Is Daniel hurt?!*"

Michael frowned. "Why would he be hurt? He's a divine beast."

A ringing sounded in Persephone's ears. The world tilted around her.

Michael looped an arm lightly around her waist as she swayed. "Easy there." He made a face. "I take it from your shocked expression that you didn't know this either?"

"No!"

"Well, I'm sure you and Artemus have a lot of questions for each other. Now, tell me where she is."

Persephone finally recovered her composure. "Where who is?"

Michael scowled. "Don't jest, woman. You know very well whom I mean. Where's Alice?"

Persephone opened her mouth.

"Before you commit a sin and lie through your teeth, know that I can feel traces of her energy in the barrier Uriel and Gabriel erected around Vatican City." Michael's voice hardened. "I know she's here."

CHAPTER EIGHTEEN

"DANIEL LENTON IS A DIVINE BEAST?!" THE MAN'S contact said on the other end of the line, aghast.

"I was surprised too." The man leaned a hip against a desk and gazed at the shadowy chamber beyond the glass wall. "But there is no denying what I saw through the eyes of the super soldiers." He frowned slightly. "His ability appears to be linked to Holy Fire."

"Holy Fire?"

"It's the first fire ever made by God, as you well know. And, as you can no doubt imagine, it is incredibly powerful. It is also deadly to demons." The man paused. "The flames that the divine beasts emit and that Drake's sword manifests originate from that Holy Fire."

"Can you manipulate it?" his contact asked curiously.

"Alas, no. It is the one element I cannot control."

Silence descended on the phone line.

"If Daniel is a beast, then that means he has a key and a gate," the mole mused.

"Ba'al has always known there was a key and a gate in

Rome. What we didn't realize was that there would be a beast here too. It shouldn't be that surprising, really."

"Wait. I thought the gate was among the artifacts Dimitri Reznak unearthed in Libya?" the mole said, puzzled. "Isn't that the reason you were so focused on attacking his convoy?"

"My dear friend, if there was indeed a gate in that collection, half of Ba'al would have descended upon it by now," the man drawled. "No, my interest in Reznak's relics is of a more, shall we say...personal nature."

His contact in the Vatican was quiet for a while. "Did your experiment work?"

The man smiled faintly. "Indeed it did. The new super soldier demons are more or less immune to the EMP bombs that Artemus and his friends used in England. And the next batch is coming along nicely." He straightened from the desk and walked across to the glass wall. "They'll be functional within the next forty-eight hours."

"I sense a but."

"Astute as always, I see," the man murmured. "You are correct. Although I am pleased with how these first-generation super soldiers have performed, I feel we could do more if we had some other specimens at hand."

"Specimens? I thought you had plenty of those."

The man smiled again. "Oh, I don't mean the cohort we stole from the Immortals. You see, the experiment tonight proved successful in more ways than I anticipated. I saw something." His smile widened. "Something very interesting."

He ended the call, put his hand against the glass, and stared avidly at what was taking place in the room beyond.

The first-generation super soldier on the table did not even flinch as his heart was wrenched from his chest by a demon and replaced with a dark, pulsating, vile mass. The grisly organ shuddered as it attached itself to its new host.

Even from where he stood, the man saw the dark lines snaking into the subject's blood vessels and flesh.

A corrupt cloud erupted around the super soldier's body. He gasped and arched his spine, his arms and legs straining violently against the demonic restraints that bound him to the metal bed. His eyes flared silver as the nanorobots inside his body fought the alien tissue invading it. A scream left his throat.

It would be the only pain he would ever experience in his unnatural life. The moment of possession by a demon.

His pupils shifted from black to yellow. He relaxed back down on the bed.

The man snapped his fingers where he still stood behind the glass wall. The restraints around the super soldier's limbs evaporated into nothingness. He sat up slowly, his ochre gaze finding and locking onto the man in the observation room.

"Welcome, brother," the man murmured.

"She's been like this all along?"

Persephone nodded. "Yes. She wakes from time to time, but mostly she sleeps."

Michael watched the motionless figure in the bed. But for the shallow rise and fall of her chest beneath the covers, she could have been one of those famous alabaster statues the Romans and the Greeks used to wax lyrical about.

Nearly three decades had passed since he'd last seen

her. She hadn't aged a single day in that time. And she was
still as beautiful as when he had first met her.

Alice. The woman Samyaza had raped to bear his
demon child. The woman Michael had been forced to
seduce so as to fulfill the prophecy God had shown him
that day.

Not for the first time, Michael wondered whether his
Heavenly Father had enjoyed the practical joke he'd pulled
on one of his strongest generals.

Because seducing Alice had not been the chore
Michael had thought it would be. In fact, truth be told,
she was the only creature for whom he had ever felt an
emotion that could loosely be regarded as sexual love, in
those short days they had been together.

She looks as delicate as the first time I laid eyes on her. He
frowned faintly as he looked upon Alice's dark hair, pale
skin, and rosy cheeks and lips. *Of course, that could very well
be because of* her.

There was movement to his right.

The air in front of the window had started to shimmer.
Light exploded across the room in the next instant,
powerful yet silent. Persephone inhaled sharply, one arm
rising to shield her eyes.

Michael did not look away.

The light wavered before taking on the form of a
woman.

She was different to the figure who lay in the bed. As
different as the sun was to the moon.

This woman was tall, with pale, long hair that glowed
and wrapped around her body like silk armor, the silvery
strands blending with the gauzy dress she wore. Her eyes
were dark and full of stars.

Persephone gasped. She lowered herself to her knees,

pressed her hands together, and bowed her head reverently to the apparition.

The latter smiled. "You may rise, child."

Persephone climbed to her feet.

The apparition's heavenly gaze switched back to Michael. "You look well, Michael."

Michael glanced at Alice before frowning at the ethereal figure in front of him. "So, this is where you've been all along."

The apparition observed the sleeping figure in the bed, her expression gentle. "It makes sense, does it not? She *is* one of the forms I chose to walk this Earth. And I *am* one of the reasons she ended up in this predicament. You are the other reason, of course."

She smiled at Michael. Persephone looked furtively between the two of them.

Michael felt his cheeks grow warm at the teasing light in the sparkling celestial eyes opposite him. He didn't have to look in a mirror to know he was blushing.

Darn this human body!

"Don't remind me," he said, trying to mask his embarrassment. "So, why are you still here? You could protect Alice from anywhere, if that was your intention for remaining with her."

The apparition glanced at Persephone. "I am not protecting her so much as keeping her company."

Michael did not miss the exchange. He narrowed his eyes. "What's going on?"

"Alice is dying."

The apparition's words rocked Michael back on his heels.

"What?" His stunned gaze found the figure in the bed. "But I—I cannot foresee her death!"

"Of course not," the apparition said. "She still carries some of my life force."

A muscle jumped in Michael's cheek as he digested this information.

"In another life, she would have been canonized a saint." The apparition crossed the room and stopped by the bed. She reached out and trailed her fingers lightly over Alice's cheek. "It pains me that she will leave this world an unknown entity."

"She doesn't need to die," Michael protested.

He knew the words he'd spoken were wrong the moment he uttered them. Life and death were a cycle that God had granted to his most fragile of creations, so they could become wise and grow closer to him. To deny it was to go against the wishes of the Heavenly Father Himself.

"Alice has already lived far beyond the years she should have. She was meant to die on the day she gave birth to Drake and Artemus." The apparition gazed benevolently at Michael, as if she could see the torment inside his heart. "Fear not, Archangel. Alice will be reborn. And her next life will be kinder than this one has been."

The apparition suddenly stilled. Michael followed her gaze and looked to the east.

She cocked her head slightly to the side, as if listening to something. "My sons are here."

CHAPTER NINETEEN

DANIEL'S HEART HAMMERED FURIOUSLY AGAINST HIS ribs. He glanced nervously at Artemus where the latter stood talking to Haruki, Otis, and Elton by the window of Persephone's private dining room. Smokey sat at their feet. The rabbit turned his head and stared at Daniel, his pupils flaring crimson.

For a moment, the priest experienced a flash of fear.

The rabbit hopped across the room, jumped up on his lap, and studied him curiously from his now limpid brown eyes. Daniel froze, shocked.

This was the closest he'd been to the hellhound since they met.

"Stay still," Callie ordered next to him.

"What—what is he—?" Daniel stammered.

The rabbit rose on his hind legs, pressed his paws against Daniel's chest, and bumped his warm, wet nose gently against his.

"There you go." Callie beamed. "You're officially a member of the family now."

Daniel blinked. "The family?"

"Welcome to the mad house," Serena Blake said drily.

She and Nate Conway had accompanied them to the Vatican.

"Amen," Drake muttered.

"That was his way of greeting you and your beast," Sebastian explained.

Before the priest could fathom what he meant, the door of the dining room banged open. Persephone stormed in, Bishop Irons on her heels. Her gaze found Serena and Nate.

"Miss Blake, Mr. Conway. It's good to finally meet you," she said curtly.

"Your Holiness," Serena murmured.

Nate dipped his head respectfully.

Daniel rose shakily, Smokey leaping to the floor to squat by his feet.

"I'm sorry," he mumbled as Persephone crossed the room. "I didn't mean to kill that—"

She wrapped him in her arms and hugged him hard.

Daniel stood rigid for a moment. Then he shuddered and closed his arms around her, his face finding the crook of her neck. He could feel her trembling in his embrace.

For a moment, he was back at the orphanage where he'd first met her, in his homeland of Ukraine. She used to comfort him just like this whenever the older children teased him about his wasted legs and his limp.

As he'd grown older and realized how little he had in common with the other boys and girls who shared his wretched fate, Persephone had come to replace his aunt as the mother figure in his life, her smiles and kind words slowly thawing his chilled, battered heart.

It was when he turned eighteen that Daniel started to see the dark aura in humans that signified a demonic possession. Scared by his new ability, he had kept it a secret from Persephone and turned to the cloth in guilt. He had left the orphanage shortly after he was ordained and accompanied Persephone as she traveled across Europe in her ever-growing role for the church. When she was appointed the supreme pontiff and moved to Rome, Daniel had vowed to dedicate the rest of his life to her.

By then, Persephone had told him of her unnatural origins and had concluded that he must be the same, since his ageing had slowed when he entered adulthood.

Daniel had never related to her the incident that had taken place on the day his uncle had died, nor had he told her his suspicions that he was unlikely to be the product of a union between a pureblood Immortal and a human; from the little his mother had told his aunt, his father had been as normal as any other man.

He had also never told her that he could detect demons, nor confided in her the strange dreams that had plagued him for the last three decades and which had had him searching for answers in hundreds of history books.

Daniel knew that he was different. Had known since the day he killed his uncle, in that small apartment in Kiev. Now, for the first time in his life, he was among people who were as different as he was.

He hadn't had time to analyze the gamut of feelings twisting through him; too much had happened in the last few hours. But he couldn't deny the resonance he was experiencing with Artemus and his companions.

Whether he liked it or not, some kind of bond had formed between him and them.

Persephone pulled back presently and cradled his face. "Are you all right, child?"

Daniel nodded, eyes blurring and emotion suddenly clogging his throat. "Yes."

Smokey bumped Daniel's leg gently with his furry head.

Persephone turned to Artemus. "What happened?"

"THERE ARE FIRST-GENERATION SUPER SOLDIERS IN Rome?" Otis said, stunned.

Artemus nodded. "Yes. They're the ones who attacked us on the way to the exhibition center."

Persephone stared. "I thought you were ambushed by demons."

"They *were* demons. Or, to be more precise, super soldiers possessed by demons." Artemus exchanged a troubled glance with Serena. "Except they weren't quite the same as the guys we fought in Chicago and England a month ago."

Artemus couldn't shake the uneasy feeling that he'd missed something crucial during their recent battle. Something that could give them an advantage over whomever their new enemy was.

"The reason we managed to defeat them swiftly back then was because of the EMP devices a friend of ours made to neutralize them," Serena explained. "They didn't work as well this time around."

"So, you're saying Ba'al has done something to make the super soldiers adapt to your technology?" Disbelief laced Elton's words. "In under a month?"

"Yes." Serena hesitated. "I hate to mention it, but these guys looked even stronger than the ones we did battle with last time."

Callie nodded grimly. "They most definitely were."

"And then there was that barrier," Nate murmured.

"Whoever was behind this latest assault created some kind of shield around us," Artemus said at Persephone and Elton's confused expressions. "It stopped people from getting in or out. It also prevented Sebastian from creating a rift so we could teleport out of there."

A wary look dawned on Persephone's face.

"I had heard of your ability to create portals in space from Elton," she told Sebastian. "I didn't realize you could produce them at will."

"They require an immense amount of divine energy," the Englishman admitted.

"And you need a strong stomach to travel through one," Otis mumbled.

"Yeah," Haruki muttered.

Silence fell across the dining room.

"I hear the convoy of artifacts you and Nate were protecting was also attacked by demons?" Persephone asked Serena.

The super soldier stiffened slightly. "Not many people are aware of that information." Lines marred her brow. "In fact, the only individuals Nate and I shared that intel with are in this room right now."

Persephone waved a hand vaguely at her suspicious stare. "Dimitri Reznak is a friend of mine. He told me what transpired during your trip when he got to Rome today, but he didn't go into the finer details."

"Why doesn't that surprise me?" Serena said in a cynical voice.

"I know you have cause for distrusting the Immortals, but not all of them are ill-willed." Persephone levelled a steady gaze at the super soldier. "They've saved our world on plenty of occasions in the past."

"They're also behind many of the conflicts that have torn human society apart," Serena countered coolly.

Persephone grimaced. "I never said they were perfect."

Nate cleared his throat in the awkward hush. "Artemus informed us that you're the descendant of an Immortal and a human?"

Persephone dipped her chin. "Indeed I am, as are many others in the Vatican."

"Tell us about the attacks on the convoy," Elton said to Serena and Nate. "We only heard bits and pieces from Callie."

The super soldiers spent the next few minutes describing what had taken place while they'd been traveling with Reznak and his Immortal guards.

"Nothing was stolen?" Drake said, surprised.

Serena shook her head. "No. Reznak went over everything with a fine-tooth comb. Not a single item was missing following those attacks." She turned to Artemus. "I want you to take a look at Reznak's artifacts. I think whatever those demons were looking for is still there."

"If Ba'al is interested in those relics, then surely this means—" Otis started.

"They may very well contain a key or a gate," Haruki finished in a hard voice.

"That's impossible," Artemus said.

Haruki frowned at him, clearly puzzled. "Why?"

"Because Daniel was in that building and he didn't feel a thing," Artemus stated emphatically.

"Have you considered that it may not be his gate or key?" Sebastian said.

Artemus sighed. "The way things have turned out so

far, the chances that there would be two divine beasts and two sets of keys and gates in this city are quasi non-existent. Besides, we've seen it over and over again. The key and the gate always end up close to the Guardian."

"What's this about keys and gates?" Daniel said, confused. "Or Guardians for that matter?"

Artemus gave the priest a surprised look before turning to Persephone. "He doesn't know?"

"No. I never saw the need to tell him." Persephone drew a ragged breath and turned to Daniel. "About this beast business. Will you tell me what happened to you?"

Daniel hesitated in the face of her stare. "I—I don't recall all the details." He glanced at Artemus. "A demon attacked me. And I killed it, somehow."

"That was not the first time you experienced something like that," Sebastian said in a self-assured tone.

Daniel's eyes grew hooded. "What makes you say that?"

"Because you never questioned your beast's awakening," Artemus replied. "Which means you had to be aware of the creature's existence at some level."

The priest's knuckles whitened in his lap.

"You're right," he said, staring at the floor. "I've always known I was different. Ever since that day."

"Ever since what day, Daniel?" Persephone asked gently.

Daniel's expression was tortured when he finally met her gaze. "The day I burned my uncle to death."

CHAPTER TWENTY

Artemus wiped the sweat from his brow, put the towel down, and picked up the glowing bar in the forge with a pair of tongs. He placed it on the anvil and hammered and thinned it for long minutes before dumping it in the slack tub. Steam sizzled up in thick waves and washed over him.

He repeated the process with another pair of metal bars, his mind returning to the previous night's conversation in Persephone's private quarters.

"I killed my uncle," Daniel had repeated hoarsely.

Persephone had drawn a sharp breath. "Wait. It was your aunt who killed her husband!"

Daniel had shaken his head. "No, it wasn't. She took the blame for it." A muscle had twitched in his cheek. "I still can't forgive myself for that. She died all alone in prison, because of what I did that day."

Persephone had reached out and taken his hand. "I read the reports the orphanage kept of that incident, Daniel. Your uncle tried to kill both of you. In fact, he beat your aunt so badly, he broke her ribs. And you were full of bruises, both old and new, when the police took you to get checked over at the hospital."

Daniel had swallowed. "He didn't just try to kill me."

Persephone had stared. Horror had slowly washed across her face. Her fingers had clenched around the priest's knuckles. "What do you mean? Did he—did he touch you?!"

"No!" Daniel had shaken his head vehemently once more. "I don't mean that." He'd faltered and swallowed. "I mean he succeeded. In killing me."

Callie's eyes had widened at that. "What?!"

"I died that day." Daniel's voice had hardened then. "Then I came back to life and killed him."

Artemus removed the cooled metal sheets from the slack tub. He wiped them down and placed them back on the anvil, the priest's shocking words echoing through his head all over again.

It wasn't the first time they'd come across the phenomenon of a beast awakening when its host was at death's door. Sebastian's initial encounter with the Sphinx had happened the night a demon broke into his mansion and killed his entire family. It was only thanks to the creature's intervention that he had survived the attack.

Callie and Haruki's own beasts had manifested themselves when the widow and the Yakuza heir had been in mortal danger.

Lines furrowed Artemus's brow.

But to actually die and return from death awakened? That's a new one on me.

His frown deepened when he recalled the look in Persephone's eyes when he and Daniel had mentioned their encounter with Michael. Though she had remained silent, Artemus's instincts told him she knew more about the archangel than she was prepared to talk about.

I wonder if he's still around. I mean, would I even know? He could be watching me right this minute.

Artemus straightened and looked around the cavern. Smokey's disgruntled words reached him in the next instant.

If he were here, I would know.

The hellhound sat a few feet away, next to an alcove where a fire burned in a crucible atop a stone pillar. He seemed fascinated by the flames.

I still have not forgiven that angel for what he did to me.

"Wait." Artemus stared. "You remember meeting Michael?!"

Smokey let out an irritated huff. *Only when you mentioned him yesterday.*

Artemus digested this thoughtfully. It had been clear to him for some time now that someone had tampered with Smokey's memories in the past.

"What did he do to you?"

You mean what did he do to us. *He is the reason we met that night, when you were six. He snatched me from my den while I was sleeping and threw me into that field with you. I was most ill-prepared for our encounter.*

"Is that why you looked so pissed?" Artemus grimaced. "I thought you were gonna kill me."

You were not the one I wanted to kill. Smokey bared his fangs. *But I did manage to bite him.*

Artemus sucked in air. "You bit an archangel?!"

Smokey sniffed. *He deserved it. The Crow agreed.*

Artemus blinked. "What crow?"

Smokey looked confused for a moment. *I...I do not know.*

"Yeah, someone's definitely messed with your mind," Artemus muttered.

He removed the individual pieces of the gauntlets he'd been making in Chicago from the leather bag on the floor and put them next to the fresh metal plates on the anvil.

"I think I'm done." Artemus cracked his knuckles. "Now, for the magic stuff."

He took a deep breath and had just started to focus his power into his hands when a voice spoke behind him.

"What are you doing?"

Artemus whirled around, startled. He clutched a hand to his chest when he saw Daniel. "Shit. Have you got cat's feet? I didn't hear you come in!"

The priest slowed to a stop, his curious eyes sweeping the cavern and the furnace. His gaze landed on the anvil. "Are those the items the others mentioned you were making?"

"Yeah. I'm about to finish them, hopefully." Artemus paused. "Have you never been down here? You look like you're seeing the place for the first time."

"No, I haven't, actually," the priest murmured. "There has never been any need for me to come all the way here before."

Artemus arched an eyebrow. "Was there a reason you came? I thought we were meeting with Persephone later, for that private tour of the Basilica Otis and Sebastian can't stop talking about."

"Your brother and your friends are planning another trip to that exhibition center before the tour. They asked me to come and get you." He frowned slightly. "They want to examine Reznak's collection."

Artemus stared. "You look like you disapprove."

Daniel hesitated. "It's not that I disapprove, per se. I

just think trouble follows you people. I would hate for the city to incur more damage than it already has because of the confrontations you seem to attract."

"Yeah, well, it's not as if we go looking for them," Artemus muttered. "And, Daniel?"

"Yes?"

"They're your people too."

Surprise flashed in the priest's gaze. He paled.

Artemus sighed. "Okay, now you look like I just told you that you have some kind of terminal disease."

"I—I'm sorry," Daniel mumbled. "I didn't mean it like that. I was just...well, taken aback."

Artemus studied the priest for a moment. "Something tells me you're not used to having friends."

"I'm not," Daniel admitted bluntly.

"Better get used to it then," Artemus said drily, "'cause we ain't goin' anywhere." He paused. "FYI, don't get into a booze match with Sebastian. That guy might look prissy but he will drink you under the table. Don't play chess with him either. He's a sore loser." A grimace twisted his lips. "And if Haruki ever gives you something that looks like water, there's a fifty percent chance it'll be homemade sake and a ninety percent chance it might make you blind." He turned his attention back to the gauntlets. "You may want to move back for this."

"Oh."

Daniel shuffled a couple of steps to his left.

CHAPTER TWENTY-ONE

Artemus latched onto the energy entwined with his soul and allowed it to fill his veins. Warmth bloomed through his body. He inhaled and concentrated it into his hands. A golden haze burst into life on his fingertips. It intensified and turned white as he began to work the metal pieces before him.

Daniel drew a sharp breath as the segments of the gauntlets levitated off the anvil and started to merge with one another with faint bangs that echoed across the cavern. The new plates joined them, slotting into place like the final pieces of a puzzle.

Artemus frowned as he recalled the details of the gauntlets from his dreams.

Not quite there yet.

He flexed his fingers lightly.

The components shimmered and blurred, the atoms and bonds holding them together shifting at lightning speed under the influence of the divine energy he was pouring into them. The metal slowly morphed, assuming a smoothness and flexibility no other metal on Earth possessed.

The finished gauntlets dropped down gently onto the anvil minutes later.

Artemus blew out a sigh, hands still tingling from the power he had just exercised. "All they need now is a good polish and they'll be—" He stopped and stared at Daniel. "Hey, are you okay?"

The priest stood ashen-faced a short distance away. His eyes were focused unblinkingly on the gauntlets.

"*It's—it's them!*"

"Them?" Artemus said, perplexed. "What do you mean, them?"

Daniel tore his gaze from the gloves long enough to flash him a dazed look. "I've been dreaming about these gauntlets for the last thirty years. I thought they were relics, so I've only ever looked for them in history books." He swallowed convulsively. "I never imagined they didn't even exist yet!"

Shock reverberated through Artemus's very bones at the priest's words.

Wait. He's seen these in his dreams too?!

A premonition burst into life in his mind in the next moment. He stared at the gauntlets.

Could they be his key?! Artemus narrowed his eyes. *No, that can't be it. A key is usually a divine weapon. This isn't from Heaven.*

The air rippled, as if an invisible wave of pressure had washed through it. Artemus's ears popped. Heat flooded the cavern.

"What the—?"

He looked at the furnace. The blaze within it remained contained.

"Artemus?" Daniel said hoarsely.

Artemus followed the priest's frozen gaze. His eyes widened.

Smokey moved away from the alcove next to the forge, his pupils similarly rounding with surprise.

They all stared at the fire in the crucible atop the stone pillar. Or, more precisely, the fire *above* the crucible. It had risen from the vessel and was rotating on its own axis in mid-air, as if dancing on invisible strings.

The flames grew steadily brighter. A shiver shook Daniel from his head to his toes.

The fire flashed toward them. Artemus gasped and took a step back.

The blaze stopped in front of him. For an insane moment, Artemus thought it was studying him curiously. It twisted and dropped toward the anvil, only to come to a stop above the gauntlets. It hovered close to them for a couple of seconds before latching on.

The flames froze for an instant.

Then they flickered before sending out tentative tongues to roam the gloves, as if exploring them.

Artemus gaped.

The fire was being slowly absorbed by the metal.

"What's happening?" Daniel mumbled.

"I don't know."

In that moment, Artemus was certain of only one thing. Whatever the fire was, it was alive.

Incandescent brightness filled the cavern without warning. Artemus winced and shielded his eyes with a hand. There was a strange humming sound, as if something was vibrating at an incredible speed. Heat wrapped around Artemus's right middle finger.

The light slowly faded.

He lowered his hand and looked blankly at the plain metal ring he now wore. It glowed for a moment, as if lit from within by flames. Yet, it felt cool.

Daniel's tone rose in alarm. "What—what is this?!"

Artemus turned.

The priest was wearing a similar ring on his left hand.

Artemus's gaze shifted to the anvil. The gauntlets had disappeared. So had the blaze that had been in the crucible.

A sense of wonderment filled him as he studied the rings he and Daniel now bore.

Could these be...?

Panic flooded Daniel's face. He was attempting to remove the metal band, without success. "It—it won't come off!"

Artemus pulled his own ring off his finger. "Oh. Mine does."

He hesitated before sliding it back on. Something told him he needed to keep it with him at all times.

A formidable energy echoed with the power inside his soul.

Artemus eyed Daniel uneasily. The surge was coming from the priest. "Hey, I think you need to calm down. You're about to—"

"I want this thing *off* me!" Daniel roared, struggling with the ring.

His pupils flashed orange behind his glasses. Fire exploded around him a heartbeat later.

"Oh, shit," Artemus muttered.

Leave him be.

Artemus glanced at Smokey. "Are you sure?"

Daniel paced the floor agitatedly, oblivious to the flames that engulfed him.

Yes. The rabbit's eyes glinted crimson as he observed the distressed man attempting to wrench the ring from his finger, to no avail. *You know what is happening, don't you?*

Artemus scrunched his face. "To be honest, I haven't a freaking clue."

The rabbit sighed. *I believe the fire in the crucible is his key and weapon.*

Artemus stared, dumbfounded. "Wait. So, does this mean the gauntlets—?"

Were a means to an end, yes. They are evidently the shells the fire needed to be able to leave this place. Which explains why he was dreaming about them.

Artemus pondered this for a moment.

Did she show me the gauntlets for this very reason?

Smokey cast a curious look his way. *Did who show you the gauntlets?*

"Nothing." Artemus's gaze dropped to the ring on his hand. "If they're meant to be his key, then why do I have one of them?"

Smokey looked as puzzled as he felt at the question. *That I do not know.*

The smithy door slammed open on the far side of the cave.

Artemus turned and made out Drake and the divine beasts on the distant gallery landing. Otis was right behind them. They raced down the stairs and headed rapidly for them.

"What's happening?" Drake shouted as they drew close.

"We felt a sudden rise in divine energy!" Sebastian added.

They skidded to a halt when they turned the corner

past the last row of armor and came in full view of the forge.

Callie bumped into their backs. "Hey, a warning would have been—oh."

Haruki and Otis came to a standstill beside her, their faces similarly surprised. They all stared at Daniel.

"What the hell is going on?" Drake muttered.

"Is this power coming from him?" Sebastian asked stiffly.

Artemus nodded.

Otis inhaled sharply. "Oh. The fire in that crucible is gone."

"Wait." A wary expression dawned on Haruki's face. "Didn't Holmes say that thing had always been here, ever since the Vatican was first built? That it had never gone out?"

"It's still here." Artemus indicated the metal bands on his and Daniel's fingers. "It's inside these rings."

The others looked at him as if he'd lost his mind.

"I thought you were making gauntlets," Drake said suspiciously.

"Has the heat gotten to you?" Sebastian asked. "How many fingers am I holding up?"

Artemus sighed. "These rings *are* the gauntlets."

A snarl of frustration made them turn to Daniel. The priest had fallen to his knees, his face a mask of sheer aggravation. His flames dimmed before snuffing out completely. The ring on his finger glowed red for an instant before resuming a dull, metallic gleam.

"It won't come off!" he wailed, gazing beseechingly at Artemus.

Artemus crossed the floor and offered him a hand. "There's a reason for that."

Daniel hesitated before taking his hand.

Artemus helped him to his feet and stiffened slightly at what he sensed through his touch. He could feel it now. The energy of the beast that lived inside the tormented man before him.

"You see, this ring contains the fire that was in that crucible," Artemus explained carefully. "And I think that fire is your key."

"My—my key?" Daniel mumbled. "My key to what?!"

"Oh, yeah." Artemus grimaced. "We never really talked about this stuff last night, did we?"

He laid a hand on Daniel's shoulder.

"The key opens a gate of Hell," he said solemnly. "And you and your divine beast are its Guardian."

Horror filled the priest's face.

Sebastian frowned at Artemus. "Subtlety is not your forte, is it?"

CHAPTER TWENTY-TWO

"They're late," Serena said in clipped tones. "Again."

"I'm sure there's a good explanation for it," Nate murmured. "I doubt it involves another attack," he added hastily at her gloomy expression.

Serena pursed her lips. The truth was, she was more than a little worried. Yesterday's incidents had made something inherently clear to her and the others when they'd regrouped at the Vatican last night.

Whoever their foe was, he was smart and powerful.

Gideon had expressed the same sentiment when she'd updated him about the first-generation super soldier demons they'd encountered the day before.

"It's happened faster than I thought it would," he had muttered.

"What has?"

"Ba'al changing something inside the super soldiers to make them resist an EMP bomb. Whoever is behind this is as skilled as I am."

Serena had frowned. "You think the guy is some kind of scientist?"

"Let's not be sexist," Gideon had said wryly. "It could be a woman."

"I have yet to see a female demon commander," Serena had said curtly. "Generals, yes. But not commanders. Artemus and the others agree with me and Nate on this. We're probably dealing with another Prince of Hell."

Gideon had grimaced on the videostream of her smart band. "That sounds...dire."

A voice recalled her to the present. "There you are."

Serena looked over her shoulder.

Jackson was crossing the rear foyer of the exhibition center. "Are they here? We're just about putting the finishing touches to the exhibit."

"They seem to be running behind schedule," Nate said diplomatically.

"Oh." Jackson stopped beside them. He gazed out across the sunny yard and lifted his face to the sky. "It's a nice day."

A comfortable silence fell between them while they waited.

"There haven't been any more demonic attacks since we got here," Serena said after a while. "I mean, on Reznak's collection."

"You think Ba'al has stopped looking for whatever you thought was among the artifacts?" Jackson asked lightly.

Serena had told Reznak and Jackson her and Nate's suspicions that morning. The two Immortals had seemed unfazed by their conclusions. Which made Serena suspect they knew more about Ba'al than they'd revealed thus far.

She frowned faintly. "I think they're biding their time, for some reason."

Movement drew her gaze to the gates. Two SUVs had just pulled up outside the exhibition center.

"There they are." Relief coated Nate's words.

He hadn't been able to spend much time with Callie the day before. Serena knew he was looking forward to her company for the next few hours.

The vehicles checked in through security, drove over sinking steel barrier posts, and parked in the bays on the left. Artemus stepped out into the sunlight with Smokey. The divine beasts joined him.

Serena was unsurprised to see Elton climb out of the second SUV with Drake and Otis; she'd suspected the auction house owner wouldn't want to miss a chance to take a close look at the artifacts Reznak had found in North Africa.

"Hey," Drake called out lightly.

Serena met his dark gaze cautiously. Neither of them had spoken about what had transpired between them yesterday, when she'd passed him the EMP bomb at the demonic barrier. She suspected he was as reluctant to broach the subject as she was.

Whatever was between them was only growing stronger. Neither of them could deny that. Whether they would choose to act upon their feelings or not was a whole other matter.

The faint roar of an engine distracted Serena from her dangerous thoughts. It grew louder, drawing everyone's gaze to the road.

Serena stiffened, wondering if another attack was coming.

A black Kawasaki sports bike barreled into view. It braked sharply outside the exhibition center's security booth.

The rider was a woman in dark leathers. Her face was obscured by a shiny red helmet.

"Uh-oh," Jackson mumbled.

Serena glanced at the professor. "What is it?"

The rider had a brief word with the security guards. They checked something on their computer and allowed her through.

Artemus and the others joined Serena and Nate on the porch. They watched the woman park the motorcycle at the bottom of the steps.

"Who is that?" Artemus said curiously.

Haruki studied the sports bike enviously. "Whoever she is, she's got a helluva cool ride."

"It is." Drake stared, looking impressed despite himself. "That's a personalized model."

"It looks expensive," Otis said.

"It looks dangerous," Sebastian stated disapprovingly.

Drake rolled his eyes. He'd taken Sebastian out for a ride on his bike once. They'd never even made it down the driveway.

"Do you know her?" Elton asked Jackson.

"You could say that."

"Blast," someone muttered behind Serena. "She's already here? I thought we'd have at least an hour before she turned up."

Reznak had appeared out of nowhere and was wearing a resigned expression identical to Jackson's.

The rider climbed off the bike, removed her helmet, and ran a hand through her short, dark hair. She was breathtakingly beautiful, with pale gray eyes that glinted like silver.

Serena froze, recognition flashing through her.

Although it had been twenty-two years, she knew who the stranger was.

Nate appeared as shocked as she was where he stood rooted to the ground beside her. "That's—"

Serena frowned. "Yeah."

What's she doing here?

Otis's eyes rounded.

"What's wrong?" Artemus asked the seraph.

"I—I think I know that lady," Otis mumbled.

The woman observed their group where they stood on the porch. Her cool gaze focused briefly on Serena and Nate before zeroing in on the man between them. Lines furrowed her brow.

She stabbed an accusing finger at Jackson. "You're in *so* much trouble, mister!"

"Oh boy. She looks pissed," the professor murmured to Reznak as the woman started up the steps. "How did she find out?"

"I have no idea." Reznak sighed. "I haven't exactly broadcast what happened yesterday to the Council."

The woman stormed past Artemus and the others, grabbed Jackson by the front of his shirt, and kissed him passionately.

"Whoa," Haruki mumbled after half a minute.

The woman pushed the professor against the wall and sank her fingers in his hair. He reciprocated, his hands rising to clasp her waist in a fierce grip as he pulled her into him.

"That's hot," Callie whispered.

Nate cut his eyes to her.

"I haven't seen you in two weeks," Callie protested. "We haven't, you know—" she raised her eyebrows and shoulders in a meaningful way, "in a while."

"Sixteen days," Haruki said dully. "It's been sixteen days since you guys last had sex."

"That's sixteen days too long," Callie stated adamantly.

Smokey sighed.

"I bet you wish you could sink into a hole in the ground right about now, huh?" Drake muttered to a scowling Sebastian.

"Are you keeping a diary?" Elton asked Haruki drily.

"It's because Artemus has been ignoring his husbandly duties." Callie cast a reproachful frown at Artemus. "Haru has needs too, you know."

"No, I do not!" Haruki snarled. He pointed an accusing finger at Artemus. "And who the hell said he's the husband in this relationship?!"

"There is no relationship," Artemus growled. "We are *not* married!"

Drake smirked. "Tell that to Akihito Kuroda and his men."

"Let's book a hotel room," Nate told Callie, his expression growing determined.

"We're on a job!" Serena snapped, her stare still on the oblivious, embracing couple at the source of the inane conversation taking place around her.

The woman finally unlocked her lips from a flushed and slightly dazed Jackson's mouth.

"What are you doing here?" Reznak asked her belligerently. "Aren't you supposed to be on a field trip with Mila and Caspian, in South America?"

"I was. I kinda sensed something was wrong, so I asked Eva and Jordan to do a little digging. They told me there'd been an incident in Rome." She turned to Jackson. "Before you ask, no, I didn't leave our daughter and son in the middle of the rainforest. Mila's in Alvarães, with Conrad, Laura, and their brood. I sent Caspian to L.A."

"I thought you'd grounded the kid." Jackson grimaced. "And you *sensed* something was wrong? Did you develop psychic abilities while I was gone?"

The woman sighed. "No, smartass. It's because we're soulmates." A deadly smile curved her lips. "Asgard is taking Caspian through his Latin revision papers. That guy is more vicious than any of the tutors Reznak hired to educate me when I was a child."

"You make it sound like I engaged monsters to teach you," Reznak protested.

The woman became aware of the battery of fascinated stares levelled at her. She turned and observed them with her laser-like eyes.

"Hi. I'm Alexa King." She cocked a thumb at Jackson. "I'm his wife." She indicated Reznak next. "And *his* goddaughter."

"Er," Artemus murmured. "Nice to meet you?"

King dipped her chin. "Likewise."

Callie nudged Artemus with an elbow.

"Oh."

Artemus made introductions. King's gaze dropped to Smokey when Artemus got to the rabbit.

The pair studied each other intently. The hellhound's eyes flashed crimson.

King smiled. "I like him."

Smokey let out a low huff, as if he too approved of the Immortal.

Serena could only stare.

Just like Jackson, Alexa King had also been in Greenland in 2017, on the night Serena, Nate, and the other super soldier children had been rescued by the Immortals.

She was, in fact, one of the most powerful warriors who had done battle with Jonah Krondike's son and his army of mutants that day.

"It's you!" Otis blurted. He gazed ashen-faced at King. "You're one of the people I've been seeing in my dreams!"

CHAPTER TWENTY-THREE

"ARE YOU SURE?" DRAKE SAID.

Otis nodded vigorously as they strolled through the exhibition center. "Positive. She's one of the Immortals from my dreams." He hesitated. "She's likely the strongest among them."

Drake stared at King where she walked alongside her husband ahead of them.

The woman hadn't said anything when Otis had made his astonishing declaration a few minutes ago. Even Jackson and Reznak had acted as if the statement hadn't fazed them. Drake could tell from Artemus's expression that his twin was thinking the same thing as he was, and likely the rest of their group.

The Immortals knew a hell of a lot more about Ba'al—and about them—than they were letting on.

Drake recalled what Serena had told him last night, when they were at the Vatican. About Reznak confessing that the Immortals were not fighting Ba'al directly and did not intend to do so in the immediate future. That it wasn't their place to stop the demonic organization intent on bringing about Hell's own version of the apocalypse on Earth. He frowned.

Whatever the Immortals' reasoning was behind why they were not leading the battle against Ba'al, there was no denying their inherent strength. Although Reznak and Jackson came across as academics with an interest in archaeology and little else, Drake could tell from the way they held themselves that they were warriors. But it was King who fascinated him the most, and he suspected Artemus too.

He could sense something from her. Some kind of energy. It was different to that which echoed through him and his brother, or even the divine beasts. Yet, Drake couldn't shake the feeling that it was a power just like theirs.

"Do you know King?" Elton asked Serena and Nate curiously. "The two of you looked like you'd seen a ghost when she turned up."

Serena hesitated. "Yes. She and Jackson were at the battle in Greenland."

Artemus slowed and stared. "Wait. You mean, in 2017? The night our powers awakened?"

"She was one of the Immortals who freed us." A muscle danced in Serena's cheek. "She also helped create the barrier that protected us from the nuclear detonation."

Sebastian stiffened at that. "By barrier, do you mean to say—?"

"A divine barrier. Like the one you showed us at the mansion, the night you turned up in Chicago." Serena frowned. "But it was really the children who focused all the Immortals' powers into that barrier in Greenland."

"Children?" Elton said, clearly puzzled.

"The ones who actually broke us free," Serena

explained. "Nate was the first super soldier child they rescued from the containment tanks where we were being held, and I was the second." She paused. "Ben was the third."

"And it was a bunch of kids who rescued you?" Callie said, surprised.

"Not a bunch." Serena's expression grew distant, as if she were reliving those dark moments once more. "Just two of them. A boy and a girl."

"Twins," Nate said. "Even though they were young, we could tell how powerful they were."

Drake and Artemus shared a startled glance.

"By the way, was it a good idea to leave Daniel at the Vatican?" Haruki asked Artemus in a low voice. "Especially now that he's found his key?"

"The Vatican is the most protected enclave in the world," Sebastian replied in Artemus's stead. "The barrier around it is virtually impenetrable. He is safer there than he is with us."

Serena and Nate stared at them.

"Wait. Daniel found his key?" Serena frowned. "When? How?!"

Drake sighed. "It's a long story."

They reached the complex's main foyer and crossed over into the east wing. It was where the exhibition of the artifacts Reznak had unearthed in Libya would be taking place the following night. A man with dark hair and eyes was directing the museum's employees in the chamber they entered a moment later.

∽

A WAVE OF AWARENESS PRICKLED ARTEMUS'S SKIN. HE slowed to a stop.

"Hey, Art," Tom greeted him from where he and Lou stood guarding the entrance to the exhibition hall.

Artemus acknowledged the super soldiers with a distracted expression. His gaze swept over the team of black-clad, armed men scattered around the periphery of the chamber before focusing on what was making his nerve endings tingle.

Scores of display cabinets of varying sizes lined the marble floors around them. Though he had yet to lay his eyes properly on the artifacts they contained, Artemus could feel the weight of thousands of years of history thickening the air.

Some of the relics were too large to be contained and stood within spaces protected by stanchions and velvet ropes.

"Ah." The man who'd been organizing the staff putting the finishing touches to the decorative banners and interactive digital stands between the exhibition pieces brightened when he spotted them. "You're finally here." He crossed the chamber, a warm smile splitting his mouth. "Mr. Steele, I presume? I'm Lionel Bach, the curator of the center."

Artemus shook the man's hand. "I didn't know my reputation had reached Rome."

"Your name is quite legendary among the art collectors in our fair city," Bach said amiably. He turned and clasped Elton's hand enthusiastically. "Mr. LeBlanc, I'm pleased you could visit too. It's an honor to meet you."

"The honor is mine, I'm sure." Elton indicated the hall. "This place is incredible."

"Thank you. We do our best." Bach acknowledged the

rest of their group with a friendly expression before focusing on Artemus once more. "Why don't I show you around the exhibition? Professor Jackson perused the artifacts yesterday and agreed with the experts Dimitri hired for the expedition in Libya about their likely origin. It will be fascinating to see if you concur with his findings too."

"How old do you think these are?" Artemus asked Jackson as Bach led their group up the left side of the hall.

"2,550 to 2,600 years. Give or take a few years."

Elton stared at the professor. "That's a pretty specific range."

King and Reznak smiled faintly.

"I know my archaeology," Jackson drawled. "Although Dimitri found these artifacts in a cave in the Libyan Desert, I'm pretty confident they originated from Sabratha."

"Sabratha?" Artemus repeated, puzzled.

"Sabratha was an ancient Phoenician port and trading post on the westernmost coast of Libya," Sebastian murmured.

"Correct." Jackson looked curiously at Sebastian. "Do you have an interest in archaeology?"

"History," Sebastian replied.

"He's practically a relic himself," Callie muttered.

Haruki grinned. Otis sighed. The Sphinx cut his eyes to his sister.

Artemus's senses hummed as he examined the items on display.

Reznak's collection was eclectic and ranged from small objects like silver coins and jewelry to large ceramics and figurines made from clay, marble, metal, and ivory. Artemus suspected most would fetch five to seven-figure sums if they ever went up for auction at Elton's place.

From Elton's zealous expression, he was thinking the same thing.

By the time they were halfway around the chamber, Artemus knew Jackson was wrong about at least a dozen of the artifacts.

"You said you found all of these in the same place, in the desert?" Artemus asked Reznak as they passed the giant, bronze statue of a horse.

"Yes. It wasn't a single cave, but rather a system of underground caverns. We believe they formed a settlement for a nomadic tribe that lived in the area at the time. We found a burial ground close by and an aqueduct leading to an ancient riverbed in the next valley."

Artemus stopped in front of a marble urn that came up to his chest. "Most of the items in your collection are around the age Professor Jackson mentioned. He's wrong about some of them, though."

Jackson arched an eyebrow. "Really?"

Bach looked intrigued, as did Reznak.

Artemus indicated the urn. "This one is at least a hundred years older than your best estimate." He strolled up the hallway. "So is this ivory—" he squinted at the eroded shape, "I'm gonna take a wild guess here and say cow?"

"That's an ox," Jackson said drily.

"Oh. Well, this one is older too."

Jackson studied the hand-sized figurine. "Are you certain?"

Artemus nodded. He turned to Bach and Reznak. "May I touch it?"

Reznak looked confused for a moment. "Will that help you figure out its origin and age?"

"Yes."

Bach had a member of staff open the display cabinet. Artemus was handed a pair of gloves. He slipped them on and carefully lifted the oxen figurine from its velvet surrounds.

The object's inherent energy seeped through his skin and sank into his flesh. Artemus didn't even have to close his eyes to read its history.

"This came from a city on a wooded plateau, not far from the sea. There was a particular herb cultivated close to it." Artemus lifted the figurine close to his face and took a cautious sniff. "Smelled a bit like sulfur?"

Jackson's eyes widened. He looked over at an equally surprised Reznak before staring at the artifact. "The only place that fits that description is Cyrene, in north-east Libya."

The professor asked for a pair of gloves and carefully took the figurine from Artemus.

"It was the Greek city that gave eastern Libya the name of Cyrenaica," Reznak explained at their puzzled expressions while Jackson studiously scrutinized the ivory figure.

Sebastian raised an eyebrow. "Which would make the herb Artemus mentioned Silphium?"

"Indeed." Admiration glinted in Jackson's eyes as he looked at Artemus. "You are correct. A closer inspection of these engravings suggest that a Greek rather than Phoenician artist was behind this particular piece." He paused. "And you can really smell Silphium off this?"

"Kinda," Artemus replied.

They went around the rest of the exhibit, Artemus pointing out the other artifacts he'd sensed were older than Jackson and Reznak's experts' assessments.

"That was truly remarkable," Bach said after they'd

completed their tour of the hall. "I would be honored if you and your friends would attend the exhibition's opening night tomorrow. I'm sure Dimitri wouldn't mind."

Reznak dipped his chin. "Not at all. It would be my pleasure to host you all."

"Sure," Artemus said. "We'll come."

He caught Drake's surprised glance.

"Thank God," King murmured with a wry expression. "You guys can keep me company. Otherwise, I shall literally die of boredom."

"How could you be bored when your insanely hot husband will be standing right next to you?" Jackson asked with a mildly affronted air.

"Because I know you and the only thing likely to excite you tomorrow night is if I suddenly turn into a statue dating back to the Byzantium era," King retorted.

The bickering couple headed out of the chamber, the rest of them following in their steps. Artemus paused on the threshold and turned to observe the exhibition hall once more. Serena and Otis returned to his side.

"So, you getting demonic vibes from any of those artifacts?" the super soldier said in a low voice.

"No," Artemus replied.

Otis stared into the hall.

Serena glanced between the two of them. "But you guys are sensing *something?*"

Artemus traded a guarded look with Otis. "It's not so much what I'm sensing as what I'm *not*."

Serena sighed. "What does that cryptic sentence even mean?"

Like Otis, Artemus's gaze locked on the bronze horse statue.

He could read nothing from it. Nothing at all.

CHAPTER TWENTY-FOUR

DANIEL COULD FEEL THE WEIGHT OF THE RING AS HE
went through the pile of documents on his desk.

He still couldn't believe the gauntlets he'd been
searching for in the tomes he'd procured from some of the
best antique bookstore owners in Europe were actually
weapons that Artemus Steele had made with his very
hands. Or that he had technically started dreaming about
them before the man was even conceived.

His gaze strayed uneasily to the metal band wrapped
around his left middle finger. Though he knew it was a
physical impossibility, he could feel it watching him.

I'm losing my mind. There's no way this thing is sentient!

He knew this was a lie the moment he thought it. Not
only because of what he'd witnessed just a few hours past
in the Vatican's smithy. But because the creature who had
lain dormant within him for all those years, the one who
now seemed to be practically ensconced behind his eyes,
had just tittered.

Daniel frowned. *I wonder if the others' beasts are jerks too.*

The titter became a full-on snigger.

The door opened, distracting him from his dark thoughts and the irritating entity inside him. Persephone entered the office ahead of Bishop Irons.

"An invitation, you say?" Persephone murmured as she crossed the floor to her desk.

"Yes, Your Holiness," Bishop Irons replied. "It is from your friend, Mr. Reznak. He is holding an exhibition tomorrow night, in the city. His new collection apparently boasts several new religious findings from North Africa. He and Mr. Bach believe you will enjoy viewing them."

"Hmm." Persephone sat down and drummed her fingers thoughtfully on her desk. "Reznak does have a knack of unearthing the most unusual relics." She looked over at Daniel. "What do you say, kid? Wanna go on a date with me?"

Daniel blinked. "Excuse me?"

Bishop Irons maintained a diplomatic silence; he was used to Persephone's casual address in the privacy of her office.

"Get your best cassock ready," Persephone told Daniel sharply. "We're going to this exhibition."

"Do I have to? You know I don't like leaving this place. And I don't have a best cassock. They're all the same."

Persephone ignored this. "It's time to spread your wings."

Daniel was about to protest when he felt a faint resonance. Something had just echoed with the energy inside him.

"They're back."

"Who's back?" Persephone said, nonplussed.

"The others." Daniel caught Bishop Irons's puzzled stare. He shuffled the paperwork on his desk awkwardly to mask his embarrassment. "I mean, Mr. Steele and his friends are in the Vatican."

MICHAEL WATCHED THE CROWD MOVING IN THE VAST square below where he perched atop the south bell tower of the Basilica. It was one of his favorite vantage points in Rome.

I'm glad Gabriel inspired Bernini to create these towers.

An immense shadow moved across the piazza, invisible to all but him. A crow swooped down from the sky and landed beside him, scattering the pigeons on the rooftop.

Its form was deceptively small compared to the dark silhouette it had just cast across the ground.

The bird eyed the feathered shapes rising raucously in the air around it with a jaundiced expression before assuming the form of a boy in dark jeans and a leather jacket. Diamond earrings glinted in his ears as he crossed his legs and settled in a more comfortable position.

Michael sighed. "What are you doing here?"

The Angel of Crows glanced at him. "Visiting. Why? Is that a crime?"

Michael narrowed his eyes at the crow's acerbic tone. "I see you're back in cranky teenager mode. Did Uriel send you?"

"No."

Michael's brow wrinkled. The crow had hesitated a millisecond too long.

"Lying is against the rules, you know."

"I'm not lying," Arael muttered. "I discussed the matter with him. He decided he would not stand in my way."

Michael was silent for a moment. He could guess why Arael had turned up. It didn't mean he had to be happy about it.

"Cerberus looks well," the crow said. "As does your son."

A smile curved Michael's mouth at that. Though his meeting with Artemus the day before had seemed infinitesimally brief, it had been more than enough for him to peer into the soul of his child and see who he had become.

"The pooch seems to be thriving. And, yeah, Artemus has grown. He's a man now."

"Time does that to a person."

Michael rolled his eyes at the crow's sarcastic words. They sat in silence for a while.

Arael finally looked to the west. "She is dying."

Michael sobered at the crow's softly spoken and unequivocal statement. Now that he knew what to look for, he could feel Alice's life force slowly ebbing away with every passing hour. She was not long for this world.

It pained him that Artemus and Drake would not get to see her before she disappeared from this realm.

Arael turned to face the square once more.

"The end of this battle is close," he said quietly. "Will you interfere or will you lay low and watch, like you have been instructed to do?"

Michael frowned. "I will always do what is best for Heaven and for all of mankind."

Though the crow remained silent, the archangel sensed his wordless approval.

CHAPTER TWENTY-FIVE

Artemus swallowed a yawn and tried to focus on Persephone's words.

They'd just visited the Vatican Museums and Library and were now inside the famous Basilica. A small army of Swiss Guards walked a discreet distance behind them. Hovering close by and making up the rest of their crowded entourage was a veritable horde of clergymen.

Much to some of the archbishops' ire, the famous church had been closed for the afternoon for their group's official tour of the Vatican. Since he'd been to Rome plenty of times before, Elton had taken the opportunity to meet up with Archbishop Holmes to discuss the Vatican's latest findings on Ba'al.

To Artemus's relief, his fears about their trip to the Holy See had yet to come true in the two days they had been in the city. Apart from showing an interest in his sword, Persephone had not commanded they surrender their weapons for a closer inspection, nor had she or members of the organization tasked with hunting out Ba'al expressed any wish to keep Otis or Drake in Vatican City.

"You know, you could at least try to look interested," Daniel said in a low voice where he dawdled next to Artemus at the back of their party.

"So, sue me. It's been a busy couple of days. Besides, churches freak me out."

Daniel's mouth grew pinched. "Don't you work with religious artifacts all the time for Elton?"

"This and that are different things."

Up ahead, Sebastian and Otis were oohing and aahing over the immense bronze pavilion beneath the central dome. Drake appeared uncomfortable where he stood beside them, Smokey looking all cute and innocent in his arms. From what Artemus could sense from his twin, it seemed Samyaza was not a fan of the Basilica.

Artemus glanced at their retinue.

I don't think some of the archbishops are fans of Samyaza either.

Haruki was studying the giant statues in the niches surrounding them. "Those bible guys were ripped."

"They sure were." Callie stared. "Shame about the togas."

Sebastian twisted on his heels and gave the Chimera and the Dragon a dark look. "The two of you realize your words echo in here, right?"

Daniel's expression grew even more disapproving.

"You getting used to the ring yet?" Artemus said to the priest as they ventured deeper into the church.

"No, I am not. I still want the blasted thing off me!" Daniel hissed. "And should we really be talking about this here?"

This earned them a stare from a cardinal.

Artemus arched an eyebrow. "Considering you dreamt about those gauntlets all those years, I would have thought you'd be thrilled to finally have them in your grasp."

"Dreaming about them is one thing. Having them surgically attached to my limb is another," Daniel snapped. "Besides, you have one of them."

Artemus narrowed his eyes. "You know, I'm beginning to realize something."

"What?"

"You divine beasts are all cantankerous bastards."

"Hey!" Callie protested.

Smokey's expression grew decidedly sullen.

Haruki glanced at Sebastian. "He's not wrong."

The Sphinx bristled. "And what, pray tell, was that look for?"

"Will you guys shut up?" Drake barked. "Those archbishops are staring at us!"

Callie sniffed. "I believe the one ruining the mood is your brother."

Persephone turned to Otis. "Are they always like this?"

The seraph made a face. "Sometimes, it's worse."

Persephone led them through a side door and into a private lobby. Stone steps appeared at the end of the narrow hall.

"Where are we going?" Artemus asked curiously.

"To the Necropolis," Persephone replied.

"Wait." Artemus stopped abruptly, causing several guards and archbishops to bump into one another. "There's a graveyard under the church?!"

"I am not sure why you look so shocked," Sebastian said. "There *is* a cemetery in your garden."

Persephone observed the archbishops and cardinals in their wake with a thoughtful look. "Gentlemen, it's going to get mighty packed if all of you come with us. Might I suggest you take your leave here?"

The clergymen looked relieved at her proposal. They headed back toward the Basilica, their cassocks swishing around their sandals.

The air inside the catacombs was surprisingly warm and humid. Short flights of stairs and narrow passages separated the many mausoleums Persephone led them through.

The burial chambers had been arranged along an ancient road, as per the Roman decree at the time that forbade burial of the dead within the city walls.

Artemus's gaze roamed the pale limestone walls, mosaics, and marble sarcophagi and altars exposed under the soft lighting that bathed the catacombs. He could feel the history of the dead all around them.

"How many bodies are buried down here?" Haruki asked.

"Over fifteen hundred," Persephone replied.

Surprise dawned on Sebastian's face. "I thought the number was lower than that."

"Officially, yes." They reached the end of the cata-combs. "We discovered another level to the Necropolis five years ago. The preservation works are still ongoing, so do mind your steps."

The light grew dim as she guided them to more stairs. The air became stuffier and warmer the farther down into the earth they descended.

Artemus's eyes widened when they reached what appeared to be an underground avenue some twenty feet beneath the official Necropolis. This road was paved, unlike the one above. The catacombs leading off it also appeared better preserved than the tombs they had seen thus far.

"We found many treasures down here." Persephone's voice echoed as she led the way along the old Roman road. "Relics that were thought to have been lost centuries past during the many wars that afflicted Europe. Some have been returned to the governments of the countries they belonged to."

Gold and silver gleamed in the gloom. Frozen figures stared at them from the decorative frescoes adorning the limestone and brick walls.

They'd just strolled past a mausoleum bearing four stone sarcophagi when Daniel suddenly stopped in his tracks. Artemus slowed and looked curiously at the priest.

The man was staring into the vaulted chamber.

Artemus joined him while the others headed farther into the catacombs. A couple of Swiss Guards paused beside them.

"It's all right," Artemus said. "You can carry on."

The guards dipped their chins and hurried along, their eyes darting furtively to the shadows surrounding them.

"What's wrong?" Artemus asked Daniel once the men were out of earshot.

"I—I don't know."

Artemus frowned. He couldn't detect any unnatural energy around them. "Are you sensing something?"

"I'm not sure," Daniel murmured. "It's my ring. It feels hot all of a sudden."

Artemus's gaze dropped to the band on the priest's finger. It was glowing slightly.

CHAPTER TWENTY-SIX

HARUKI WALKED OUT OF THE LOBBY AND STOPPED ON the busy avenue outside. The meeting he had arranged with the investors interested in doing business with the Kuroda Group had gone better than he'd expected. If things progressed according to plan, he would likely close the deal by the end of the month. Satisfaction filled him at that thought.

With this, the Kuroda Group and their wider syndicate would venture further with their legitimate business enterprises.

Dad will be happy. So will Kanzaki-san. A bout of melancholy danced through Haruki then. *Yashiro would have been proud too.*

"Hey, you done?"

Haruki turned. Callie was coming out of the building, a snoozing Smokey in her arms.

"Yeah." He'd been surprised to discover that Callie's meeting was in the same high-rise as his. "How did it go?"

"Quite well, considering. Our European shareholders have been grumbling for a while, so I thought things would get dicey with the company's board of directors. They seemed surprisingly agreeable all of a sudden."

Smokey opened a lazy eye.

Haruki was willing to bet a lot of money the hellhound's presence had something to do with Callie's successful meeting.

"Wanna hit the shops?" Callie said.

Haruki hesitated. "Shouldn't we go back and help them?"

Callie grimaced. "Do I look like I want to spend the rest of my day digging up tombs? Besides, I need to get a dress for tonight. And I spotted the cutest little outfit for Smokey when we were headed here. We can't have him attend the exhibition *au naturel*."

Smokey went limp in Callie's arms. Haruki could tell the hellhound had resigned himself to whatever grim fate awaited him.

They started up the sunny avenue.

"You realize *au naturel* is the pooch's default state, right?" Haruki murmured.

Callie ignored him. "Wait till you see the suit I've got my eye on."

Haruki exchanged an uneasy look with the rabbit. "You're gonna dress him in a suit? He's gonna be the laughing stock of the party."

Smokey huffed in agreement.

Someone bumped lightly into Haruki.

"Excuse me," the stranger murmured.

Haruki stopped. He twisted on his heels and stared at the figure who'd walked around them and was now headed down the road.

It was a boy with dark hair and eyes. Diamond earrings

glinted in his ears as he tucked his hands in the pockets of his leather jacket.

"Haru?"

Haruki startled.

A frown marred Callie's brow. She followed his gaze. "Is something wrong?"

The boy had disappeared in the crowd circulating along the avenue.

"I—" Haruki hesitated. "No. It's nothing."

Whatever it was he thought he'd felt when the stranger had walked into them was already fading from his mind.

ARTEMUS PRESSED HIS HANDS AGAINST THE LIMESTONE wall and closed his eyes.

"Haven't you already done that one, like, a dozen times?" Drake said irritably.

"Yeah, I have. I still got nothing." Artemus looked over at his brother. "What about you?"

"If there's anything demonic down here, it's incredibly well concealed."

Sweat beaded Drake's forehead. He wiped his skin with the back of his sleeve and tugged at his collar. They'd been in the lowest level of the Necropolis for nearly three hours.

"I concur," Sebastian said where he was exploring the floor once more. "I cannot sense anything either."

Artemus glanced at the ring on his finger. Unlike Daniel's, it hadn't reacted to anything in the catacombs yesterday.

It was with some reluctance that Persephone had allowed them to return to the Necropolis with the priest, after delivering strict instructions that they were not to interfere with any of the ongoing renovations.

"The cardinals will have my head if you disturb anything down there," she'd said morosely that morning at breakfast.

Unfortunately, whatever it was Daniel had felt the day before had yet to manifest itself. His ring remained stubbornly cold and dull.

They'd explored the mausoleum with the four stone sarcophagi for a whole hour before deciding to split up and move on to the adjacent chambers. Daniel and Otis returned presently from where they'd been investigating the tombs on the other side of the avenue.

"You guys found anything?" Artemus asked.

Otis shook his head tiredly. "No."

"Maybe it was just a fluke," Daniel said. "Or the ring felt an echo of something that's no longer here."

"Persephone did say some of the items had been dispatched to other countries," Drake murmured.

"My gut's telling me the ring is right," Artemus said in a stubborn tone. "There's something down here."

"We better hurry," Otis said. "The party's in two hours."

Drake caught Artemus's frown. "We can come back in the morning."

Artemus cast a final look at the catacombs as they started up the stairs.

They were missing something. He was certain of it.

SERENA OBSERVED THE ELEGANTLY DRESSED CROWD queuing up outside the exhibition center. She and Lou had been assigned front door security until the start of the event. It was six-twenty and the venue wasn't meant to open for another forty minutes.

"I'm surprised there are so many people here already," Lou murmured. "I didn't realize Bach had invited this many guests."

"According to Jackson, Reznak's exhibitions are pretty famous," Serena said. "He's had heads of state and royalty attend them before."

Drake had called her a short time ago to say that they were on their way. Serena found herself feeling strangely restless as she waited for their arrival. A wry grimace twisted her lips when she realized she was drumming her fingers impatiently against her thigh.

Christ, when did I start missing those guys so much?

Serena knew this was only a half-truth. The one she truly wanted to see more than anyone was Drake.

Her smartband flashed with a message, averting the dangerous direction her thoughts had just taken.

"Everything okay?" Lou asked with a frown.

He and Tom had been on edge since they'd discovered there were first-generation super soldiers in the city.

"That was Nate. Artemus and the others are at the south gates."

❦

NATE STARED. "YOU CLEAN UP NICE."

Tom grinned. "Yeah. You guys look neat. Like a bunch of penguins."

Artemus grimaced where he stood next to Sebastian and Otis. They'd just alighted from one of the SUVs that had brought their group from Vatican City to the exhibition center.

"I already feel bad enough wearing this suit without you guys harping on about it."

Callie stepped out of the second vehicle with Haruki and Drake, her cane in hand. She was wearing a sparkling, emerald gown that highlighted her eyes and had piled her hair up in an elegant chignon.

She strolled up to Nate and kissed him lightly on the mouth. "Hey, big guy."

"Hey, yourself."

Callie grinned and twirled around. "You like it?"

Nate swallowed and dipped his chin. "I like it. A lot."

"Sheesh, get a room you two," Haruki muttered.

Tom's gaze dropped to the leash in Callie's grip. It lowered farther to the rabbit at the other end of it.

His grin widened. "The bunny's wearing a tux."

Smokey's eyes flashed red. He glared at the super soldier.

Tom chuckled. "He doesn't look happy."

"I strongly suspect he will eat his outfit before the party is over," Sebastian stated.

Callie narrowed her eyes. "He'd better not. That thing cost a few hundred bucks."

"I tried to stop her," Haruki said to Smokey. "I really did."

You did not try hard enough, Dragon!

Police sirens sounded in the distance. Persephone's security escort appeared at the head of the armored vehicle she'd traveled in. Bach and Reznak came out of the back door of the exhibition center just as the black town car pulled to a stop outside the building. King and Jackson were close behind them, the Immortal warrior wearing a crimson pantsuit that matched her husband's wine-red cummerbund and jacket lapels. She looked as comfortable in her outfit as Smokey did in his.

Captain Rossi and his team of Vatican policemen fanned out around Persephone's vehicle. Daniel and Bishop Irons climbed out of the rear ahead of her.

Bach bowed his head respectfully. "Your Holiness, it's a pleasure to meet you."

"The pleasure is mine." Persephone smiled regally as the curator pressed a kiss to the back of her hand. "Thank you very much for your kind invitation, Mr. Bach."

She greeted Reznak with a friendly slap on the back and spoke to King and Jackson as if she knew them.

They were heading inside the exhibition center when something made Artemus stop in his tracks. He studied the rooftop of the building across the road.

"What is it?" Haruki said.

"I thought I saw something."

Artemus stared into the night. There was nothing there.

CHAPTER TWENTY-SEVEN

DANIEL FIDGETED WITH HIS CRUCIFIX.

Though he knew he belonged at Persephone's side in his capacity as her personal aide, he was nonetheless conscious of the stares he was drawing. It didn't help that the hours he'd spent in the catacombs with Artemus earlier that day had tired his legs and made his limp more noticeable.

"Relax," Drake murmured. "You look like you're gonna puke."

Callie lifted a champagne flute from a passing waiter's tray and offered it to him. "Here, have a drink."

"I don't drink," Daniel protested.

He took the glass nonetheless.

They finished touring the center and headed for the hall where the main exhibition was taking place. The sound of the crowd grew louder as they entered the chamber. The place was packed wall-to-wall with people.

Daniel hung back and twisted the stem of his glass nervously before downing the entire drink in a single, giant gulp. He winced as the alcohol struck his taste buds and burned his throat.

Someone replaced his empty glass with a full one.

"Thank you," Daniel mumbled.

He flashed a distracted smile at the waiter who'd served him and had just taken a step toward the others when he froze. He whirled around so fast some of the champagne sloshed over the rim of the flute and dripped onto his hand.

The man with the tray of drinks and canapes had disappeared into the crowd. Daniel's heart thudded dully against his ribs as he searched for him frantically with his gaze.

There was no way the priest could mistake those eyes.

SERENA AND LOU STROLLED A DISCREET DISTANCE behind the Pope's security escort while the curator and Reznak showed her around the exhibition.

"And here we have a figurine of El, the mighty god of the Canaanites," Bach said presently.

Persephone paused and studied the gilded statue under the spotlight critically. "Hmm. He's shorter than I thought he'd be."

Reznak sighed. "This is just a representation."

"Well, they should have revered him with a bigger statue."

"Size isn't everything," Artemus said.

"You would know, obviously," Persephone countered.

Haruki snorted into his drink. Otis flushed.

Artemus frowned.

"I meant your weapon," Persephone continued in a

voice dripping with innocence. "It's noticeably bigger than it first appears to be."

Callie swallowed a grin. Elton looked like he wanted to disappear into the ground. Jackson's shoulders shook where he stood behind Bach. King smiled faintly next to her husband.

"You're not making this any better," Artemus told Persephone between gritted teeth as the guests who'd overheard them looked over in confusion.

Lou exchanged an amused glance with Serena. "Man, this whole trip was worth it just to hear that."

Serena grinned. She felt a gaze on her face a moment later.

Drake stood a short distance away. He met her eyes briefly before disappearing into the crowd, his tall, suited figure drawing admiring stares from the female guests.

"Wow," Lou said wryly. "Your tongue is practically rolling out of your mouth."

"It is not," Serena protested.

"Is too."

There was motion in the crowd.

Daniel appeared through the throng of people. The priest walked over to Artemus, pulled him to one side, and whispered urgently in his ear.

ARTEMUS STIFFENED. "ARE YOU SURE?"

Daniel nodded, his eyes gleaming anxiously behind his glasses. "Positive. Michael is here."

Artemus's pulse accelerated as he scanned the crowded hall. He concentrated. Bar the others, he couldn't feel another divine energy close by.

Then again, I didn't the other night either. He must be masking his presence.

"Stay close to me," he told Daniel curtly.

Drake came up behind them just as they caught up with the rest of their group.

"What's wrong?" his brother said.

"Daniel just saw Michael."

This earned Artemus and Daniel a battery of shocked stares.

"Are you certain?" Sebastian observed the packed chamber with a frown. "I do not detect any other divine energies in the room except for ours."

"I think he's hiding it, the same way demon commanders can mask their auras."

Drake's expression hardened. "If Michael is here, it can only mean one thing."

"Something is about to go down," Haruki said grimly.

Otis looked around nervously.

Artemus caught Persephone's curious stare from where she stood some dozen feet ahead of them. "Be ready for anything."

Smokey's eyes glittered with a red light. Callie dipped her chin stiffly.

They started up the hall toward Persephone.

AN UNDERCURRENT OF TENSION THRUMMED THROUGH Serena as she watched Artemus and the others join the Pope's entourage. She could tell they were on their guard.

Someone tapped her on the shoulder.

She turned, her hands dropping instinctively to the

weapons on her thighs. Her apprehension eased slightly when she saw the person standing behind her.

"Can I help you?"

Bishop Irons glanced nervously from her to Lou. "Would you mind taking a look at something?"

"Sure," Lou said. "What is it?"

Bishop Irons hesitated. "I could be wrong, but I think I just saw some of the first-generation super soldiers who attacked Artemus and his friends the other day."

Serena traded a startled look with Lou. "Show us."

Bishop Irons nodded and guided them briskly toward the exit.

The noise of the crowd faded as they crossed over into the west wing. They navigated a couple of turns and slowed to a halt in the third corridor they came to.

A display case lay broken halfway down the passage. A set of double doors stood open on the left, several feet ahead of it. The chamber beyond was shrouded in darkness.

"Stay back," Serena warned the bishop in a low voice.

The clergyman nodded jerkily.

Serena and Lou approached the doors with their weapons drawn. It was as they crossed the threshold that Serena realized something was very wrong. Her stomach lurched. She froze in her tracks.

"Wait." Serena turned to look at Irons. "How do you know what the first-generation super soldiers look—?"

Her legs went out from under her so suddenly she could only gasp.

She fell to the ground, her ears ringing. Lou collapsed beside her, his body striking the marble tiles with a dull thud a mere second after hers.

For a moment, she wondered if they'd both been shot.

She stared into Lou's stricken gaze where he lay opposite her in the dim light washing through the chamber's doorway. She could feel no penetrating injuries in her body. Though they were both conscious, it was clear neither of them could move.

Serena gritted her teeth, summoned the unearthly power that now lived inside her, and managed to turn her head slightly to look at the bishop.

Irons smiled. "You are not the only ones who can disarm super soldiers."

Her eyes widened when she saw the device in his hand.

There was movement in the shadows. Yellow pupils flared into life around them.

CHAPTER TWENTY-EIGHT

FEAR DANCED THROUGH DANIEL AS THEY REJOINED Persephone. He could sense something in the air. It was as if the pressure in the hall were steadily dropping.

Some kind of energy was gathering around them. And it wasn't coming from the angels and the divine beasts next to him. The creature inside his soul stirred as it too detected the change.

A pulse of heat shot through Daniel's core.

"And this statue dates back to the 5th century BC," Bach said as they stopped in front of a giant bronze horse.

The hot feeling throbbing inside Daniel intensified. The ring on his finger started to grow warm.

THE DRAGON STIRRED. *SOMETHING IS COMING.*

Haruki had to concur with his beast. The temperature in the room had just dropped by several degrees.

Callie's hand tightened on her cane. Sebastian removed

his pocket watch from his vest. A low growl escaped Smokey. Artemus and Drake reached for their knives.

Their energies intensified as they prepared to transform.

Reznak and Elton stared at them, their puzzled expressions indicating they'd picked up on the change that had come over their group.

"Is everything all right?" Jackson asked Haruki.

King was scanning the hall around them with narrowed eyes.

"No," Haruki replied in a strained voice. "Be ready to take cover."

Artemus turned to Persephone. "You need to leave."

Rossi tensed beside her.

Unease filled Persephone's face. "What's going on, Artemus?"

"I don't know. But whatever it is, it's gonna be bad." Artemus frowned at the Vatican policeman. "Get her out of here."

Rossi hesitated before nodding. "Your Holiness, if you could step this way."

Haruki felt a presence at his back. He twisted on his heels.

The boy who'd bumped into him that morning in the street was standing behind him. He was dressed in a waiter's outfit that matched his dark hair and eyes.

"Your friends are in trouble."

The boy's voice was low and rich, with a melodious twang that reverberated through Haruki's mind like liquid silver. He could sense immense power behind it.

The words the stranger had uttered finally registered.

"Which friends?" Haruki said, startled.

"Serena and Lou. Ba'al has them."

King scrutinized the boy. "Do I know you?"

The stranger's eyes warmed as he gazed at her. "You look well, warrior."

King blinked, surprise widening her pupils.

"Follow me," the boy ordered.

King looked from Haruki to the stranger.

"I'm coming with you," she stated in an adamant voice.

Jackson sighed at the sight of his wife's stubborn expression. "Be careful."

King pressed a kiss to his mouth and fell into step beside Haruki as he started after the boy.

It was only after they'd exited the hall that the Yakuza heir realized none of the others had noticed the stranger.

~

"DANIEL, COME WITH ME," PERSEPHONE SAID anxiously.

The priest did not reply.

Artemus looked over his shoulder.

Daniel stood frozen to the ground. An orange glow was pulsing through the ring on the priest's hand. The same radiance shimmered in his unfocused pupils.

The lights in the exhibition hall flickered and dimmed. Surprised murmurs rose from the crowd. They stared at the chandeliers and spotlights hanging from the high ceiling.

Daniel turned stiffly, his body moving as if he were a puppet on strings. His gaze locked on the bronze horse to his left.

Artemus's stomach dropped. He could feel something

from the statue now. A faint echo of malevolence. From Otis's widening eyes, so could the seraph.

The pressure in the chamber plummeted. The air grew icy. Some of the guests gasped, their breaths pluming in front of their faces.

Artemus's attention was drawn to a spot some fifteen feet above the unsettled crowd. He could detect an undercurrent of corrupt energy pooling there.

It felt strangely familiar.

"Uh-oh," Callie murmured.

Artemus finally recognized where he knew the sinister force from. His knuckles whitened on his knife.

The force was identical to the one he'd sensed two days back, when they'd been attacked on their way from the airport.

"Shit," Drake said. "It's that demon cloud!"

Smokey shook himself into his dark hellhound form. Shocked cries rose from the guests who witnessed the rabbit's transformation.

"It's too late!" Artemus barked at Rossi. "Stay behind us." He glanced at Otis. "You know what to do!"

Otis nodded and shifted to the center of their group while the captain and the other policemen crowded Persephone against the wall.

The air in the room trembled.

A ball of darkness exploded into existence a few feet beneath the ceiling, its appearance heralded by a thunderous boom that made Artemus's teeth vibrate in his jaws. The sphere grew exponentially until it became a maelstrom of shadows. Distorted apparitions appeared in the inky mass. Mouths opened on eldritch shrieks. Crimson eyes flashed with an evil light.

The crowd froze for a moment. Panicked shouts broke

out as the guests finally came to life. They turned and fell over one another as they bolted for the exit.

Divine energy pulsed across the chamber as Artemus and the others transformed.

"Here it comes!" Drake shouted.

The cloud descended upon them with a savage roar.

It struck the barrier Otis instinctively projected to protect them.

A SHIVER RACED THROUGH NATE. HE AND TOM WERE guarding the exhibition center's back door. He stiffened, startled by the eerie sensation suddenly gripping him.

He could sense something from inside the building. Something that was resonating with the divine power he now possessed.

"Nate?" Tom frowned. "Is everything—?"

Nate's smartband flashed with a red alert.

So did Tom's. "What the—?"

The back door opened. A boy dressed in a waiter's outfit walked out, Haruki and King on his heels.

"What's happening?" Nate indicated the message broadcasted by the Immortal leading their security team. "Are we under attack?"

"Yes!" A muscle jumped in Haruki's jawline. "It's Ba'al. They've captured Serena and Lou!"

Tom cursed. Alarm twisted Nate's stomach.

The boy threw a set of keys at him. "Take the car."

Nate automatically caught them. He looked at the black Corvette in the courtyard.

It hadn't been there a moment ago.

King stared at the Kawasaki bike parked next to the sports car. "I could have sworn I left that at the hotel."

"Head east." The boy frowned at Nate and Haruki. "You'll know how to find her."

Nate and the Dragon exchanged a startled look.

"Go. You don't have much time."

CHAPTER TWENTY-NINE

SAMYAZA'S STRENGTH ECHOED THROUGH DRAKE AS HE drew upon the dark force inside his soul. The runes on his shield blazed red and gold. The flames on his broadsword swelled and multiplied.

Bloodlust filled him. He clenched his jaw and visualized the golden lasso his mother had bestowed upon him to bind his inner demon. The devil roared in rage as he tightened the rope. Drake smiled savagely.

That's right, asshole. I'm the one in charge of this little power play.

"Where's Haruki?" Callie looked around. "Wait. Please tell me he's not inside the storm?!"

Her anxious gaze found Otis.

The seraph hesitated before shaking his head. "I—I cannot sense his presence."

"He and my wife left a couple of minutes ago," Jackson said stiffly. "A kid told them your super soldier friends were in trouble."

Artemus stared. "A kid?"

Alarm widened Callie's eyes. "Nate's in trouble?!"

Jackson shook his head. "No. It's Serena and Lou." His wary gaze swept across the invisible wall protecting them. "How long can this thing hold?"

"As long as I'm conscious," Otis said, his tone resolute.

Drake beat his wings until he reached the summit of the divine barrier.

Sebastian rose beside him, his eyes and hands glowing with divine power while the flames on his triple-thonged whip lashed the air angrily, the weapon reacting to the demonic energy filling the hall.

Callie scowled. "Together!"

Her ribcage swelled to gargantuan proportions as she took a deep breath. A river of fire roared out of her jaws when she exhaled.

The flames penetrated the barrier and smashed into the storm.

Drake sensed Artemus's anxious eyes on him as he and Sebastian dove for the narrow opening the Chimera had created. She followed them into the vortex.

Darkness swallowed them.

Drake snarled and swung his fiery sword at the apparitions that charged toward them.

DREAD GNAWED AT ARTEMUS WHERE HE STOOD INSIDE Otis's divine shield. He had never felt so helpless in his life. Smokey paced the floor beside him, faint growls and whines rumbling from his chest. The hellhound's fretful gaze darted to the bright flashes of light piercing the demon cloud surrounding them.

"Can they defeat it?" Reznak said above the noise of the storm.

Artemus fisted his hands. "I think so."

Persephone's alarmed shout made him turn around. "Daniel!"

The priest was on his knees in front of the bronze statue, a tortured expression distorting his face. He looked to be in unbearable pain.

His eyes flared orange behind his glasses. A cry left his lips.

Flames burst into life around him.

Persephone sucked in air. Rossi and the Vatican policemen gasped and crowded around her. It was their first time witnessing the priest's powers.

Daniel curled his hands into fists and smashed them down onto the marble tiles with an animal roar. The floor cracked and warped.

The ring on Artemus's hand started to grow warm.

DANIEL COULD FEEL THE BEAST'S AGITATION CHURNING his blood. It was angry at something. Something inside the statue in front of him.

The ring on his left middle finger trembled. His eyes widened as it transformed into its original shape, the metal extending to wrap smoothly around his hand and wrist. Flames ignited on the glove. They intensified, turning a brilliant white.

Heat bloomed inside his soul.

A jet of pale fire arced jaggedly into the air from the gauntlet. It rotated on itself for a moment before forking into two. One of the tongues struck the bronze horse with a bang and disappeared inside it.

The second latched onto the ring on Artemus's hand and sank into the metal.

ARTEMUS'S HEART SLAMMED AGAINST HIS RIBS AS HE stared at the band on his finger. It was changing back into the gauntlet it had once been. The whole thing burst into flames a second later.

He blinked. Though it looked and felt fierce, the fire did not burn him.

The blaze engulfing the glove spilled over onto his broadsword. The blade shifted, growing thinner and sleeker along the edges. Power blasted through Artemus from the weapon.

OTIS STARED, ASHEN-FACED, FROM THE FIRE SWALLOWING the gauntlet and sword in Artemus's hand to the priest consumed by divine flames. He could feel both their energies growing exponentially.

"I think I can fight it now!" Artemus said.

His eyes flared gold and orange.

Smokey huffed anxiously as the angel shot up into the air and dove for the barrier. He vanished inside the storm cloud.

A sinister force throbbed across the space within the protective dome seconds later. Otis's stomach lurched. His gaze swiveled to the source of the malicious wave washing across his skin.

A glow appeared in the bronze horse's breast. It

expanded until the entire statue shimmered with a pale light.

Rossi moved Persephone and Bach hastily away from the artifact. Elton, Jackson, and Reznak took several steps back.

Otis's ears popped as the sculpture imploded on itself with a loud whoomph.

EXHILARATION SWEPT THROUGH THE MAN.

The bronze horse had collapsed into a seething globe of darkness some two feet wide. It floated in mid-air where the statue once stood, the inky tendrils at its surface fluttering wildly while it sought to protect what lay within it from the circle of flames attacking it.

The man could almost see the artifact taking shape inside the shadowy sphere. Power slowly filled the demon inside him, dark energy leaching from the object into his blood.

Finally! I almost have you in my grasp once more.

CHAPTER THIRTY

DANIEL CLIMBED UNSTEADILY TO HIS FEET. HIS BODY felt tight, as if the creature inside him were straining to burst through his skin. A wave of revulsion twisted his gut as he gazed at the strange black cloud enclosed by a globe of fire.

A voice boomed inside his head. *We must destroy it.*

Daniel startled. He knew instinctively that the voice belonged to his beast. Just as he knew that the creature was right.

Whatever had been concealed inside the statue was something they were meant to wipe off the face of the Earth.

"What is it?" he mumbled, watching the flames stab at the dark, writhing globe.

It is a weapon. One that will break the seal suppressing the powers of a formidable demon. Now, do as I tell you.

Daniel found himself automatically obeying the creature's next words. He raised his left hand toward the malevolent manifestation. A shiver raced down his spine as the flames on the gauntlet blazed white hot. He could feel the potent force of the weapon he was wielding.

Daniel suddenly knew what he had to do. He flexed his fingers.

The fire around the black cloud responded to his wordless command. The conflagration thickened, flames interlacing with one another to form an impregnable barrier.

A series of gasps reached his ears. They were followed by dull thuds. Someone swore.

"I wouldn't do that if I were you."

Daniel whirled around. He froze.

Fear wrapped cold fingers around his heart.

Bach had Persephone in his hold. Three Vatican policemen lay on the ground behind them, bodies jerking and crimson jets pulsing from the jagged tears in their necks. Rossi dropped to his knees and pressed his hands against the closest man's wound while Jackson and Reznak used their jackets to apply pressure to the other policemen's throats.

Anger and outrage twisted through the priest. He could tell it was already too late. The officers were dying.

Elton had removed a gun from inside his suit and was aiming it steadily at Bach, his expression flinty. "How the hell did you manage to hide your aura?"

The curator's eyes flashed with an ochre light. "Oh, come now. I am one of Satanael's strongest commanders. Masking my true nature is but child's play."

His claws sank into Persephone's flesh where he clasped a hand around her throat. Blood bloomed on her skin. She clenched her teeth, her expression defiant.

Rage flooded Daniel. He took a step toward them.

Stop. You are not strong enough to face him yet.

Frustration churned Daniel's stomach at the beast's

warning. Though Bach had yet to change into his full demon form, he could tell the man was not lying. Just as his beast had said, the curator was a fearsome foe.

A suffocating energy burst into life around them, forcing him and Otis back several steps.

Persephone gasped as Bach cast her violently aside. Elton caught her in his arms and stumbled to the ground.

Alarm stiffened Daniel's body. He stared at the orb levitating where the bronze horse once stood. The flames were being consumed by the darkness. An object was slowly emerging from within it.

A savage smile split Bach's mouth. The whites of his eyes turned obsidian. His body swelled as he stepped toward the mutating sphere, the demon inside him finally materializing.

Otis cursed.

Daniel glanced at Artemus's assistant. Surprise jolted him.

Something was happening to the young man. His eyes were glowing faintly. So were his right hand and the middle of his forehead.

The shadows wreathing the orb dissolved into nothingness, revealing the object that had taken shape inside it.

It was an inky, nine-pronged crown tipped with glistening, red-black pearls. The artifact throbbed and pulsed, as if made of corrupt flesh.

Pleasure brightened Bach's wicked eyes. He clasped the crown and laid it reverently upon his head. Dark tendrils snaked from the object and sank into his skull.

A hiss of satisfaction left the demon. He shuddered, his pupils flaring crimson.

Daniel took a step back as Bach grew another three

feet, his towering shape casting them in shadow. He could feel the demon's powers growing.

Horns sprouted from Bach's forehead. Jet-black wings emerged from his back.

"Ah." He closed his eyes briefly. "It is so refreshing to take this form once more. It has been far too long." He turned and observed the storm battering the divine barrier around them with his red eyes. "It seems I was correct in my suspicions. The only thing that could make the crown manifest its presence was if the air was full of enough divine energy to resonate with it." A mocking smile tilted his lips. "My spirit cloud has proved a useful distraction to draw away your friends." His loathsome gaze shifted to Daniel and Otis. "Of course, the two of you helped as well. Alas, you are no match for me, so please don't do anything stupid."

A harsh wind thumped violently against Daniel's skin as Bach beat his wings and rose some ten feet above the ground. The demon stopped and hovered for a moment before reaching out to his right. A boom split the air next to his clawed hand. A dark line flickered into existence. It thickened and tore in two.

Bile rose in Daniel's throat at the evil force emanating from the red rift that emerged between the wavering boundaries. Bach pushed his arm inside the breach. He bared his teeth, his expression smug.

Trepidation swamped Daniel.

The demon was removing an enormous black broadsword from the crimson crack. It was made from the same material as the crown and radiated pure malice.

"*King Paimon!*" Otis spat.

Daniel looked at the seraph. His voice sounded different.

Bach focused on Otis. "I see you recognize me, Seraph."

The demon's growl reverberated in Daniel's very bones. His shape blurred in the next instant. The priest blinked and gasped.

The demon was floating mere inches in front of him, his foul breath washing across his face.

"Since you appear to have come upon your key, what say you and I go find that gate of yours, eh, Guardian?" Bach said with a monstrous grin.

He swung his sword at Daniel's left wrist. The beast inside Daniel roared.

Sparks erupted between them. Someone grunted.

Bach and Daniel's gazes dropped to where Otis had grabbed the demon's blade barehanded. Surprise flared in Bach's eyes. He frowned at the seraph.

A third eye had appeared on Otis's forehead. His skin had turned the color of silver and the consistency of stone. Divine light shone from his right hand where he clasped Bach's sword.

Daniel wasn't sure who was the most shocked out of the three of them.

The storm cloud outside the divine barrier started to dissipate. Bach looked up, displeasure darkening his face. It was evidently not of his doing.

Artemus and the others appeared from within the fading wisps of darkness, their expressions confused as they gazed at their disappearing enemy.

Drake's eyes rounded when he spotted the demon.

Artemus gaped. "What the—?"

Bach moved. The rift expanded to accommodate his giant form as he darted toward it.

Winged shapes dropped toward the demon. Artemus

and Drake were almost at the rift when someone flashed into view in front of it.

The apparition's voice echoed around the hall and rattled the chandeliers. "*No.*"

Artemus and Drake drew back sharply, their wings thrumming the air with heavy beats.

Daniel's eyes widened. It was Michael.

The archangel gazed at the two brothers steadily where he floated in space. "You must not go after him."

Artemus scowled. "Get out of my way!"

"If you chase after Paimon now, all will be lost, Artemus."

Artemus stiffened at Michael's warning.

The rift closed with a sound like thunder. Deafening silence fell around them in the aftermath.

Daniel looked around.

The exhibition hall was a scene of chaos. Smashed display cabinets and broken glass were strewn everywhere, the remains of Reznak's priceless collection lying haphazardly amongst them.

The air trembled as Otis lowered the divine barrier.

"Wow." Callie glanced from Michael to Artemus. "So, that's your dad, huh? I can kinda see the family resemblance."

"I can't," Artemus snapped.

He alighted on the ground and resumed his human form, Drake in his wake.

Michael landed beside them. He raised a hand to his heart. "Your words wound me, son."

Artemus narrowed his eyes at the archangel's dry tone.

The fire surrounding Daniel slowly fizzled out. A wave of lassitude swept over him. He wobbled slightly. Otis put an arm around his shoulders and steadied him.

"What kind of time do you call this, you silly man?!" someone barked. "And why, pray tell, are you dressed like that?"

Elton had helped Persephone back on her feet. She was glaring at Michael as if he had committed an unforgivable sin.

Michael looked down at his server's outfit. "I'm incognito." He scratched his cheek as he met Persephone's irritated glower. "And I want to say something trite like 'Hammer Time', but I suspect that will only upset you more."

Persephone mumbled something rude under her breath.

"He is most *definitely* your father," Sebastian told Artemus.

"Without a doubt," Drake murmured.

Artemus studied Michael and Persephone with a cold expression. "So, I was right. You two really *do* know each other!"

CHAPTER THIRTY-ONE

Haruki clung to King as she stormed along the busy highway, the Kawasaki's engine roaring hotly between their thighs. The Corvette was twenty feet ahead of them. The sports car veered sharply in and out of the traffic headed east, tires squealing and raising smoke from the asphalt as it performed controlled slides and skids.

King stuck close to the vehicle, her speed never falling below a hundred miles an hour.

"Any idea where we're headed?" she shouted over her shoulder.

"I can kinda sense something. An echo of divine energy somewhere up ahead. Nate can probably feel it too."

That kid back at the exhibition hall was right. Haruki couldn't suppress the sliver of unease that shot through him at the thought. *How did he know we would be able to detect Serena's location this way?*

He was about to ask King if she knew the boy from somewhere when movement in front drew his gaze. An eighteen-wheeler had started changing lanes, the vehicle moving ponderously into their path. Haruki cursed.

There wasn't enough space to get past it.

The Corvette's taillights flashed red. The car zipped jerkily to the right, rose on its inside wheels, and darted back into the outside lane. It mounted the wall of the concrete barrier in the median strip with its raised tires, skimmed past the eighteen-wheeler with a couple of feet to spare, and shot ahead with a burst of speed.

Haruki's eyes widened as the Kawasaki closed in rapidly on the back of the truck. "Er, I think you should—"

"Hang on!" King yelled.

Haruki's grip tightened reflexively on the Immortal's waist as she braked. She dropped back fifteen feet, accelerated again, and killed the throttle abruptly. The front wheel of the motorbike lifted off the asphalt.

King aimed it at the barrier.

Haruki's stomach lurched as they climbed the concrete wall and landed atop it with a bounce.

King ignored the fast-moving traffic shooting past in the opposite expressway and punched the throttle again. They pelted down the foot-wide barricade, flashed past the eighteen-wheeler, and soared into the air in front of it.

Haruki caught a glimpse of the driver's shocked face before they touched back down on the asphalt with a sharp jolt.

"You can let go now," King said a while later.

Haruki flushed and loosened his hold on the Immortal's waist. "Sorry."

The Corvette came into view thirty feet in front of them.

The traffic was getting lighter the closer they got to

the outskirts of the city. The wind stung Haruki's eyes as they sped along the highway. He could feel Serena's presence growing closer across the divine ties that now linked them. A wry smile curved his mouth.

Whether Nate and Serena liked it or not, there was no denying that their bond with the angels and the divine beasts was only getting stronger with the passage of time. He was aware from talking to Callie that Serena in particular had resisted embracing their unnatural alliance. The Yakuza heir could guess as to the reason behind her initial opposition.

There was no mention of super soldiers in Catherine Boone's journals. As such, Serena probably felt she and Nate had no direct role to play in the prophecies written by Otis's mother.

Haruki knew in his bones this wasn't true, as did the others. Nate and Serena's fates were tied to theirs. From a conversation he once overheard between Artemus and Drake, he was conscious of Artemus's strong feelings on this subject.

The angel had once told Elton that he could only see Nate and Serena ever leaving them if they did so of their own free will, rather than on the orders of the Vatican or the Immortals.

And there's also the matter of Serena and Drake.

Though none of them had spoken about it, everyone could sense what was going on between the super soldier and the dark angel.

Unlike Nate, who had entered into a relationship with Callie as if it were the most natural thing in the world, Serena's love affair with Drake was likely to take a more tortuous and explosive path.

Haruki's smile widened to a grin. He knew Artemus

was getting a kick out of watching his brother struggle with his feelings for the aloof super soldier.

The Corvette took the next exit.

Haruki sobered up and closed his eyes. It took a handful of seconds to feel out Serena's location. She was somewhere on their left. So far, the super soldier's energy had remained stable, with none of the fluctuations that would suggest she was agitated or actively fighting.

Haruki wasn't sure whether that was a good thing or a bad thing.

The streetlights grew sparser as they entered an area of dense woodland.

"By the way, do you know who that kid was back there?" Haruki said as the Corvette angled onto a road snaking up a hill.

King did not reply straightaway. "I have an inkling."

Haruki waited.

"Are you going to tell me?" he said after a moment.

"No."

Irritation shot through him. "Why not?"

"Because you are not meant to know yet."

Haruki stared at the back of the Immortal's head. "What do you mean?"

"Everything will become clear in the future." She paused. "If you survive this trial, that is."

Haruki frowned. "What trial?"

"I'm afraid I cannot say more on the subject. You'll just have to wait and see."

Haruki blew out a sigh. "You Immortals are annoyingly cryptic."

King smiled. "We've been around a while."

Haruki grew curious at that. "If you don't mind me asking, just how old are you?"

"Around three hundred and fifty years. I do not know my exact date of birth."

"Wow," Haruki mumbled. "So, you're like one of Reznak's relics, huh?"

Cool silence fell between them.

"It's a good thing you're a divine beast, or you'd be roadkill right now," King muttered.

The Corvette slowed before turning onto a winding, pothole-ridden access road. Nate killed his headlights after a quarter mile and pulled onto the side of a drive. King decelerated and rolled the Kawasaki to a stop behind the vehicle.

A pair of wrought-iron gates rose at the end of the road. Thick woodland and overgrown shrubs crowded the driveway beyond it.

Haruki could sense Serena's life force somewhere beyond the trees. His gaze moved to the dilapidated board to the right of the entrance. A grimace twisted his face when he read the sign.

"Great. Just great."

CHAPTER THIRTY-TWO

SERENA'S EYES SNAPPED OPEN. IT TOOK A SECOND FOR her vision to clear. A grimy, water-stained ceiling appeared some ten feet above her. Memory returned in a rush of sounds and images.

The super soldiers!

She tried to sit up. Cold bands tightened painfully around her wrists and ankles, holding her immobile. Serena lifted her head carefully, her heart hammering against her ribs.

Her stomach dropped when she saw the restraints that bound her to a metal gurney. The straps writhed and trembled, living darkness given form. She didn't have to feel the sickening energy rolling off them to know they were of a demonic nature.

She frowned as she recalled the EMP bomb Bishop Irons had used to immobilize her and Lou. Though the device hadn't looked anywhere as sophisticated as the ones Gideon had made for them, it had performed its function well.

It must be the frequency of the pulse. Ba'al must have modi-

fied the nanorobots in their super soldiers to make them immune to the bomb Gideon created and invented one that resonates with our own. She closed and opened her fists slowly. *At least I have control over my body again, even if I cannot move freely.*

"Serena?" someone mumbled on her left.

She looked around.

Lou was strapped to a bed next to her. The super soldier was gazing at the chamber they found themselves in.

"Where the hell are we?" He strained against his restraints. "And what the heck are these things?!"

"Those are demonic ties. I wouldn't bother fighting them if I were you."

Apprehension filled Serena as she studied their murky surroundings.

They were in some kind of windowless chamber. Paint peeled and flaked from the damp, dirty walls around them. Abandoned medical equipment lay scattered across the debris-strewn floor.

There was an office of sorts behind some glass windows ahead. A pair of metal doors stood ten feet to the right of it.

It was the only entry and exit she could see to their prison.

"Oh shit," Lou said leadenly.

Serena had to twist her head to follow his alarmed gaze. She clenched her jaw.

Damn it.

Rows of tanks lined the wall behind them. Some two dozen first-generation super soldiers floated amidst the murky liquid inside the pods. Tubes punctured the backs of their necks and the vessels at their elbows, the lines pulsing with wisps of darkness. The men's eyes were closed and their limbs relaxed.

"They're in stasis. We have to keep them that way when we do not need them."

Serena's head whipped around.

A shadowy form had taken shape in the gloom next to the office. It approached the metal beds slowly.

Irons's shiny face appeared in the feeble light of the naked bulb suspended from the ceiling. "They start to malfunction if they are left to their own devices, you see."

Serena narrowed her eyes at the clergyman. "You're a demon."

"Not yet. I would otherwise not have been able to enter the divine barrier at Artemus Steele's mansion and, more to the point, the one around the Vatican." Irons raised his hand and looked at it strangely, as if the appendage did not quite belong to him. Beads of sweat dotted his forehead and upper lip. "But I will be a demon soon. Now that my master has awakened, I can take my true form, like he promised I would."

Serena stared. The bishop's eyes were slightly unfocused, as if he were under the influence of something.

"Your master?" she repeated slowly.

Irons inclined his head gravely. "My king. Paimon, one of the greatest commanders of Hell's army. I believe you know him as Lionel Bach."

Lou sucked in air. "That bastard?! He's the one behind all of this?"

Irons blurred and vanished. Serena blinked.

A choked noise sounded on her left.

The clergyman was standing by Lou's bed, one hand clasped tightly around the super soldier's throat. Dread swamped Serena. She hadn't seen him move.

"You will do me the decency of addressing him as King Paimon, please," Irons told Lou in an eerily casual voice.

Lou's face reddened as he fought the bishop's hold and thrashed against the bonds that held him down.

"Let him go!" Serena yelled.

For a moment, Irons looked like he hadn't heard her. He blinked and abruptly released the super soldier.

"Pardon me," he murmured. "I do not know what came over me."

A creepy giggle left his lips. He started to laugh maniacally.

Serena exchanged an uneasy glance with Lou. *He's insane!*

Her breath plumed in front of her face. Serena tensed. The temperature inside the room had dramatically dropped. Her eardrums throbbed as the pressure plummeted next. Her gaze was drawn to a spot some fifteen feet from the bottom of her bed.

The air trembled. A dark line flashed into existence halfway between the floor and the ceiling. It lengthened and thickened before ripping open. Serena dug her nails into her palms when she saw the demons who stepped out of the crimson rift.

There were eight of them.

"Funny story," Irons said in a conversational tone. "Lionel Bach was actually a very successful entrepreneur and businessman."

One of the demons walked over to Lou's bed. The super soldier stiffened.

"He was fascinated by the occult and spent an inordinate amount of time and money collecting rare texts on demonology in the 1960s."

Irons paused and shuddered. Serena's eyes widened.

Something was happening to the clergyman. His skin was darkening and quivering, strange lumps appearing beneath the oily, glistening surface.

"One day, Bach got his hands on an authentic copy of the *Ars Goetia*."

Irons groaned and arched his back at an impossible angle before bowing it forward. Bony protrusions erupted from his spine, piercing his cassock. His nails thickened and lengthened to wicked talons, the claws on his feet tearing through his sandals.

"The silly man used the book to summon Paimon. You see, he thought he could make my master dance to his tune."

Irons's body swelled and grew until his head almost touched the ceiling. The whites of his eyes shifted to black. His pupils flared with a sulfurous light.

"My master was most amused." Irons's voice was now a guttural growl. "Unfortunately for Bach, he took a liking to his soul. So, he stole it for himself."

The growths on Irons's skin erupted into pus-weeping tumors. Serena gagged as the stench of rotting flesh filled the chamber. Her breath froze in her throat when he reached inside the chest of the demon who stood by Lou's bedside and ripped the creature's heart out.

The demon swayed and fell to the ground with a grunt. His body transformed into the human he had once been, his eyes open and lifeless.

Serena and Lou's gazes locked on the beating mass of corrupt flesh in Irons's palm.

Another demon approached Lou. He ripped the super soldier's shirt open, scoring cuts across his skin.

"What are you doing?" Lou mumbled.

Irons handed the dead demon's heart across to the second fiend. He smiled at Lou.

A sudden premonition chilled Serena's blood. "Get away from him!"

Lou glanced at her in confusion. Irons smiled at her, the glee in his hateful eyes confirming her worst fears.

"This will only hurt for a moment," the demon told Lou.

He sank his talons inside the super soldier's chest.

Lou went rigid. He arched his back and screamed.

CHAPTER THIRTY-THREE

MOONLIGHT STREAMED THROUGH THE FILTHY, CRACKED windows of the abandoned asylum sitting atop the wooded hill, the pale glow washing across the flaking paint and damp patches on the walls and dispersing some of the shadows crowding the empty cells they passed. Disused gurneys and medical kit littered the floor, along with dead branches and decomposing debris that had washed inside the building.

Haruki eyed the deserted corridor they were navigating nervously. From the state of the place, it had been empty for some time.

A bang sounded behind him. He jumped and whirled around.

Tom stepped around the wheelchair he'd bumped into. "Sorry."

Haruki pressed a hand to his racing heart. "Christ, be careful."

"Are you all right?" Nate asked.

"No," Haruki mumbled. "This place gives me the creeps. And I hate hospitals in general."

They turned the corner and entered another corridor. A low howl echoed down the passageway toward them.

Haruki stiffened. "What was that?!"

"It's just the wind," King said.

Her gaze dropped to her arm. Haruki realized he was clutching it in a white-knuckled grip. He let go abruptly.

She observed him with a steady stare. "You're a bit of a scaredy cat, aren't you?"

Haruki bristled. "I am not! Wait till you see my dragon."

A frosty silence fell across the passage.

King's expression grew flinty. Nate sighed.

"Dude, keep it in your pants," Tom muttered. "She's a married woman."

"What?" Haruki's eyes rounded. "Wait. I didn't mean it like that!"

The Dragon stirred. Haruki stilled.

Nate froze beside him.

They had both felt the strong demonic power that had just erupted somewhere inside the building. Underlying it was a current of divine energy. The golden threads churned agitatedly, reflecting the distress of the soul it was bound to.

A distant scream echoed out of the depths of the asylum.

SERENA CURSED AND STRAINED AGAINST THE TIES binding her, muscles bunching with super-human strength to no avail. The corrupt bands only bit into her flesh, stinging her skin and drawing blood.

"Do not be impatient." Irons flashed his glistening

fangs at her. His hand was still embedded inside Lou's chest. "Your turn will come soon enough."

Lou was convulsing on the gurney, face flushed a deep purple and back bowing off the metal surface. The other demons watched avidly, their yellow eyes gleaming with hunger.

Rage and anguish stormed through Serena. Lou was going to die. And there was nothing she could do about it.

Something moved in the shadows behind the demons.

Someone was standing there. Pale hair glittered in the gloom as the apparition moved closer. Serena's eyes widened. Irons and the demons seemed oblivious to the woman's presence.

The specter ignored the monsters in the room and approached the bed, her star-filled eyes on Serena. The last time the super soldier had seen her had been inside Drake's soul.

Do you really believe there is nothing you can do? Artemus and Drake's mother smiled gently. *You are stronger than you think you are, child. Believe in yourself.* She placed a gentle hand on Serena's chest. *Believe in your bond with your allies.*

Serena blinked. The woman had disappeared. Only the warmth of her palm remained where she'd touched her.

Lou's screams reverberated in Serena's ears. Her heart clenched in despair.

Can I really do it?

Drake's face rose in front of her. Determination surged through her. She gritted her teeth.

Guess there's only one way to find out.

Serena took a shallow breath, closed her eyes, and focused inward.

A light flickered into existence in the darkness behind her eyelids. It pulsed warmly, golden tendrils wavering in the gloom. Serena could almost feel it watching her.

Help me. Please.

For a second, nothing happened.

Heat exploded inside her chest in the next instant. The blaze expanded, filling her with the most glorious power. Serena snarled and flexed her muscles. The demonic restraints trembled and snapped.

Irons whirled around.

Serena bolted upright and leapt from the bed. She closed the distance to the demon in the blink of an eye and grabbed his wrist, a pale light fluttering across her skin.

"Take your filthy hands off him!"

The doors crashed open.

Divine energy resonated inside Serena in tune with two of the figures who rushed inside the chamber.

HARUKI STOPPED A FEW FEET INSIDE THE DIMLY LIT basement, King, Nate, and Tom at his side. He took in the tanks at the back of the room and the demons turning to face them, before zeroing in on the giant figure looming over a bed and the woman beside it.

Serena's eyes shone with a faint, golden glow as she yanked the demon's hand out of Lou's body. The same luminescence lit her body with a pale aura.

Tom wrinkled his nose in disgust. "Jesus, what is that smell?!"

Nate hurled a flat object and a knife over the heads of the demons charging toward the doors. "Serena!"

She jumped, caught the disc, and slapped it on her

chest. Her nanorobot suit deployed a second before she grabbed the falling dagger and stabbed it into the giant demon's eye.

The monster howled in outrage.

Motion drew Haruki's gaze. A demon was lunging across the floor toward him. Heat bloomed in his core. The Dragon growled as he transformed.

The demon closed in on him, dark talons swinging for his eyes.

Haruki turned his head sharply. The claws glanced off the silver scales covering his left cheek and the ivory horn framing his jaw. A savage smile dawned on his lips.

He glared at the demon. "Bad move, asshole."

Haruki took a deep breath and exhaled a jet of white-hot flames. The monster shrieked and stumbled backward, flesh charring as he was engulfed by divine fire.

Haruki unleashed the Sword of Camael and stabbed the creature in the heart.

"Man, that's *so* cool!" Tom gushed. "Hang on a sec!"

The super soldier ducked beneath a clawed hand, hit his assailant's gut with enough force to leave an imprint of his knuckles on the fiend's flesh, and kneed him in the stomach.

King blocked a strike to her belly, clasped the arm of the demon who'd attacked her, and sent him flying up and over her head. The creature struck the ground with an "Oomph!" that turned into a tortured groan; King had just stabbed one of her heels into his groin.

Tom winced. "Ouch."

A demon sailed past them and crashed into a metal gurney, courtesy of a punch from Nate. The same light shimmering around Serena was dancing across the super soldier's body and in his eyes.

Another wave of divine energy washed across Haruki's skin.

The Dragon straightened. *Oh.*

Haruki turned and stared at King. It was coming from the Immortal.

The Dragon seemed in awe of what he was sensing. *She is powerful.*

The air quivered around King. The ground started to shake. It cracked beneath her feet.

A violent force exploded around the Immortal, forcing them back several steps and sending the disused equipment crowding the basement skittering across the floor and crashing into the walls.

She was gazing unblinkingly at the back of the room, her expression deadly. She reached over her shoulders and removed a pair of Sai daggers strapped to her back.

Haruki looked around.

The first-generation super soldiers were waking up.

SURPRISE SHOT THROUGH SERENA. SHE RECOGNIZED THE power emanating from King.

It was the same incredible force she'd felt twenty-two years ago, on the night she and the other super soldier children were rescued from the research facility in Greenland.

The Immortal's attention was focused on the tanks at the rear of the chamber, where her old foes were awakening.

Serena's gaze shifted to Irons.

The demon was holding a clawed hand to his face and glaring at her with his good eye. A dark liquid oozed out of his injured socket and dripped onto his fingers. He bared his fangs and swung his fist.

She blocked his wrist with her hands. Shock flashed in Irons's ochre pupil.

Serena's mouth split in a fierce smile. Divine energy surged in her blood. She front-kicked the demon in the thigh, gripped his throat as he sagged, and struck him in the face with her palm.

Bone crunched beneath her hand. Foul blood spurted from Irons's nose. The demon howled and staggered back a couple of feet.

Lou moaned on the bed, his eyelids fluttering weakly. The dark marks scorching his chest had turned a livid red.

"Is he okay?!" Tom called out anxiously from where he engaged a demon.

"No." Serena narrowed her eyes at Irons. "But he will be."

The bishop looked wildly around the basement.

Four of the demons he'd brought with him were out for the count. At the rear of the room, the first-generation super soldiers were stepping out of their life pods, their pupils mutating to yellow and the whites of their eyes turning silver.

A triumphant grimace lit Irons's face. A rift burst into life beside him.

Oh no, you don't!

Serena scowled and bolted toward the demon. Irons stepped inside the breach and vanished.

She skidded to a stop in front of the fading crimson crack. "Shit!"

Movement drew her attention to the gurney. Lou was trying to sit up.

"Don't." Serena strode to his side and pushed him down gently on the bed. "You're hurt."

Lou winced and gingerly touched the bruises on his chest, his face pale. "Damn. I feel like I've been hit by a two-ton truck." His gaze landed on the lifeless, dark heart lying on the floor, where the demon who'd been holding it had dropped it. "What the hell was that bastard trying to do to me anyway?"

Serena studied the corrupt mass thoughtfully.

"I think that's how they transform the super soldiers into demons," she said slowly. "By replacing their heart with one of their own."

Horror filled Lou's face. He shuddered.

"Hey, asshole, how long are you gonna lie there help-lessly for?" Tom yelled as he narrowly avoided a punch from a demon.

Lou flipped his middle finger at the super soldier.

Serena stared from the radiance dancing across her fingertips to the scarlet wounds on Lou's body. *I wonder...*

She hesitated before touching his skin lightly.

"Hmm," Lou mumbled. "What are you doing?"

"I'm not sure."

Serena concentrated. Golden sparks arched from her hand and entered Lou's body. He stiffened.

A gasp left his lips a moment later. "Oh wow."

The marks on his chest were disappearing, the nanorobots inside him galvanized by the divine energy she was pouring into them. The color returned to his face.

Serena lifted her hand.

Lou sat up and pressed his fingers against his heart, his expression stunned. "I feel...okay." He looked at her blindly. "In fact, I feel more than okay. What did you do to me?"

Serena faltered. "I think I...accelerated your healing."
She flexed her hand in astonishment.

"That's a very touching moment you two, but a little help would sure be appreciated right about now!" Tom shouted as a super soldier demon lifted him into the air and flung him against the wall.

CHAPTER THIRTY-FOUR

BACH DROPPED ONTO ONE KNEE AND BOWED HIS HEAD before the wavering portal, the dark energy emanating from within it washing over him in waves that pressed uncomfortably against his skin.

The voice of Ba'al's supreme leader boomed across the chamber. "I see you have found your crown, Paimon."

"Yes, my liege."

The weight of his newfound weapon sat heavily on Bach's head. Though he was one of Hell's most powerful soldiers, even he had to concede to Ba'al's supreme leader.

He was Satanael's right hand, after all, and the most trusted of his brethren.

The room Bach knelt in was in the basement of his home. Constructed from steel-reinforced concrete, it was able to withstand the pressure that Ba'al's supreme commander projected by his mere presence.

The demons and spirits Bach ruled over stayed well away from the chamber. To draw too close to it when he was in communion with Ba'al's leader was to risk losing their sanity.

"Good. Very good." Ba'al's leader paused. "I take it this means you ran into Artemus Steele and his companions?"

"Indeed I did, my liege."

"And, yet, here you are," Ba'al's leader mused. "Did you run away from the fight, Paimon?"

Bach narrowed his eyes slightly at the floor. "I chose to make a strategic retreat."

Silence fell across the chamber. For a moment, Bach wondered if he had been too impudent with his words.

"I have always admired the way your mind works, Paimon," Ba'al's supreme leader muttered. "You were a king among kings. I gather this means you have a plan of attack?"

Bach smiled faintly. "Indeed I do, my liege."

Dozens of dark tanks lined the wall behind him. Suspended in the murky liquid inside, blissfully unaware of what he had in mind for them, the super soldier demons slept.

ARTEMUS EXITED THE RIFT AFTER DRAKE AND OTIS. Sebastian stepped out behind him and closed the portal with a motion of his hand.

Following the chaos at the exhibition center, they'd decided the safest and fastest route to Vatican City was via a shortcut. Rossi had stayed behind with Reznak and Jackson to deal with the aftermath of the unholy battle that had taken place inside the building.

The only fatalities of the incident were the three policemen Bach had felled before his transformation. It was thanks to the quick response of Reznak's Immortal security team that the rest of the guests had been safely evacuated after their initial panic.

Considering what went down in that hall, it's a miracle no one else died.

Artemus frowned, more troubled than he'd care to admit. He suspected the only reason the casualties numbered but a handful was that Bach had been so focused on finding his crown.

From what Daniel had revealed, it was a weapon that enabled the demon king to unseal his full powers.

Artemus looked at his hand. The gauntlet had resumed the form of the ring once more. He flexed his fingers and recalled the glorious force that had spread through him from the weapon.

The divine flames the gauntlet had emitted had enabled him to fight the spirit cloud Bach had generated. He didn't completely understand the glove's power. And he couldn't help but feel that it was a borrowed gift.

Artemus was still staring at the ring when the door to Persephone's study burst open.

Holmes strode in, his face pale. "Your Holiness, are you all right?! Elton called and told me what happened."

Persephone waved a hand weakly where she leaned against her desk, Daniel hovering close to her. "I'm okay. Just a bit dizzy from traveling through that portal." She cast an uneasy look at Sebastian. "That was quite something."

"What was that radiance?" Elton mumbled, ashen-faced.

It had been his first time inside a rift too.

"That was Heaven's light," someone said behind them.

Artemus turned.

Michael stepped out of thin air next to the fireplace.

He had discarded his waiter's outfit and wore his long coat once more. A boy in dark jeans and a leather jacket appeared beside him. Diamond earrings glinted in the stranger's ears. He wore a wine-red belt with a silver buckle and a delicate bracelet on his left wrist.

"Who is that?" Callie said curiously.

"I don't know, but I like his T-shirt," Drake muttered.

Smokey's eyes brightened when he saw the stranger. He jumped from Callie's arms and transformed into his dark hellhound form as he scampered toward the boy.

Holmes blanched. The archbishop had never witnessed the rabbit's transformation before.

The hellhound bumped the boy's thigh affectionately with his body.

The stranger smiled and stroked Smokey's head. "Hello, Cerberus. It has been a while, my friend."

Artemus stared. The boy's voice had a strange musical undertone, one that resonated with the divine power inside him.

"Arael, it's good to see you again," Persephone said warmly.

The boy's expression turned apologetic as he faced the Pope. "I'm sorry you had to go through that."

Persephone shrugged. "From Michael's timing, I divined it was meant to be."

"Arael?" Sebastian looked from Persephone to the boy, surprise lighting up his eyes. "As in, the Angel of Crows?"

The stranger dipped his head solemnly. "Indeed, my dear Sphinx."

Holmes wobbled slightly, close to fainting. Elton got hold of a chair and forced the elderly clergyman down on it.

An echo of anger swirled within Artemus as he faced Michael. "Why did you stop me from going after Bach?"

Michael watched him with an unreadable expression. He glanced at Drake. "Because your brother would have fallen to Hell."

Shock widened Artemus's eyes. Drake stiffened beside him.

"Drake is stronger than that," Artemus protested. "And I would have been there for him."

A sad light danced in Michael's eyes. Arael's face grew troubled.

"Drake is strong. I am not denying that." Michael paused. "But Samyaza is stronger."

"Drake isn't alone," Artemus insisted. "We can protect him."

"Yeah," Callie mumbled.

"Artemus is correct," Sebastian stated.

Otis nodded.

Michael studied them with a melancholic air before gazing at Artemus. "If Drake falls to Hell, you will too, Artemus."

Michael's words echoed in the stunned silence that befell them.

Artemus's heart thumped rapidly against his ribs. He knew the archangel was not lying.

"Is that a foregone conclusion?"

Everyone looked at Daniel.

"Do Catherine Boone's predictions mention this as being something that cannot be avoided?" the priest said doggedly. "That Drake's downfall is inevitable?"

Michael's expression grew enigmatic once more. "Nothing is certain in this world."

"Then there is still a chance," Daniel countered in a determined tone.

Persephone stared at the priest.

"What is it?" he murmured self-consciously.

"Nothing." She smiled faintly. "It appears you have finally found your purpose."

"There's one thing I don't get," Elton said. "If Otis's powers can stop demons from approaching him, then how come Bach wasn't rejected by the barrier?"

Otis rubbed the back of his head awkwardly. "I've been thinking about that. I believe it might have been because I didn't deem him to be an enemy until he was inside the barrier. Everything happened so fast back there, so I'm not one hundred percent confident that is the right answer."

"I suspect you are correct," Sebastian said. "It could also be because his demonic transformation only truly occurred after he found his crown." He eyed Michael and Arael with a jaundiced look. "Of course, the ones who know for certain are standing right there."

"I'm afraid we cannot reveal that which we know," Arael stated firmly. "We are not to interfere in matters at hand."

"I thought you did that already when you told Haruki about what happened to Serena and her friend," Michael said wryly.

The Angel of Crows narrowed his eyes at the archangel. "Oh yeah? What about you stopping Artemus and Drake from chasing Paimon?"

Michael scratched his cheek. "You know as well as I do that that needed to happen for what will follow."

"Why?" Otis asked nervously. "What follows?"

"I'm afraid we cannot divulge that either," Michael replied.

"Has anyone heard from Serena and Nate?" Callie asked Holmes, concern clouding her face.

The archbishop shook his head. "No. And no one has seen Bishop Irons either."

"I am sure Serena and the others are all right," Sebastian reassured a depressed-looking Callie.

Arael cocked his head slightly to the east, as if listening to something no one else could hear. "They are fine."

Callie brightened. "You know where they are?! Can you take us there?"

"No."

Callie visibly deflated at the boy's flat refusal.

"Is this one of those predestined things again?" she muttered in a morose voice.

Arael smiled faintly. "You are correct. But do not fret. The warrior is with them."

"What warrior?" Artemus said.

"He means Alexa King," Persephone murmured.

She was observing Artemus and Drake with a calculating expression.

Michael frowned at Persephone. "No."

Persephone sighed. "You don't even know what I was going to say."

"Oh, I know all right," the Archangel said grimly. "You can't."

Artemus glanced between the pair, now utterly confused. "Can't what? What is it?"

Persephone's face grew determined. "It's one of the reasons I invited Artemus and Drake to Rome, Michael. And I suspect it was preordained, since I feel so strongly about it. I thought I still had time, but it appears that I am fast running out of that precious commodity."

Drake furrowed his brow. "What are you talking about?"

"*You cannot take them to see their mother!*" Michael said vehemently.

Artemus's heart contracted painfully. Drake paled.

"Oh." Michael's face fell. "Damn. Did I just let the cat out of the bag?"

A heavy sigh left Arael. "This is why you suck at poker."

CHAPTER THIRTY-FIVE

HARUKI PARRIED A BLOW FROM A SUPER SOLDIER DEMON, headbutted him in the face, and swiped his legs out from under him with his powerful tail.

He thrust his blade into the monster's chest as the latter fell to the ground. A frown wrinkled his brow as a silver wave of nanorobots swarmed up his sword, stopping it from plunging fully into the demon's body.

Haruki reached for the source of his powers. The Dragon inside his soul growled. The flames on the divine blade flared white as they poured energy into it.

The nanorobots retreated. The sword started to sink into the super soldier's flesh. The yellow light in his pupils dimmed as it finally punctured the demonic heart within.

Another super soldier leapt on Haruki from behind. He grunted and bowed his spine. The bony spikes on his back lengthened and cast off his attacker.

"These guys are seriously pissing me off!" Lou snarled. "My knife can't even cut through their skin!"

"It's the demon inside them," Serena said grimly. "It's using the nanorobots to shield itself."

Fire boiled in Haruki's stomach. He took a deep breath and released a river of flames. The jet swallowed two super soldier demons.

It slowed them down but did not stop them.

"Looks like the only way we can kill them is by stabbing them in the heart with a divine weapon," Haruki said tensely.

"Well, that's not an option for all of us," Tom muttered.

King observed the enemy surrounding them with a pensive frown. "Let me try something."

She bolted into a running jump, roundhouse-kicked one of the super soldier demons in the head, and brought him to the ground. She locked a hand around the monster's throat before glancing at Nate.

"Would you mind holding him down?"

Nate straddled the struggling super soldier's legs and trapped his arms to his sides.

Surprise jolted Haruki when he felt the energy radiating from King intensify. Tremors shook the basement.

Nate clenched his jaw and leaned into the destructive force pressing against him. King knelt behind the demon and gripped the thrashing monster's head. A look of intense concentration came over the Immortal.

The unearthly energy blasting from her body started to abate.

No. Haruki stared. *She's focusing it in her hands.*

He blinked. For a moment, he thought he'd seen a pale light flutter across the Immortal's skin.

King clenched her jaw.

"Holy crap," Tom said dully.

The Immortal's fingers had dented the creature's flesh.

The muscles in her arms bunched. She snarled and twisted the monster's head sharply.

The demon's neck snapped with an audible crack. The silver sheen faded from his eyes. His body relaxed in death.

King rose and dusted her hands, oblivious to their shocked stares. "Now we have two ways to defeat them." She studied Serena and the others. "I suggest the four of you work to immobilize them while Dragon boy and I finish them off."

Tom recovered first. "Oh. So, we'll be like your four musketeers."

"Don't," Lou warned.

Tom brightened. "Or maybe Tonto to your Lone Ranger."

King narrowed her eyes.

"Make him shut up before she kills him," Serena hissed at Lou out of the corner of her mouth.

"You don't like that?" Tom's chagrined expression suddenly cleared. He slammed a fist against his palm. "I know! How about Robin to your Batman?"

"Dude, you got a death wish?" Haruki mumbled as he took in King's glacial frown.

Lou turned to the Immortal. "You have my permission to hurt him."

DRAKE HEADED AFTER PERSEPHONE AS SHE STRODE across the dark Vatican gardens, his brother at his side and his mind still abuzz with what Michael had revealed a short while ago.

"They were never meant to meet Alice," Michael had reiterated. "Especially not now."

"Is that her name?" Drake had mumbled. "Alice?"

Artemus had swallowed convulsively next to him.

Drake had felt his younger twin's distress across the bonds that linked them. Smokey had whined and padded the floor agitatedly between the two of them.

Michael had cast a frown their way before looking disapprovingly at Persephone.

"Yes, that is her name." Persephone had returned the Archangel's gaze steadily. "Why are you so adamant that they not meet? And how certain are you they shouldn't? Because something tells me it's vital that they see her at least once."

"She's dying," Michael had ground out. "This will only cause them more pain."

Color had drained from Artemus's face. "What did you just say?"

Drake had fisted his hands, his throat choking with anguish. "Our mom is dying?"

A miserable light had darkened Persephone's eyes.

"It's true," she'd said quietly. "Alice is dying."

Artemus had stiffened before striding over to Persephone and grabbing her shoulders. "Take us there! Take us to see her *right now!*"

Drake had clenched his jaw, the agony swirling through his brother resonating with his own torment, his heart an icy lump in his chest.

Daniel had frowned and taken a step toward Artemus. "Let her go."

"Artemus," Elton had murmured in a distressed voice.

A sad smile had tilted Persephone's mouth. She'd

placed a hand over one of Artemus's and dipped her chin. "Come with me."

"NO!" Michael had roared.

Drake's eardrums had throbbed then. The windows had rattled and an ink pot had trembled and moved across Persephone's desk.

A hush had fallen across the study once the archangel's powerful voice had died down.

Arael had stepped in front of Michael and pressed a hand to the archangel's chest. "Let it be."

Michael had scowled at the Angel of Crows. "I—"

"If you stop them now, your son will forever resent you."

Michael had faltered at that. He'd gazed at Artemus, a defeated expression washing across his face.

The rooftop of a building appeared between dense magnolia bushes up ahead. Roses climbed the walls of the old, dilapidated monastery sitting in a shallow bowl in the land. A single light burned in a window on the second floor.

"How long has our mother been here?" Artemus asked stiffly.

Drake knew his brother was still upset with Michael. Deep down inside, he understood why the archangel had wanted to protect them from the truth. If their mother was truly dying, then they were about to lose her for the second time in their lives.

"They came here after I was elected as Pope," Persephone replied. "The divine barrier around the Vatican protects them from unwanted attention."

Drake and Artemus faltered.

"They?" Drake repeated.

Persephone flashed a guarded glance their way. "You'll

see what I mean soon enough."

She opened a side door and entered the building ahead of them.

It was dark and cool inside. From the little Drake could see, the monastery appeared unlived in.

"This place is off limits to everyone but me," Persephone explained, confirming his suspicions. "When Alice wakes up, I have food brought over from the Palace."

Drake shared a troubled look with his twin. The more they heard about this mysterious Alice, the more daunting she sounded.

Persephone led them past a kitchen and up a flight of stairs. Light glowed under a door at the end of the passage at the top.

Drake's heart raced as they neared it.

"Go in," Persephone said quietly. "I will wait for you downstairs."

Drake glanced at Artemus while Persephone turned and retraced her steps. His twin nodded, his eyes glistening in the gloom.

Drake took a shallow breath and twisted the doorknob, his own vision blurry with tears. A familiar energy warmed his skin as he opened the door and crossed the threshold with his brother.

Artemus stopped and inhaled sharply.

A woman lay motionless on a narrow bed on the far side of the room.

She looked to be in her mid-twenties, with midnight-black hair as fine as silk. The only color on her alabaster skin was the flush of pale pink across her cheekbones and her rosy lips. She was achingly beautiful and looked as fragile as the finest crystal.

Fresh flowers sat in a glass vase on the side table next to her.

Artemus grabbed Drake's arm. Drake startled and glanced at him before following his stunned gaze. His stomach lurched.

The pale light illuminating the room was not coming from a lamp.

Instead, it emanated from the woman who stood by the window to their right. Eyes full of stars gazed steadily upon them.

The apparition smiled. "Hello, Drake. Hello, Artemus."

CHAPTER THIRTY-SIX

ARTEMUS COULD FEEL DRAKE'S PULSE THUMPING WILDLY against his fingers. He didn't know what had possessed him to take hold of Drake's arm.

In that moment, he'd wanted some kind of physical contact. Any kind of contact to keep him grounded. To remind him that none of this was a dream.

Drake bore a shocking resemblance to the woman lying in the bed. Whereas his own features were a mirror of the specter by the window, bar his eyes, which he had inherited from Michael.

"Are you—?" Drake swallowed, his voice hoarse with emotion. "Are you Alice?"

The apparition shook her head slightly, her pale hair glimmering with divine radiance. "No." She walked over to the bed and took the unconscious woman's hand in one of her glowing ones. "This is Alice." She turned to them. "I am Theia."

Her name danced in Artemus's ears and resonated with the very marrow of his soul. He could sense the immense power behind it.

Drake clutched Artemus's hand where it lay on his arm.

"Theia?" he repeated numbly. "As in the goddess?!"

Theia dipped her head. "I am also known as a Titaness in your mythology. They are one and the same thing."

Blood drained from Artemus's face. *Our mother is a goddess?!*

"I—how—?" he stammered.

Theia let go of Alice and crossed the floor. She stopped in front of them and raised gentle fingers to their cheeks.

Artemus shuddered at the tranquil warmth that seeped into his body from her touch. He slid his hand over hers where it lay on his skin. Divine energy pulsed from her core to his.

A sad smile curved Theia's lips.

She told them then. Of Alice's simple origins as a farmer's daughter in a small town in Idaho. Of her attraction to the church from an early age and how she had taken her vows at the age of eighteen. Of the pure and untainted spirit that made her soul shine brightest among all others. Of how she had gained the attention of Theia, who had been looking to bind herself to a mortal coil so as to walk the Earth once more, one of the innumerable hosts she had gifted with her specter over the millennia.

She told them of how Samyaza had taken possession of a man one night and sought out Alice in the abbey where she dwelled. Of how he had raped her, unaware that the reason he had been drawn to her in the first place was due in part to Theia's divine presence.

Of how Theia, in the moment when she could have fought off and hurt Samyaza, had been shown the future and had realized that this was all meant to be.

She had numbed Alice's body and mind during the

assault, so that she would not recall the atrocities she had suffered at Samyaza's hands.

She told them of how Michael had come upon the ravaged form of the naked, young nun in the woods behind the abbey and taken her to a remote cabin, where he had healed her before seducing her, so as to fulfill Heaven's prophecy and impregnate her womb with another child. One whose soul would be bound to the life that was already there.

Samyaza's heir. The key to the Apocalypse Satanael intended to unleash upon the Earth and Heaven itself.

"Alice's body was too weak to enable her to survive her labor," Theia explained. "She should have died the day she gave birth to you. She has lived on borrowed time these past twenty-eight years, flitting into consciousness for a few days every so often." A kind expression lit her face as she studied the silent figure in the bed. "I do not begrudge giving her some of my time. It is but an infinitesimal fraction of the existence of a being like me."

Artemus gazed blindly at Alice before staring at Theia. "But—but Michael and Persephone said she's dying!"

He clenched Drake's hand tightly and felt his twin grip his fingers just as strongly.

"She is," Theia murmured. "Her time has finally come. She was only waiting to meet you before she left this realm." The goddess turned toward the bed. "Hello, Alice."

Drake gasped. Artemus trembled. The woman in the bed had opened her eyes and was looking at them.

"Hello, Theia," she said softly. She stared unblinkingly at Artemus and Drake. "Is this—?"

Theia nodded. "They are our sons."

A dazzling expression lit Alice's face. She struggled to sit up, the covers falling to her waist.

Artemus and Drake were at her side in a heartbeat. They helped her gingerly to sit on the edge of the bed. Tears fell unfettered down Alice's face as she studied them where they knelt at her feet, her gaze roaming their features hungrily.

"So handsome." She caressed their cheeks with a shaking hand. "You never told me our sons were this dashing."

She flashed a tremulous smile at Theia.

Artemus closed his eyes briefly, his own face wet with tears.

"There is so much I want to tell you," Alice said. "So much I want to know."

A low sob escaped Drake. Artemus reached across and took his twin's hand.

Alice smiled and gazed at their intertwined fingers. "But I see enough to know that you will be all right." Her eyes darkened then, her expression growing serious. She glanced at Theia, as if listening to words they couldn't hear. "We don't have much time." She hooked an arm around their necks and drew them to her chest. "What-ever happens, know that you are loved." She pressed a kiss to their cheeks and hugged them tightly. "That Theia and I treasure you above all else. That Michael cares deeply, for both of you. That Samyaza, although now a demon, was an archangel first and foremost." She drew back and stared at them fiercely. "Remember this well. The two of you are unique and the first of your kind. No child has ever been born of an archangel, a goddess, and a human. Your powers are unknown, your potential limitless."

"Alice is correct," Theia murmured. "Though I can see

your futures to some extent, I cannot see all of it. Your paths are still unwritten."

The air quaked slightly. Artemus's eyes widened. Something was drawing close. A powerful demonic force.

Theia looked to the east. "They are coming." The goddess frowned faintly. "You need to go."

Artemus and Drake hesitated before climbing to their feet.

"How long do you have?" Artemus asked Alice shakily.

Alice smiled again, her eyes gleaming with unshed tears. "I have all the time in the world."

"Liar," Drake whispered brokenly.

Alice chuckled. "I shall look forward to your future conquests. Something tells me the world should watch out for my boys." She rose and embraced them tightly one last time. "I love you, Drake. I love you, Artemus. Now, go and fulfill your destinies."

Artemus and Drake stopped on the doorstep of the bedroom and turned to face the two women.

"Will we see you again?" Drake asked.

Alice beamed. "In a future life."

Theia smiled. "We are always with you."

It was as they were crossing the gardens with Persephone that Artemus pulled Drake to a stop. "I won't let you fall to Hell." He wiped his wet cheeks and gazed hotly at his twin. "But if you do, know that I will follow you and bring you back."

Drake stared at him for a moment. Then he closed his arms around him and hugged him tightly.

"I will do my utmost to make sure that never has to happen," he whispered, burrowing his face in Artemus's neck.

Persephone took a tissue out from inside her sleeve and blew her nose. Drake sighed and let go of Artemus.

"If you don't stop crying, Daniel will think we did something to you," he told her drily.

They all stiffened as a distant scream rendered the air. It had come from the direction of St. Peter's Square.

Bright sparks tore across the sky, revealing the invisible barrier high above Vatican City.

"They're here," Artemus said grimly.

CHAPTER THIRTY-SEVEN

BACH FOCUSED THE POWER FLOWING FROM HIS CROWN into his hands. The corrupt energy blasting from his fingers intensified, smashing into the divine barrier outside the Holy See. Flashes lit the air where darkness met light.

Elation coursed through the demon. He could feel the shield weakening.

His spirit cloud roared as it swept through St. Peter's Square, swallowing up the souls of the people it killed and fortifying its strength, the bodies of the dead falling prey to the demons pouring out of the rifts opening up across the piazza.

Movement on the other side of the barrier drew Bach's gaze.

Two figures darted into view some thirty feet in front of him, their white and black wings in sharp contrast to one another as they came to an abrupt halt in mid-air.

Bach bared his fangs at the angels and beat his own midnight wings.

They shadowed him as he rose, their faces fierce and their eyes throbbing with divine energy.

The Sphinx and the Chimera appeared from the direction of Vatican Palace, the seraph and the hellhound on their heels.

A CROWD OF PEOPLE RAN OUT AFTER OTIS AND SMOKEY.

Artemus turned, alarmed.

Elton, Persephone, and Holmes slowed at the head of the large group of Swiss Guards and Vatican policemen who'd followed them outside. Rossi's face blanched as he took in the army of demons outside the divine shield.

Artemus dove and hovered above them.

"Gather everyone in Vatican City and go to the smithy!" he yelled. "The iron there should keep the demons out!"

Holmes swallowed. Elton nodded grimly. Rossi led them back toward the palace, the policemen and guards crowding protectively around Persephone.

"Where's Daniel?" Artemus asked Sebastian.

The Sphinx soared beside him, his eagle wings thrumming the air while his weapon transformed into the fiery, triple-thonged whip of Raguel. "I do not know. He was with us a moment ago."

Drake joined them.

"Can the two of you reinforce that barrier?" he asked Sebastian and Otis grimly. "It'll buy Persephone and the others time to get to safety."

The seraph and the Sphinx traded a guarded look.

"I'm not sure," Sebastian admitted.

Artemus clenched his jaw. "Try."

Smokey shook himself out into the giant, three-headed Cerberus. Angry noises rumbled from his throats as he paced the ground, his golden eyes zeroing in on the enemy gathering outside the divine shield.

"You'll get your chance soon enough, pooch," Artemus muttered.

Callie's knuckles whitened on the Scepter of Gabriel, her divine flames an orange glow lighting up her chest and belly. "Be ready, brother."

Yes, sister.

DANIEL WANDERED DAZEDLY THROUGH THE BASILICA.

One minute, he'd been trying to keep up with Sebastian and Callie as they rushed toward the source of the powerful demonic force they'd sensed gathering outside Vatican City, the next his feet had led him inside the sacred church.

His beast trod the darkness behind his eyes. It was agitated and angry. Not just because of the enemy it could discern, but because of something else. Something that was resonating faintly with its own divine power.

Daniel's ring throbbed with an echo of heat.

He found himself drawn to the door that would take him to the Necropolis.

OTIS IGNORED THE DEMON ARMY SWARMING THE PIAZZA and placed his hands against the invisible wall he could sense before him. Sebastian mimicked his actions where he floated some twenty feet above him.

Artemus and Drake stayed close to them, their anxious

gazes sweeping the ochre-eyed masses gathering a short distance from their location.

A shiver coursed down Otis's spine as the divine energy within the barrier resonated with the power within his soul.

Whoever made this was incredibly strong.

He clenched his teeth and concentrated. A tide of warmth erupted inside his body. The middle of his forehead heated up.

Divine light exploded across his fingertips.

"*Together!*" Sebastian shouted, power glowing in his eyes and on his hands.

BACH SCOWLED WHEN HE FELT A RESISTANCE IN THE divine wall.

He swooped down to where Artemus's assistant and the Sphinx were fortifying the defensive barricade and concentrated his own demonic force into his hands. A dark jet erupted from his clawed fingers and palms.

It struck the barrier with a bang.

The seraph and the Sphinx glared at him, brows furrowed and gazes flaring with Heaven's light as they attempted to repair the damage he had caused to the shield.

Bach snarled and drew on the wicked power of the crown. The weapon thickened and grew, thorns sinking farther into his head as it delivered the corrupt energy he so craved. A torrent of darkness swept through the demon, filling his blood and flesh with unholy strength.

The jet pouring from his fingertips swelled. A crack

tore through the space where it met the barrier, the sound deafening as it echoed around the piazza.

A golden fracture appeared where once there was none. It grew inch by slow inch, its length extending upward across the surface of the divine shield.

Alarm filled the seraph and the Sphinx's faces as they tilted their heads and followed the rising breach with their gazes, their dismay reflected in the eyes of the angels and divine beasts at their side.

Bach grinned savagely. His muscles bunched with unholy strength as he poured even more power into the dark jet. The crack widened.

The demon opened a rift on his right and extracted his dark broadsword.

~

GLOOM SWALLOWED DANIEL WHEN HE REACHED THE lowest level of the Necropolis. He started up the ancient, paved road, his body moving without his volition.

Something was calling to him. Something the creature inside him loathed with every fiber of its being. Something not of this world.

Something evil.

His legs took him to the mausoleum Artemus and the others had searched that very morning.

The hairs lifted on his nape as he stepped inside the vaulted chamber. Apprehension crawled across his skin, raising goosebumps in its wake.

~

THUNDER CLAPPED REPEATEDLY IN ARTEMUS'S EARS. THE

noise was coming from the jagged fissures snaking across the barrier.

"Get back!" he yelled at Otis and Sebastian. "The barrier is coming down!"

The seraph stumbled behind Callie and Smokey. The Sphinx flapped his wings and shot back to Drake's side.

Dread surged through Artemus as the fabric of space fluttered all around them, his trepidation mirrored by the others across their bond. He twisted in mid-air.

Golden sparks erupted in the night as the divine shield around Vatican City dissipated into nothingness. Darkness slowly replaced it, the spirit cloud summoned by Bach rising to block out the night sky and the stars.

The demon army stormed the Holy See.

DANIEL'S STOMACH CHURNED AS A CORRUPT ENERGY washed across his skin from above. He knew instinctively that the barrier protecting the Vatican had just fallen.

Paimon is here. He seeks to destroy the Holy See, and to capture us and our gate.

Coldness filled Daniel at the sound of his beast's voice. He knew the words it spoke were true.

There was motion on his left. His gaze gravitated to the second sarcophagus inside the mausoleum. Dust trembled off the ancient stone coffin as it started to vibrate on its stand.

It is time, old friend.

Daniel swallowed. From the tales he'd heard of the other beasts' awakening, he knew what the creature meant.

"I'm—I'm not ready!" he stammered.

His beast frowned. *Do not falter now, child. You killed a demon when you were but a pup. Trust in yourself. Trust in what we can do together.*

Cracks tore across the surface of the stone sarcophagus. A cloud of shadows erupted around it. Daniel took a step back, stunned by the vile energy it was emitting.

Time slowed. His breath bloomed in a ghostly mist in front of his face as the temperature inside the mausoleum plummeted. Blood thumped in his veins, the heavy beat echoed by the heart of the creature within him.

Thump.

The coffin exploded silently inward, the pressure wave of the detonation throbbing against his eardrums. Solid matter dissolved into writhing darkness.

Something gleamed within the evil, billowing mass now floating above the stone stand. Daniel's eyes rounded.

It was an iron casket.

The metal box shuddered and rattled alarmingly where it hovered in mid-air, as if struggling to contain whatever lay within it.

Thump-thump.

The ring on the priest's hand started heating up. It transformed into the gauntlet in the next instant. He looked down and froze at what he saw.

A line of golden, archaic symbols had appeared on the surface of the metal, the scripture extending from the tip of his middle finger to his wrist.

A second explosion ripped through the mausoleum, forcing him back another couple of steps. The iron casket had come apart, metal pieces twisting and blackening as they fell slowly to the ground.

An object wrapped in a mantle of corruption levitated where it once stood. It was a bronze urn.

A voice that did not belong to Daniel tumbled out of his lips, framing words he did not recognize. The first symbol on the gauntlet flared with light before flashing crimson.

Thump-thump. Thump-thump.

The earth shook beneath Daniel's feet. Flames burst into life around his body. Power filled him.

The bronze vessel started to darken.

CHAPTER THIRTY-EIGHT

THE WIND WHIPPED AT HARUKI'S HAIR AS THE Kawasaki stormed through the streets of Rome. He could see a distant haze of darkness growing across the sky to the west, in the direction of Vatican City. An echo of his divine companions' dread resonated across the bond that linked them.

"Hurry!" Haruki shouted at King, the Dragon's growl underscoring his voice.

The Immortal punched the throttle. The motorbike accelerated, overtaking the Corvette and the stolen SUV racing ahead of them.

Lightning flashed across the sky as they shot across the Via Acciaioli and barreled the wrong way up a bridge spanning the Tiber River. Red-tinged clouds erupted into existence above them, the rippling mass twisting and boiling with eerie shapes.

Static danced across Haruki's skin, raising the hairs on his arms and nape. He clenched his teeth at the suffocating demonic energy throbbing through the atmosphere.

Hang in there, you guys!

Indistinct screams reached his ears a moment later. They grew louder. For a moment, Haruki thought they belonged to demons.

A panicked crowd bolted into view at the head of the street they were traveling down. He scowled.

Nope, those are people.

King cursed and swerved sharply to avoid the human wave flowing across their path. She braked to a stop and jumped off the Kawasaki, the Corvette and the SUV screeching to an abrupt halt inches from the motorbike's rear tire.

"It's gonna be faster if we run the rest of the way!" she yelled at Haruki and the super soldiers.

The Immortal took the lead as they moved swiftly through the fleeing masses and headed for St. Peter's Square, their weapons in hand. The Basilica came into view when they turned the corner at the top of the road. They slowed to a halt, their eyes widening.

"Holy shit," Tom mumbled.

"You can say that again," Lou muttered, his face pale.

King's knuckles whitened on her sai daggers.

Haruki's heart thudded wildly in his chest as he gazed at the unholy battle unfolding before them. What he was witnessing bore an uncanny resemblance to the biblical scenes depicted in several of the paintings hanging in the Vatican Museums, where the forces of Light faced the forces of Darkness.

Except, in this instance, Darkness was winning.

Loud clashes tore the air as Artemus and Drake engaged a giant demon with horns and inky wings some thirty feet above the piazza, their movements so fast their figures shivered in and out of focus. The monster they fought wore a black crown pulsing with corrupt energy.

The same energy that was radiating from the wicked broadsword he wielded. Sebastian darted around the three figures, lightning balls leaving one hand while he lashed his whip at the winged creatures attempting to attack Artemus and Drake from behind.

Below them, Callie and Smokey fought the army of monsters and misshapen hellhounds advancing across the square. Though they were vastly outnumbered, the divine beast and the hellhound fought with all their might, their eyes glowing savagely and their attacks unrelenting despite the blood dripping from their wounds.

Otis stood a few feet behind them, his gaze and hands shimmering with divine light as he defended their backs, the demons battering in vain at the divine shield protecting him. Though he had yet to assume the full, winged form of the powerful seraph, his third eye had manifested in the center of his forehead and his hair and skin had changed color.

Serena swore beside Haruki.

More demons were emerging from the crimson rifts that had opened up around the piazza, the creatures' loathsome gazes locking on the dark-winged commander who had summoned them before moving to the enemy in their midst.

"We have a problem," King said.

"You mean, besides the forces of the Underworld gathering around us?" Tom muttered in a sickly tone.

King pointed. "Yes."

Haruki's stomach dropped when he looked in the direction she was indicating.

The dome of darkness in the sky was extending rapidly around Vatican City, its walls falling to enclose the Holy See in a violent storm cloud.

"They're gonna get trapped inside!" Serena yelled above the roar of the tempest.

She headed toward the divine beasts and the angels, Haruki one step behind her.

"Wait!" King barked.

They stopped and turned toward the Immortal. She was staring north. They followed her gaze.

"Are those—?" Nate started.

"Super soldiers," Lou finished grimly.

A crowd of silver-eyed super soldier demons was approaching the square.

Instinct made Haruki look over his shoulder. He clenched his teeth.

"There are more coming the other way."

Serena observed the two groups converging on them with a conflicted expression, her fingers clenching and unclenching on the handle of her blade.

Haruki unleashed his divine sword. "We're gonna have to make a stand here." He shared a troubled glance with the super soldier. "It's the best way to help Artemus and the others, and to protect Vatican City."

"I agree," King said.

Nate's face hardened as he dragged his gaze from where Callie was fighting the creatures surrounding her and Smokey, her divine flames turning the creatures into ash clouds while the bloodied Scepter of Gabriel left her hand and twisted through the air, the weapon piercing the monsters' hearts and heads at lightning speeds before returning to her grasp.

Serena stared at Drake where he battled the giant demon in the sky with Artemus, her face full of hesitation still.

"Your lover will be fine," King said.

Serena stiffened. "He's not my lover."

King arched an eyebrow. "Why not?"

"Yeah, why not, Serena?" Tom muttered in a saccharine tone.

Serena narrowed her eyes at the super soldier. Lou sighed.

A distant curse reached them.

A pale broadsword brimming with divine light hummed down from the sky. It landed with an explosive bang before sliding across the ground in a shower of sparks and an ear-splitting screech of metal against stone.

King stepped on it with one foot, halting its progress.

Haruki's eyes rounded. "Isn't that—?"

King stooped and lifted the blade. She studied the weapon with a thoughtful expression before casting it back in the direction it had come from. "I believe this is yours!"

The blade slid through a breach in the storm cloud closing around the square.

Artemus caught the Sword of Michael as it winged past him, a stunned look on his face. "Er, thanks!"

A shadow dropped down on the angel. He swore and leapt out of the way of the giant demon's blade before disappearing from view, the black dome sealing him and the others inside the Holy See with the army of fiends.

King turned and met Haruki and Serena's shocked stares. Nate looked similarly dumbfounded.

"What?" the Immortal said with a puzzled frown.

"Nothing," Haruki muttered.

He transformed into his divine form. *She lifted Artemus's sword as if it weighed less than a toothpick!*

An appreciative sound rumbled out of the Dragon. *The female warrior impresses me more and more. Pity she is wed. I would have suggested we mate with her. Our offspring would be quite something to behold.*

Haruki dropped the Sword of Camael.

"You okay, buddy?" Tom said with a curious glance as the blade clattered noisily onto the cobblestones.

"Hmm, yeah," Haruki mumbled, his cheeks flaming as he grabbed his holy weapon.

CHAPTER THIRTY-NINE

DUST ROSE AROUND DANIEL IN SPIRALING CIRCLES AS HE translated the divine sigils carved on the gauntlet on his hand, the motes flaring red before fading to wisps of ash as they were engulfed by the divine flames roaring from his body.

The priest shuddered and gazed upon the evil structure taking shape before him. Where the urn once floated was a rectangle of growing darkness.

It was a doorway, yet unformed and still sealed.

Daniel was aware that Hell waited beyond it. Just as he knew that he, and the allies who were fighting the forces of darkness somewhere above him, could not afford to lose this fight.

To do so would mean the end of mankind and the world as they knew it.

The divine beast's voice rumbled up his throat, fierce and self-assured as it framed the sacred words. It was as if the creature never doubted their ability to win the battle they were engaged in.

Daniel closed his eyes and welcomed the potent power

rising inside him. It grew stronger with every symbol they translated and carved away at the troubled feelings that still lingered in his mind.

Fear that he was only as strong as his crippled body. Doubt that he truly belonged to the circle of divine beings he had befriended these past few days. Despair that he would end up disappointing the creature who had chosen to bond its soul to his and the woman he considered his mother.

All his insecurities dissolved in glorious fury as his and the divine beast's spirits started to merge.

And when the final translation tumbled from his lips and the gate to Hell manifested its full form, Daniel finally saw the one who had been with him all the years that he had been alive, even during the dark chapters of his childhood.

Golden eyes welcomed him with a savage flash as their souls became one. The beast's holy name resonated through his consciousness, its identity breathtaking in its magnificence.

Daniel opened his eyes. Wings sprouted from his back, feathers blazing where they brushed against the ceiling of the mausoleum. The gauntlet transformed into a weapon of living fire, the key achieving its ultimate incarnation. The flames extended from his hand and wrapped around the gate like a lasso, the air around them throbbing with the intensity of the heat they emitted.

Muted shrieks erupted from the hellish portal.

Daniel started to ascend, a divine conflagration filling the chamber in the wake of his passage.

A HEAVY WEIGHT LANDED ON ARTEMUS'S BACK. CLAWS tore at his armor, frantic talons attempting to rip the suit from his body. He cursed, spun in mid-air, and thrust his sword through the heart of the winged creature who'd attacked him.

Metal glinted on his left. Artemus gasped and moved out of the way of the black blade arcing toward his arm.

Sparks erupted when the tip of Bach's sword scraped across his holy suit of armor. Artemus beat his wings and glared at the demon commander as he shot out of the range of his corrupt blade.

Bach smiled, his wicked fangs glistening. "I expected this fight to be more challenging." He looked to where Drake was battling a ring of winged demons a short distance away. "So far, I am disappointed, Son of Michael."

"Yeah, well, sorry for failing to meet your expectations, asshole."

Artemus gripped his sword, dove behind the demon, and swung the blade. Bach turned at lightning speed and parried his strike.

A fiery whip wrapped around the monster's right wrist, the triple thongs locking in place with a hiss that scorched his skin.

Bach observed a scowling Sebastian where he hovered above them. "Oh my. Is that all the power you possess, my dear Sphinx?"

The demon's smile widened a second before he tugged his arm. Sebastian cursed as he was dragged through the air and cast savagely toward the ground. He landed in the midst of a group of yellow-eyed fiends and hellbeasts and disappeared beneath them.

A roar left Artemus's lips. He barreled into the demon commander's flank and carried the monster all the way across St. Peter's Square toward the storm cloud that thundered around Vatican City, divine power boiling inside his veins. The darkness writhed as they collided with it, the noise of the impact rolling across the piazza.

Bach started to laugh. Artemus pulled away from the demon, suspicion narrowing his eyes.

"Did you really think that would stop me?" the demon asked in an amused voice.

Ropes of living night shot out from the spirit barrier and wrapped around Artemus's arms and legs in the blink of an eye. "Shit!"

He struggled against the demonic bonds as he was pulled inexorably toward the storm cloud. Crimson eyes flashed hungrily in the whirling shadows.

"*Artemus!*" Drake yelled.

The dark angel carved off the heads of the remaining monsters who'd ambushed him with a single swing of his sword, his blade pulsing with crimson flames. His shape blurred as he closed the distance to Artemus and Bach, his face a mask of fury.

Artemus's heart twisted with fear when he sensed Samyaza's corrupt energy intensifying inside his twin.

Drake, stop!

His brother's voice reached him. *I'm okay!*

Artemus gritted his teeth and focused his powers on his armor. The demonic restraints roared as he attempted to wrench himself out of their grasp, the spirits within the storm cloud screeching in rage.

Heat throbbed through his ring.

Artemus glanced at it, startled. An orange light flickered across the metal. Fire burst through the surface a second later. The ring transformed into the gauntlet, flames racing across the glove to engulf his broadsword. Power surged through Artemus.

The spirits shrieked and pulled back, the inky restraints holding him prisoner falling away.

Bach swung his blade. Artemus lifted his sword and blocked the blow, metal clanging violently against the weapon's corrupt matter.

They both froze.

Artemus blinked, stunned by the powerful divine energy that had just resonated with his own. His gaze gravitated to the Basilica.

Daniel?!

"What is that?" Bach growled.

A loud detonation rocked Vatican City, halting Drake's flight as he drew close to them. The dark angel stopped and turned, surprise widening his crimson-rimmed, gold eyes.

A hush fell over the piazza as everyone looked toward the rooftop of the church.

Awe filled Artemus, his blood thumping in tandem with the heartbeat of the incredible beast that had just awakened and manifested its presence, the creature's glorious power reverberating through his very bones.

The spire of the church glinted as it twisted and spun toward the sky. It stopped shy of striking the dome of darkness shrouding Vatican City and started to drop, its descent as slow and as graceful as its ascent had been.

It plummeted to the ground amidst the cloud of debris that was all that remained of the cupola of the Basilica, the metal spike skewering several demons before it finally crashed onto the cobblestones of St. Peter's Square, dark blood oozing along its length from the bodies it had impaled.

In the place where it once stood soared a being of pure fire.

Flames fluttered off the edges of the beast's blazing wings as they thrummed the air with strong beats, their span so wide they reached beyond the breadth of the Basilica.

The creature's eyes burned gold and crimson as he observed the monsters crowding the square below it. Wrapped within a lasso of flames extending from his left hand was a doorway throbbing with the corrupt energy of Hell.

"The gate!" Bach twisted away and darted toward the dark portal.

His army followed, a mass of yellow-eyed fiends and beasts moving in a wave toward the Basilica, the monsters scaling the walls of the sacred church.

The Phoenix spread his wings and roared at the approaching enemy.

CHAPTER FORTY

PERSEPHONE STUDIED THE CROWD OF CLERGYMEN AND nuns assembled in the smithy anxiously. Though Rossi's men and the Swiss Guards had managed to gather everyone within the enclave and get them to the cave, they were not out of danger yet. Fear swamped the air, a palpable wave reflected by the terror she could see in the eyes staring up at her.

"Why don't you lead them in prayer?" Elton suggested quietly where he stood beside her on the stone landing. "It will calm them down."

"I agree," Holmes murmured.

Persephone swallowed and dipped her chin.

"Let us pray, brothers and sisters," she said loudly, her words echoing against the stone walls around them.

She knelt on the floor, bowed her head, and pressed her palms together. A mumble of voices joined hers as she started to recite the Lord's Prayer. They gathered in strength as the men and women fell into the rhythm of the familiar verses. Dust trembled off the ceiling above their heads, the only sign of the terrible battle raging across Vatican City.

Persephone was leading them into their third prayer when someone started banging on the door.

"Help! Help me!" a voice yelled from outside. "It's Bishop Irons!"

Persephone froze before climbing hastily to her feet, Holmes and Elton rising beside her. She was reaching for one of the bolts when Holmes laid a hand on her arm, halting her action. She looked at him, surprised.

"Where's Captain Rossi, Patrick?" the archbishop called out.

Silence reached them from the other side of the door.

"Captain Rossi?"

Persephone's eyes widened. Irons's voice sounded strange.

"Yes," Holmes said in a guarded tone. "May we speak with him, please?"

Elton removed his gun from inside his jacket. Persephone's heart started pounding for a whole other reason.

It had been several hours since the bishop had disappeared from the exhibition center. Not only would the man have had to walk past the Vatican policemen and Swiss Guards who had elected to stay outside the smithy to guard its door, he would also have had to navigate the hordes of demons swarming the enclave to get there.

A violent thud shook the door.

Persephone gasped and took a step back. Elton and Holmes moved protectively in front of her.

Something heavy smashed repeatedly against the entrance, the strikes echoed by startled yelps rising from the crowd behind her.

"Iron!" Elton shouted over his shoulder. "Get everyone to grab a piece of—"

The hinges and bolts exploded off the stone wall. A rivet struck Elton in the temple, drawing a surprised grunt from his lips as he fell. Deadly shards of metal winged past Persephone and sailed over the balustrade before clattering amongst the armor in the smithy below.

The door followed, carrying Holmes to the stairs and sending him tumbling down the steps. A stray splinter traced a bloodied line across Persephone's right cheek as it shot by her face.

Fear formed a cold knot in the pit of her stomach when she beheld the monster framed in the doorway. *Irons was the mole all along!*

A rank odor rose from the weeping tumors crawling across the demon's flesh. His single ochre eye flared as it found her, the other an empty orbit filled with congealing obsidian blood and pus. He clasped the top of the doorframe with his claws and dipped his head to enter the room, the bony spikes on his back scraping against the lintel.

A growl of frustration escaped him.

He stopped on the threshold and glared at the iron-filled armory below, his loathing for the metal holding him at bay, just as Artemus had predicted.

Anger surged through Persephone when she saw Rossi. The captain lay with his arm twisted at an unnatural angle behind Irons, the bloodied and battered bodies of his men and the Swiss Guards littering the passage beyond. Some still showed signs of life, their chests moving raggedly with their breaths while blood pooled across the stone beneath them.

Elton moaned and stirred on her left. Persephone's

gaze landed on the gun beside him before shifting to the stairs beyond the weapon. They were only half a dozen feet away. She had but to run down them and she would be safe. Her nails curled into her palms.

Persephone stepped over to Elton and picked up the gun.

Irons bared his fangs as she raised it at him with trembling hands.

THE POWER OF THE PHOENIX SANG THROUGH DANIEL'S veins as he disengaged the weapon he wielded from the fiery ropes binding Hell's gate. That the restraints would hold the portal in check until he could subdue it was something he never doubted.

His beast was one of the strongest creatures in Heaven.

Bach's demonic shape blurred into view some dozen feet before him. The demon exposed his teeth in an angry snarl, the divine flames too dangerous for him to draw any closer.

A series of heartbeats echoed that of his and his beast's soul.

They sought their brethren with fierce eyes, pleasure filling them as the bond they had formed with their new family finally cemented into the unbreakable tie that would unite them forever more.

"I SUSPECTED AS MUCH, BUT TO SEE HIM IN PERSON IS something else," Sebastian breathed.

His heart raced as he gazed at the fearsome creature looming over the Basilica, the beast's energy throbbing through him.

Callie and Smokey stared.

"Is he what I think he is?" Callie mumbled.

Artemus landed beside the obelisk where they'd gathered, in the middle of the square. "Yeah, that's the Phoenix."

Drake dropped down next to his brother. "He may be powerful, but he's still going to need our help."

Otis joined them, his third eye and hands pulsing with white light.

A tide of corrupt energy blasted through the square. Sebastian's eyes widened.

Bach's crown had swelled to twice its size. So had the demon's body.

The monster roared as he glared at the being holding Hell's gate prisoner. His bellow echoed to the sky, a declaration of war that propelled the monsters trying to reach the portal forward.

A savage light flared in Daniel's eyes. A line of flames erupted from his left hand. It grew until it assumed the shape of a gigantic bow. He drew the string and released it toward the sky.

Arrows of fire shot from the weapon.

They whistled upward before falling toward the sea of demons surrounding him, a rain of divine fire. Fiends and hellbeasts screeched and burst into clouds of glowing ash as the shafts pierced them.

Dread dawned on Bach's face. A quarter of his army had just been decimated.

The bow disappeared. In its place sprouted an immense axe of living flames some one hundred feet long. The weapon hummed as Daniel twisted it above his head a couple of times before unleashing it upon the monsters crawling across what remained of the rooftop of the Basilica.

The demons' screams faded as they exploded into dust.

Daniel smiled savagely as the enemy's numbers were halved once more. He stilled a moment later. His smile faded.

He stared in the direction of Vatican Palace, a cold expression of fury washing across his face. The axe shrank and vanished. A sphere of flames exploded into existence in his left palm.

He cast it at Bach and his remaining troops.

The ball expanded until it became a wall of living fire some two hundred feet high. It roared across the Basilica and burst onto the square.

ALARM TWISTED ARTEMUS'S STOMACH.

"Shit!" He shot into the air and looked wildly at Sebastian. "We need to get out of here! Open a rift!"

"Don't," Otis ordered calmly. "There is no need to fear the fire. The Flame of God will not hurt us."

Artemus stared at the seraph. His voice had taken on the same musical undertone as Michael and Arael's.

The conflagration grew closer, demons and hellbeasts bursting into nothingness in its wake. Artemus hesitated. He landed on the cobblestones just as the inferno swept over their group.

The flames danced harmlessly across their bodies, leaving nothing but a warm breeze and a faint scent of spices in its passage.

PERSEPHONE WHEEZED AND GRASPED AT IRONS'S WRIST where he'd wrapped his talons around her neck. Foul blood oozed from the bullet holes in the demon's body, the holy water burning gaping wounds into his flesh.

Elton's empty gun lay beneath her dangling feet where she'd dropped it.

A bellow sounded behind her. Holmes bounded up the stairs, an iron spear in his hands. Trailing in his steps were a horde of armed priests and nuns.

Irons let go of Persephone and batted them aside with a powerful strike of his clawed hand. Holmes crashed into the wall with a grunt. The spear clattered to the floor and was lost beneath the men and women who landed pell-mell beside him.

Irons's gaze found Persephone once more. She took a step back, her heart thudding erratically against her breastbone.

A hiss of displeasure escaped the demon. He looked down.

Rossi had crawled across the threshold of the smithy and was hanging on grimly to Irons's left leg with his unbroken arm, his battered face full of determination despite his injuries. Irons's talons glinted as they headed for the policeman's eyes.

Heat washed through the cave.

The demon froze. He straightened and looked toward the fire in the forge at the far end of the smithy. The blaze flickered and danced blamelessly in its hearth.

A distant boom reached Persephone's ears. It grew louder. The ground trembled beneath her feet. She stiffened when she saw the orange glow growing at the end of the passage leading to the smithy.

A voice sounded in her head, startling her. It was Daniel.

A tide of fire crashed against the stone walls of the corridor. The flames boiled over angrily as they filled the passageway and raced toward the smithy.

Persephone swallowed and did as Daniel had instructed. She turned to face the blaze and stood her ground.

Irons shrieked, his arms rising protectively to cover his face.

Persephone saw the demon explode into a cloud of crimson ash a second before she closed her eyes.

The fire swept over her as gently as a warm summer rain.

CHAPTER FORTY-ONE

A EUPHORIC FEELING TORE THROUGH HARUKI AS HE battled the army of super soldier demons. The power of the beast who had just awakened resonated with the heavenly energy inside his soul. He could feel the Dragon's satisfaction as they welcomed the newest member of their divine family.

Holes tore through the storm cloud surrounding Vatican City, the spirits screaming as they vanished under a river of flames. The Basilica came into view as the demonic barrier fell.

Haruki grinned when he finally saw the formidable creature looming above the church.

A rueful sigh left the Dragon. *That bird liked to show off even when we were in Heaven.*

King paused beside Haruki. "Is that—?"

"Hey, guys, anyone else seeing some dude with giant wings of fire over there?!" Tom yelled from the other side of the piazza.

He swore and swooped beneath a fist.

"That's Daniel, isn't it?" Serena called out.

She blocked a kick to her belly. Nate grabbed the neck of the super soldier demon who'd attacked her and flung him aside, his skin fluttering with a golden light.

"Daniel?" Lou arched an eyebrow. "As in the priest who burst into flames during that fight?"

"Yeah," Haruki said. "That's his awakened form."

"He's the Phoenix," King murmured.

"You're kidding?" Tom said leadenly. A demon smacked him in the face. "Hey, asshole, I'm kinda having an important conversation here!"

He punched the monster in the jaw.

"Do you need a hand?" someone called out.

Sebastian shot into view above their heads. The ground shook as Smokey landed amidst them, crushing several silver-eyed demons beneath his giant paws.

A weak smile twisted Tom's mouth as he looked up at the beast. "Oh. Er, hi there, pooch. Long time no see."

Smokey turned one of his heads and cast a golden stare at him.

Tom gasped as the hound of Hell licked him, giant tongues sweeping up his body and head and leaving a trail of thick saliva in their wake. His eyes widened in horror as he pulled the gooey substance from his face and hair.

"He likes you," Sebastian declared.

Smokey huffed and wagged his tail.

Lou snorted.

"If you experience a warm tingling sensation, it is the acid drool," Sebastian added.

~

RAGE FILLED BACH AS HE BEHELD THE CREATURE WHO'D

defeated over half of his army and destroyed his spirit cloud.

With the angels and the Chimera disposing of the remaining demons and hellbeasts in the square below, the Phoenix had turned his attention to the gate of Hell. The fiery ropes binding the doorway thickened as he poured power into it. Light flashed in his crimson-gold eyes. He flexed his fingers.

Faint howls echoed from the portal as it started to shrink.

Bach snarled and shot toward the divine beast, scarlet rifts exploding around the piazza as he called to Ba'al.

Two figures flickered into view before him, blocking his path. The demon drew back sharply and narrowed his eyes at the two angels.

Artemus scratched his cheek. "So, a little birdie told us you don't like fire."

Drake grinned, his eyes flaring. Red flames exploded on his dark sword. Divine fire swallowed up his twin's pale blade, the weapon shifting into an even more powerful form.

"*You dare defy me?!*" Bach raged, his voice booming across the square.

Artemus shared a surprised glance with his brother. "Well, yeah."

They charged the demon.

AN OVERPOWERING DIVINE ENERGY ERUPTED OUTSIDE the Basilica.

Surprise darted through Daniel. His gaze found the

figure at the source of the incredible force throbbing through the air.

The seraph was rising from the ground, his pale wings barely flickering as he soared. Demons shrieked in fury as he shut down the rifts Ba'al had opened with gentle waves of his hands, his third eye and fingers blazing with white light.

"*Damn you!*" Bach roared.

The smell of burning flesh filled the air as Artemus and Drake's swords carved across his body, the divine flames effortlessly penetrating his thick demon skin.

Daniel concentrated on the portal, confident the angels would hold the monster at bay. The darkness shrouding the gate started to contract. Rising from its midst was the bronze urn.

The corrupt energy of Hell faded when the doorway finally closed.

Daniel caught the relic as it fell. He could hear the faint screams of the demonic souls still trapped inside it.

Otis appeared opposite him, his divine gaze serene. Daniel bowed his head and wings respectfully to the Seal of God.

"There is one more left," he murmured.

They turned toward the giant demon hovering in the air some thirty feet away.

Bach panted and glared at the angels attacking him. Dark lines scored his body where their blades had scorched him. The monster blocked a blow to his head. He stiffened when he spied the relic in Daniel's hands.

Terror widened his eyes. "*Nooooo!*"

Bach twisted and dove for the crimson crack that burst into existence a few feet from him. Artemus cursed.

"No, you don't!" Drake snarled, diving after the demon.

Otis waved a hand. The rift vanished before Bach could reach it.

Ancient words of power rumbled up Daniel's throat. The divine spell sparked from his mouth and tore through the air, leaving a sparkling trail in its passage. The demon screamed as it wrapped around him like a mantle.

Artemus and Drake drew back, surprise dawning on their faces.

Bach's crown and sword grew smaller. So did his body. The demon cursed and struggled violently as the golden cloud dragged him relentlessly toward Daniel, his form warping as it thinned and diminished at an exponential rate.

His head disappeared inside the urn first. His incensed shriek faded to a dim echo as the relic swallowed his body next.

Satisfaction coursed through Daniel and the beast within him.

It is done.

They turned and handed the urn to Otis. The seraph closed his hands around the artifact. He concentrated.

His third eye flashed with dazzling brilliance. Light exploded between his palms. He parted them a moment later.

The urn that had been inside his grasp slowly crumbled into gold dust that faded into the night.

There was movement in the square below. Persephone ran out of Vatican Palace, Holmes and Elton in her wake. They staggered to a stop when they saw the devastation around them, their faces turning ashen with shock.

"Mother," Daniel whispered.

He dove across what remained of the Basilica and landed in front of Persephone. Emotion choked him as he wrapped his arms around her, his wings shrinking and his flames vanishing. Persephone hugged him back just as fiercely, tears streaming down her face.

"I heard you!" she sobbed. "I heard your voice!"

In the sky above, the two angels vanished in the direction of the Vatican's gardens. The seraph gazed after them, his expression sad.

CHAPTER FORTY-TWO

Persephone gazed pensively out her study window. Police barriers surrounded St. Peter's Square in the distance. Sunlight gleamed on hundreds of cameras and news vans crowding the streets beyond the barricade, where tourists rubbed shoulders with reporters.

Everyone was talking about the mysterious damage Vatican City had incurred two nights ago.

The craters dotting the cobblestones of the piazza and the scorch marks burnt into the colonnades framing the holy space had been streamed countless times across news channels and social media. As for the ruins of the Basilica's iconic roof, it had made headlines around the world for the second day running.

It was Michael and Arael who had made it so that no footage existed of the actual battle that had taken place that night. The memories of the people who had witnessed the arrival of the demons in St. Peter's Square had also been wiped clean. As for the Vatican staff who had been inside the enclave at the time, Bach's attempt to destroy the Holy See and secure Hell's gate had become a distant, vague dream for many who wished to forget it.

The official story was that a small meteor shower had struck the Basilica and St. Peter's Square in the early hours of that morning. NASA and the European Space Agency had even shown images of the incandescent rocks as they streamed through space. Persephone had no doubt that a certain archangel with blue eyes was behind that little stunt.

The world was not ready to know about Ba'al yet.

"The latest conspiracy theory going around is that this was a misguided attempt by a small South American nation to kidnap you for ransom purposes," Daniel murmured.

He perused a selection of newspapers at his desk.

"That's mild compared to what the Chinese are saying," Holmes said morosely.

"Alien attack?" Daniel hazarded.

"No," Holmes muttered. "The undead."

Persephone sighed and strolled back to her desk. "Do we have any estimates of the costs of the repairs yet?"

A guilty look darted across Daniel's face.

"Hmm, no," the priest mumbled, looking as if he wanted to crawl into a hole in the ground.

It was only after the battle that the full extent of the damage he had caused to the sacred church following his transformation into the Phoenix had become manifest. The gaping, thirty-foot hole in the floor of the Basilica spanned all the underlying levels as far down as the newly found Necropolis.

They still had not deciphered the identity of the Roman family whose sarcophagi had occupied the mausoleum where the urn had been hidden.

Persephone pursed her lips and sighed again. "It was better that the Basilica be destroyed, than Rome and the world be invaded by the forces of Hell."

"I agree," Holmes said. "And Ba'al's mole in the Vatican is no more."

Persephone shuddered as she recalled the deadly encounter in the smithy.

It was Otis and Sebastian who had deduced the final identity of Bishop Irons. They suspected he'd been Bishop Sperion, one of the spirits that King Paimon once commanded.

From what they and the Vatican archives' experts knew of the *Ars Goetia*, the book that made up the first portion of *The Lesser Key of Solomon*, an infamous grimoire on demonology, King Paimon had been one of seventy-two demons sealed in a bronze vessel by King Solomon. The same bronze vessel that had been hidden inside an iron casket in a sarcophagus under the Basilica for hundreds of years.

The truth of the matter was likely even stranger than that.

Paimon's abilities had included the power to control spirits, as well as command the elements. His one Achilles' Heel had been fire.

As for the divine barrier around Vatican City, Michael and Arael had spent the rest of that night erecting it once more. It was the primary reason for their presence in Rome.

Although they had borne witness to the fierce battle that had raged across the Holy See that fateful night, they had been true to their promise to God and had not interfered.

The door to the study opened. Artemus and his companions walked in, Elton in their wake.

"We're all packed," Artemus said quietly.

Persephone rose shakily to her feet. She came around the desk and hugged each of them in turn. Even Smokey got a kiss on his cute bunny nose where he perched in Callie's arms.

"I don't even know where to begin," Persephone murmured as she stepped back and looked at them. "You saved the Holy See and the world."

A wry smile curved Drake's lips. "Seems we're doing that more and more these days. Saving the world." His expression sobered. "Thank you for agreeing to have Alice's final resting place be here."

Persephone swallowed the lump in her throat and dipped her chin wordlessly. The identity of Artemus and Drake's mothers had shocked their close-knit group of friends and all those who had learned the startling truth. What it meant for the future of their battle against Ba'al no one yet knew. Alice had been buried in the gardens of the abandoned monastery the day before, in a simple ceremony they had all attended.

As for Theia, neither Drake nor Artemus had seen her since the morning she had left their side, following the night they had mourned their human mother's passing. Nor had Michael put in an appearance since.

Persephone, Daniel, and Holmes escorted Artemus and the others through the palace and into the courtyard outside, where their escort waited to take them to the airport.

Rossi stood close by, his broken arm in a cast. He was one of the few policemen who had wanted to retain their memories of what had taken place the night Hell almost came to Vatican City. He shook their hands and bade them goodbye, his face solemn.

"Will we see you in Rome again?" Persephone asked Artemus.

"Maybe," Artemus said.

Persephone nodded a greeting to Serena and Nate where they stood next to an SUV. With their mission officially over, the super soldiers were returning to Chicago.

One of the new super soldier demons' bodies had been shipped to Gideon Morgan so that he could analyze what Ba'al had done to them.

"Don't be a stranger," Callie told Daniel with a smile.

The priest had decided to stay in Rome instead of going to Chicago with them. His ears grew red with embarrassment as Callie gave him a hug and kissed his cheek. Smokey bumped his chest with his furry head, his eyes flashing crimson.

Artemus was the last one to climb inside a vehicle. He gazed at Persephone, his expression conflicted.

She smiled. "I'll tell Michael to drop by your place if he wants to talk."

Artemus opened his mouth. He closed it soundlessly, dipped his head, and slipped inside the SUV.

CHAPTER FORTY-THREE

ARTEMUS BLINKED HIS EYES OPEN. PALE DAYLIGHT peeked through a gap in the curtains covering the east-facing windows of his bedroom. He glanced at the antique clock on the nightstand.

It was six-thirty a.m.

He rolled over, plumped his pillow, and settled back down to sleep. A low growl erupted at his feet a moment later.

"Go back to sleep, Smokey," Artemus mumbled, burrowing under the covers.

The growl grew louder. The rabbit's fuzzy weight suddenly got heavier.

Artemus sat up. "For the love of God, what is—?"

He froze, senses on high alert. Smokey had assumed his dark hellhound form. He was baring his fangs at the shadows next to the door.

Someone was standing there.

Artemus grabbed the knife under the pillow.

The figure sighed and stepped out of the gloom. "There's no need for that."

Artemus's eyes widened. "Michael?!"

"Hey, kid." The archangel arched an eyebrow at the hellhound. "And you, would it be too much to ask you not to greet your commander with such animosity every time we meet?"

Smokey stopped growling, made a disgruntled noise, and shrank back to his bunny form. He turned his butt to the archangel, his expression mutinous.

Artemus swallowed as he gazed at his father. "What are you doing here?"

It had been a week since their return from Rome. Despite Drake and the others' reassurances that Michael would turn up at some point, Artemus had almost given up on ever seeing his father again.

Now that he was there, Artemus didn't know what to say to him.

"By the way, why were you standing in the dark?" he mumbled.

"I was watching you sleep."

Artemus stiffened. "That's creepy. Never do that again."

"Oh, come on," Michael protested. "I missed out on lots of things when you were growing up. I need to catch up on all the precious moments."

Irritation shot through Artemus. He could tell the archangel was teasing him. He moved the covers off his legs and climbed out of bed.

"Trust me, watching an adult male sleep shouldn't be one of those moments," Artemus muttered darkly as he removed a change of clothes from a dresser. "It's the kind of crap that will land you in jail."

He headed for the bathroom.

Michael started to follow. "Want me to scrub your back?"

Artemus scowled and whirled around. "No, you dirty old man!"

He slammed the bathroom door in the grinning archangel's face. Smokey started growling again.

By the time Artemus walked out into the bedroom, Michael had disappeared. A sharp pang shot through him.

"Where'd he go?" he asked Smokey.

The bunny rolled his eyes. *I do not know. But my instincts tell me he will be back again, like a nasty rash you cannot rid yourself of.*

Artemus found himself smiling faintly at that. At least his and Drake's mothers had had more gravitas in their bearing.

Pain twisted his heart as he thought of Alice and Theia.

He still hadn't come to terms with everything that had happened in Rome, nor had he fully absorbed what it meant to have a goddess as one of his parents.

Nate was putting breakfast together when he got downstairs.

Artemus made himself a cup of coffee and handed one to the super soldier. "Are the others up yet?"

"Drake is out for a run and Serena went to get a paper," Nate said. "Haruki and Callie are still asleep."

"And Sebastian?"

"He never came back last night."

Artemus frowned as he took a seat at the kitchen table.

Otis and Sebastian had had their heads buried in Catherine Boone's journals ever since their return from

Rome. They had barely left Otis's apartment above the shop.

Drake and Serena returned to the mansion presently.

"Well, they're still talking about that meteor shower," Serena said as she sat down with the newspaper.

"Oh yeah?" Drake poured himself some orange juice from the refrigerator and mopped his forehead with his workout towel. "You'd think they'd be on to something else by now." He grabbed a piece of bacon from Serena's plate and munched on it unconsciously. "You heard anything from Gideon yet?"

"No." Serena frowned and pointed. "You have a crumb."

"Where?" Drake said, swiping at his mouth with the back of his hand.

She reached up and removed the offending morsel from his lower lip. "Got it."

They froze and stared at one another in shocked silence as they processed what had just transpired. Their heads swiveled around as one.

Artemus and Nate were grinning at them.

"You guys should just date," Nate said.

"Yeah, that or get a room," Artemus drawled.

Smokey tittered under the table. Drake and Serena scowled.

The front door banged open in the distance. Footsteps stormed across the foyer and headed toward the kitchen. Otis and Sebastian appeared, their clothes in mild disarray and their expressions flustered.

"The next Guardian is in Chicago!" Otis blurted out.

Artemus stared. "What?"

"Jackson helped us decipher the code," Sebastian explained. "We have been translating the journals all night.

Otis is correct. Catherine Boone writes of a Guardian in Chicago. She is yet to awaken."

"It's a girl?" Serena asked.

"Yes." Otis nodded vigorously. "Everything that my mother envisioned has taken place. From our awakenings to the events in Rome. It's all there. We're still deciphering the rest of it!"

"What's with all the commotion?" someone mumbled sleepily.

Haruki strolled into the kitchen, Callie on his heels.

"The next Guardian is in Chicago," Drake muttered.

Haruki's eyes rounded.

Callie gaped. "What?!"

The doorbell rang. They all startled and stared at one another.

"It couldn't be," Callie mumbled.

Artemus led the way into the foyer, his heart thumping wildly. He stopped in front of the entrance and hesitated. He couldn't feel anything from the other side.

The bell rang again. They all jumped.

"Open it," Haruki said hoarsely.

Artemus swallowed, gripped the knob, and yanked the door open.

Michael was standing on the threshold.

"Oh, hey. I kinda forgot to mention something." He looked past Artemus's shoulder. "Great, you're all here."

The archangel reached out to his right and pulled something out of thin air. Artemus's jaw dropped open.

"You have a new tenant," Michael announced with a grin.

A heavy-lidded Daniel blinked at them blankly from where he dangled in Michael's grasp. He had a toothbrush in his mouth and was frozen in the act of moving it. He squinted at them blearily, his eyes unfocused without his glasses.

They widened when he registered Artemus and the others' presence.

"What are you guys doing in our communal washrooms?" Daniel mumbled around his toothbrush.

"I'm sorry to have to break it to you, kid, but this isn't Rome," Michael told him jovially.

"Well, now we know what a priest wears beneath his cassock," Callie said flatly.

"I think it's kinda cute," Serena murmured appraisingly. "Homely, even."

"He looks better without his glasses," Haruki stated.

Color bloomed on Daniel's cheeks. He covered his plaid shorts and white vest primly with his hands, spat his toothbrush out, looked around with a scowl, and glared at the archangel holding him in his grasp. "Where the hell am I?!"

"In Chicago, where you belong," Michael said blithely.

Daniel's eyes rounded.

"No, I don't!" he snapped.

"No, he doesn't!" Artemus barked.

A thud sounded somewhere on the upper floors of the mansion.

Artemus looked at the ceiling before narrowing his eyes at the archangel. "What was that?"

"That was Arael moving Daniel's stuff in."

As if on cue, the Angel of Crows appeared beside Michael and stepped down lightly onto the porch.

"You're in the room next to Artemus," Arael told a shocked Daniel. "Persephone has secured you a position at a local church. Here's your official letter of introduction."

He removed an envelope closed with the Vatican's seal

from inside his jacket and placed it in the priest's limp hand. Daniel spluttered, speechless for a moment.

"*Persephone knows?!*" he finally blurted out.

"Well, yeah." Michael shrugged. "This was her idea, after all."

Daniel paled.

"She's been hinting heavily all week that your rightful place is in Chicago, but you apparently have selective hearing, so she asked us for a favor," Arael explained, adding insult to injury. He turned and handed a second envelope to Artemus. "Persephone told me to give you this."

Artemus looked at the envelope as if it were poison. "What is it?"

"It's a bill for damages caused to Vatican City," Arael said smoothly. "She is willing to forget about it if you agree to Daniel staying here."

Artemus sucked in air, outraged. He snatched the envelope from Arael's grasp and tore it open. "What the hell does she mean, a bill for damages?! Her adopted son there caused most of the—"

He stopped and swallowed convulsively when he registered the figure at the bottom of the single sheet of paper inside.

Sebastian peered over Artemus's right shoulder. "My goodness."

Drake took the bill from Artemus's loose fingers. A whistle left him as he and Serena studied it.

"Wow," Haruki said over Drake's shoulder. "That's a lot of numbers."

"It would take you fifteen—" Serena started.

"Eighteen," Callie interjected.

"—eighteen years to pay that." The super soldier laid a

heavy hand on Artemus's shoulder. "I would give in if I were you."

"Take me back to Rome!" Daniel told Michael between gritted teeth. *"Take me back to Rome, right now!"*

His eyes flashed orange. Flames burst into life around him.

"No can do, kiddo." Michael beamed. "We'll be off, then."

He dropped Daniel on the porch and shot toward the sky, Arael at his side.

Artemus recovered his senses. He marched outside and shook his fist at their disappearing figures, face crunching up in a glower.

"Get back here this minute, you shitty father!"

Thunder boomed in the clear morning sky. A bolt of lightning pierced the heavens and split one of the gravestones in the cemetery in half.

The blood drained from Artemus's face.

"Oh, look," Michael said with a chuckle from somewhere above him. "The Old Man is back into his smiting again."

THE END

AFTERWORD

Thank you for reading FORSAKEN! HALLOWED GROUND, the next book in LEGION, will be coming soon. Want to find out when HALLOWED GROUND will be released? Sign up to my newsletter for new release alerts, giveaways, and plenty more. You also get a FREE boxset as a thank you for joining my mailing list.

➤ http://bit.ly/1YndWmB

If you enjoyed FORSAKEN, please consider leaving a review on your favorite book site. Reviews help readers find books!

Want exclusive sneak peeks at my upcoming books? Join my VIP Facebook Group for this and more.

Have you read HUNTED, the first book in the SEVEN-TEEN series, the prequel to LEGION? Turn the page to read an extract from HUNTED now!

HUNTED EXTRACT

PROLOGUE

My name is Lucas Soul.

Today, I died again.

This is my fifteenth death in the last four hundred and fifty years.

~

CHAPTER ONE

I woke up in a dark alley behind a building.

Autumn rain plummeted from an angry sky, washing the narrow, walled corridor I lay in with shades of gray. It dripped from the metal rungs of the fire escape above my head and slithered down dirty, barren walls, forming puddles under the garbage dumpsters by my feet. It gurgled in gutters and rushed in storm drains off the main avenue behind me.

It also cleansed away the blood beneath my body.

For once, I was grateful for the downpour; I did not want any evidence left of my recent demise.

I blinked at the drops that struck my face and slowly climbed to my feet. Unbidden, my fingers rose to trace the cut in my chest; the blade had missed the birthmark on my skin by less than an inch.

I turned and studied the tower behind me. I was not sure what I was expecting to see. A face peering over the edge of the glass and brick structure. An avenging figure drifting down in the rainfall, a bloodied sword in its hands and a crazy smile in its eyes. A flock of silent crows come to take my unearthly body to its final resting place.

Bar the heavenly deluge, the skyline was fortunately empty.

I pulled my cell phone out of my jeans and stared at it. It was smashed to pieces. I sighed. I could hardly blame the makers of the device. They had probably never tested it from the rooftop of a twelve-storey building. As for me, the bruises would start to fade by tomorrow.

It would take another day for the wound in my chest to heal completely.

I glanced at the sky again before walking out of the alley. An empty phone booth stood at the intersection to my right. I strolled toward it and closed the rickety door behind me. A shiver wracked my body while I dialed a number. Steam soon fogged up the glass wall before me.

There was a soft click after the fifth ring.

'Yo,' said a tired voice.

'Yo yourself,' I said.

A yawn traveled down the line. 'What's up?'

'I need a ride. And a new phone.'

There was a short silence. 'It's four o'clock in the morning.' The voice had gone blank.

'I know,' I said in the same tone.

The sigh at the other end was audible above the pounding of the rain on the metal roof of the booth. 'Where are you?'

'Corner of Cambridge and Staniford.'

Fifteen minutes later, a battered, tan Chevrolet Monte Carlo pulled up next to the phone box. The passenger door opened.

'Get in,' said the figure behind the wheel.

I crossed the sidewalk and climbed in the seat. Water dripped onto the leather cover and formed a puddle by my feet. There was a disgruntled mutter from my left. I looked at the man beside me.

Reid Hasley was my business partner and friend. Together, we co-owned the Hasley and Soul Agency. We were private investigators, of sorts. Reid certainly qualified as one, being a former Marine and cop. I, on the other hand, had been neither.

'You look like hell,' said Reid as he maneuvered the car into almost nonexistent traffic. He took something from his raincoat and tossed it across to me. It was a new cell.

I raised my eyebrows. 'That was fast.'

He grunted indistinct words and lit a cigarette. 'What happened?' An orange glow flared into life as he inhaled, casting shadows under his brow and across his nose.

I transferred the data card from the broken phone into the new one and frowned at the bands of smoke drifting toward me. 'That's going to kill you one day.'

'Just answer the question,' he retorted.

I looked away from his intense gaze and contemplated the dark tower at the end of the avenue. 'I met up with our new client.'

'And?' said Reid.

'He wasn't happy to see me.'

Something in my voice made him stiffen. 'How unhappy are we talking here?'

I sighed. 'Well, he stuck a sword through my heart and pushed me off the top of the Cramer building. I'd say he was pretty pissed.'

Silence followed my words. 'That's not good,' said Reid finally.

'No.'

'It means we're not gonna get the money,' he added.

'I'm fine by the way. Thanks for asking,' I said.

He shot a hard glance at me. 'We need the cash.'

Unpalatable as the statement was, it was also regrettably true. Small PI firms like ours had just about managed before the recession. Nowadays, people had more to worry about than what their cheating spouses were up to. Although embezzlement cases were up by a third, the victims of such scams were usually too hard up to afford the services of a good detective agency. As a result, the rent on our office space was overdue by a month.

Mrs. Trelawney, our landlady, was not pleased about this; at five-foot two and weighing just over two hundred pounds, the woman had the ability to make us quake in our boots. This had less to do with her size than the fact that she made the best angel cakes in the city. She gave them out to her tenants when they paid the rent on time. A month without angel cakes was making us twitchy.

'I think we might still get the cakes if you flash your eyes at her,' mused my partner.

I stared at him. 'Are you pimping me out?'

'No. You'd be a tough sell,' he retorted as the car splashed along the empty streets of the city. He glanced at me. 'This makes it what, your fourteenth death?'

'Fifteenth.'

His eyebrows rose. 'Huh. So, two more to go.'

I nodded mutely. In many ways, I was glad Hasley had entered my unnatural life, despite the fact that it happened in such a dramatic fashion. It was ten years ago this summer.

Hasley was a detective in the Boston PD Homicide Unit at the time. One hot Friday afternoon in August, he and his partner of three years found themselves on the trail of a murder suspect, a Latino man by the name of Burt Suarez. Suarez worked the toll bridge northeast of the city and had no priors. Described by his neighbors and friends as a gentle giant who cherished his wife, was kind to children and animals, and even attended Sunday service, the guy did not have so much as a speeding ticket to his name. That day, the giant snapped and went on a killing spree after walking in on his wife and his brother in the marital bed. He shot Hasley's partner, two uniformed cops, and the neighbor's dog, before fleeing toward the river.

Unfortunately, I got in his way.

In my defense, I had not been myself for most of that month, having recently lost someone who had been a friend for more than a hundred years. In short, I was drunk.

On that scorching summer's day, Burt Suarez achieved something no other human, or non-human for that matter, had managed before or since.

He shot me in the head.

Sadly, he did not get to savor this feat, as he died minutes after he fired a round through my skull. Hasley still swore to this day that Suarez's death had more to do with seeing me rise to my feet Lazarus-like again than the gunshot wound he himself inflicted on the man with his Glock 19.

That had been my fourteenth death. Shortly after witnessing my unholy resurrection, Hasley quit his job as a detective and became my business partner.

Over the decade that followed, we trailed unfaithful spouses, found missing persons, performed employee checks for high profile investment banks, took on surveillance work for attorneys and insurance companies, served process to disgruntled defendants, and even rescued the odd kidnapped pet. Hasley knew more about me than anyone else in the city.

He still carried the Glock.

'Why did he kill you?' said Reid presently. He braked at a set of red lights. 'Did you do something to piss him off?' There was a trace of suspicion in his tone. The lights turned green.

'Well, broadly speaking, he seemed opposed to my existence.' The rhythmic swishing of the windscreen wipers and the dull hiss of rubber rolling across wet asphalt were the only sounds that broke the ensuing lull. 'He called me an ancient abomination that should be sent straight to Hell and beyond.' I grimaced. 'Frankly, I thought that was a bit ironic coming from someone who's probably not that much older than me.'

Reid crushed the cigarette butt in the ashtray and narrowed his eyes. 'You mean, he's one of you?'

I hesitated before nodding once. 'Yes.'

Over the years, as I came to know and trust him, I told Reid a little bit about my origins.

I was born in Europe in the middle of the sixteenth century, when the Renaissance was at its peak. My father came from a line of beings known as the Crovirs, while my mother was a descendant of a group called the Bastians. They are the only races of immortals on Earth.

Throughout most of the history of man, the Crovirs and the Bastians have waged a bitter and brutal war against one another. Although enough blood has been shed over the millennia to fill a respectable portion of the Caspian Sea, this unholy battle between immortals has, for the most, remained a well-kept secret from the eyes of ordinary humans, despite the fact that they have been used as pawns in some of its most epic chapters.

The conflict suffered a severe and unprecedented setback in the fourteenth century, when the numbers of both races dwindled rapidly and dramatically; while the Black Death scourged Europe and Asia, killing millions of humans, the lesser-known Red Death shortened the lives of countless immortals. It was several decades before the full extent of the devastation was realized, for the plague had brought with it an unexpected and horrifying complication.

The greater part of those who survived became infertile.

This struck another blow to both sides and, henceforth, an uneasy truce was established. Although the odd incident still happened between embittered members of each race, the fragile peace has, surprisingly, lasted to this day. From that time on, the arrival of an immortal child into the world became an event that was celebrated at the highest levels of each society.

My birth was a notable exception. The union between a Crovir and a Bastian was considered an unforgivable sin and strictly forbidden by both races; ancient and immutable, it was a fact enshrined into the very doctrines and origins of our species. Any offspring of such a coupling was thus deemed an abomination unto all and sentenced to death from the very moment they were conceived. I was not the first half-breed, both races having secretly mated with each other in the past. However, the two immortal societies wanted me to be the last. Fearing for my existence, my parents fled and took me into hiding.

For a while, our life was good. We were far from rich and dwelled in a remote cabin deep in the forest, where we lived off the land, hunting, fishing, and even growing our own food. Twice a year, my father ventured down the mountain to the nearest village, where he traded fur for oil and other rare goods. We were happy and I never wanted for anything.

It was another decade before the Hunters finally tracked us down. That was when I learned one of the most important lessons about immortals.

We can only survive up to sixteen deaths.

Having perished seven times before, my father died after ten deaths at the hands of the Hunters. He fought until the very last breath left his body. I watched them kill my mother seventeen times.

I should have died that day. I did, in fact, suffer my very first death. Moments after the act, I awoke on the snow-covered ground, tears cooling on my face and my blood staining the whiteness around me. Fingers clenching convulsively around the wooden practice sword my father had given me, I waited helplessly for a blade to sink into my heart once more. Minutes passed before I realized I was alone in that crimson-colored clearing, high up in the Carpathian Mountains.

The crows came next, silent flocks that descended from the gray winter skies and covered the bloodied bodies next to me. When the birds left, the remains of my parents had disappeared as well. All that was left was ash.

It was much later that another immortal imparted to me the theory behind the seventeen deaths. Each one apparently took away a piece of our soul. Unlike our bodies, our souls could not regenerate after a death. Thus, Death as an ultimate end was unavoidable. And then the crows come for most of us.

No one was really clear as to where the birds took our earthly remains.

'What if you lived alone, on a desert island or something, and never met anyone? You could presumably never die,' Reid had argued with his customary logic when I told him this.

'True. However, death by boredom is greatly underestimated,' I replied. 'Besides, someone like you is bound to kill himself after a day without a smoke.'

'So the meeting was a trap?' said Reid.

His voice jolted me back to the present. The car had pulled up in front of my apartment block. The road ahead was deserted.

'Yes.' Rain drummed the roof of the Monte Carlo. The sound reminded me of the ricochets of machine guns. Unpleasant memories rose to the surface of my mind. I suppressed them firmly.

'Will he try to kill you again?' said Reid. I remained silent. He stared at me. 'What are you gonna do?'

I shifted on the leather seat and reached for the door handle. 'Well, seeing as you're likely to drag me back from Hell if I leave you high and dry, I should probably kill him first.'

I exited the car, crossed the sidewalk, and entered the lobby of the building. I turned to watch the taillights of

the Chevrolet disappear in the downpour before getting in
the lift. Under normal circumstances, I would have taken
the stairs to the tenth floor. Dying, I felt, was a justifiable
reason to take things easy for the rest of the night.

My apartment was blessedly cool and devoid of immortals hell-bent on carving another hole in my heart. I took a
shower, dressed the wound on my chest, and went to bed.

➤ Get HUNTED now!

BOOKS BY A.D. STARRLING

Hunted (A Seventeen Series Novel) Book One

'My name is Lucas Soul. Today, I died again. This is my fifteenth death in the last four hundred and fifty years. And I'm determined that it will be the last.'

Warrior (A Seventeen Series Novel) Book Two

The perfect Immortal warrior. A set of stolen, priceless artifacts. An ancient sect determined to bring about the downfall of human civilization.

Empire (A Seventeen Series Novel) Book Three

An Immortal healer. An ancient empire reborn. A chain of cataclysmic events that threatens to change the fate of the world.

Legacy (A Seventeen Series Novel) Book Four

The Hunter who should have been king. The Elemental who fears love. The Seer who is yet to embrace her powers. Three immortals whose fates are entwined with that of the oldest and most formidable enemy the world has ever faced.

Origins (A Seventeen Series Novel) Book Five

The gifts bestowed by One not of this world, to the Man who had lived longer than most. The Empire ruled by a King who would swallow the world in his madness. The Warrior who chose to rise against her own kind in order to defeat him. Discover the extraordinary beginnings of the Immortals and the unforgettable story of the Princess who would become a Legend.

Destiny (A Seventeen Series Novel) Book Six

An enemy they never anticipated. A brutal attack that tears them apart. A chain of immutable events that will forever alter the future. Discover the destiny that was always theirs to claim.

The Seventeen Collection 1: Books 1-3

Boxset featuring Hunted, Warrior, and Empire.

The Seventeen Collection 2: Books 4-6

Boxset featuring Legacy, Origins, and Destiny.

The Seventeen Complete Collection: Books 1-6

Boxset featuring Hunted, Warrior, Empire, Legacy, Origins, and Destiny.

First Death (A Seventeen Series Short Story) #1

Discover where it all started...

Dancing Blades (A Seventeen Series Short Story) #2

Join Lucas Soul on his quest to become a warrior.

The Meeting (A Seventeen Series Short Story) #3

Discover the origins of the incredible friendship between the protagonists of Hunted.

The Warrior Monk (A Seventeen Series Short Story) #4

Experience Warrior from the eyes of one of the most beloved characters in Seventeen.

The Hunger (A Seventeen Series Short Story) #5

Discover the origin of the love story behind Empire.

The Bank Job (A Seventeen Series Short Story) #6

Join two of the protagonists from Legacy on their very first adventure.

The Seventeen Series Short Story Collection 1 (#1-3)

Boxset featuring First Death, Dancing Blades, and The Meeting.

The Seventeen Series Short Story Collection 2 (#4-6)

Boxset featuring The Warrior Monk, The Hunger, and The Bank Job.

The Seventeen Series Ultimate Short Story Collection

Boxset featuring First Death, Dancing Blades, The Meeting, The Warrior Monk, The Hunger, and The Bank Job.

Blood and Bones (Legion Book One)

The Seventeen spin-off series is here!

I am darkness. I am light. I am wrath. I am salvation. I am rebirth. I am destruction. I belong to Heaven. I belong to Hell. P.S. I like bunnies.

Fire and Earth (Legion Book Two)

L.A. is teeming with demons. Only one man and his ragtag team of supernatural misfits can stop them.

Awakening (Legion Book Three)

Knowledge is power...

Forsaken (Legion Book Four)

They thought they knew who their enemy was...

Mission:Black (A Division Eight Thriller)

A broken agent. A once in a lifetime chance. A new mission that threatens to destroy her again.

Mission: Armor (A Division Eight Thriller)

A man tortured by his past. A woman determined to save him. A deadly assignment that threatens to rip them apart.

Mission:Anaconda (A Division Eight Thriller)

It should have been a simple mission. They should have been in and out in a day. Except it wasn't. And they didn't.

Void (A Sci-fi Horror Short Story)

2065. Humans start terraforming Mars.

2070. The Mars Baker2 outpost is established on the Acidalia Planitia.

2084. The first colonist goes missing.

The Other Side of the Wall (A Short Horror Story)

Have you ever seen flashes of darkness where there should only be light? Ever seen shadows skitter past out of the corner of your eyes and looked, only to find nothing there?

AUDIOBOOKS

Hunted (A Seventeen Series Novel) Book One

Warrior (A Seventeen Series Novel) Book Two

Empire (A Seventeen Seres Novel) Book Three

First Death (A Seventeen Series Short Story) #1

Dancing Blades (A Seventeen Series Short Story) #2

The Meeting (A Seventeen Series Short Story) #3

The Warrior Monk (A Seventeen Series Short Story) #4

ABOUT THE AUTHOR

AD Starrling's bestselling supernatural thriller series **Seventeen** combines action, suspense, and a heavy dose of fantasy to make each book an explosive, adrenaline-fueled ride, while **Legion**, the spin-off series, has been compared to Jim Butcher's **The Dresden Files**. If you prefer your action hot and your heroes sexy and strong-willed, then check out AD's military thriller series **Division Eight**.

When she's not busy writing, AD can be found eating Thai food, being tortured by her back therapists, drooling over gadgets, working part-time as a doctor on a Neonatal Intensive Care unit somewhere in the UK, reading manga, and watching action flicks and anime. She has occasionally been accused of committing art with a charcoal stick and some drawing paper.

Find out more about AD on her website www.adstarrling.com where you can sign up for her awesome newsletter, get exclusive freebies, and never miss her latest release. You'll also have a chance to see sneak previews of her work, participate in exclusive giveaways, and hear about special promotional offers first.

Here are some other places where you can connect with her:
Sign-up to AD's Newsletter
Follow AD on Bookbub
Follow AD on Amazon
Join AD's Facebook VIP Fan Group